CN00519223

Travel by Night

Sophie Morton-Thomas

www.darkstroke.com

Discover us online:
www.darkstroke.com

Join us on instagram:
www.instagram.com/darkstrokebooks/

Include **#darkstroke** in a photo of yourself
holding this book on Instagram and
something nice will happen.

For Jimbo, Tilly, Felix and little Raffy

Acknowledgements

Firstly, I would like to thank Laurence and Steph Patterson at darkstroke books for having taken me on and giving my story a chance. In particular, Laurence for pulling apart my many semi-coloned sentences and having patience with my dire IT skills. I would also like to thank the rest of the darkstroke and Crooked Cat community for their new-found support and enthusiasm for my book.

To the Crime and Thriller Writing MSt cohort at Cambridge University, especially Tracey Morton, I would like to say a very big thank you for your encouragement through my moments of self-doubt! Thank you also, Sophie Hannah, Midge Gillies and Elly Griffiths.

Thank you to the New Voices Competition run by Adventures in Fiction for giving the first few pages of Travel by Night a special mention in your 'particularly strong contenders' list for your prize – this gave me the confidence to continue writing the book, and to finish it.

Tilly, thanks for your laughter at my dialogue which proved it needed a little more work.

Felix, thanks for the ideas for the next book…

To my mum and sister Charlotte, thanks for your continuing support as I battled to work as a teacher, student and mum as well as writer. Thanks to my friend Lisa Grindon for your support too.

And last but not least, thanks to Jimbo for taking your daily two hour walks (sometimes in the rain) with Raffy over summer's lockdown, without which this book would not exist.

About the Author

Sophie Morton-Thomas is a British writer based in West Sussex, where she lives with her husband and children. She is an English teacher by day and a Master's student and writer in her free time. Travel by Night is her debut novel.

Travel by Night

Prologue

Yalina

June 30th 2007
South Yorkshire

I know he is waiting. I can hear the gravel crunching under his wellies, the outside tap is dripping like a metronome. *Drip, drip, drip.* Time stands completely still for a moment, then lurches forward, and now he won't wait any longer. I feel a slap to my cheek: the bitter, biting wind of South Yorkshire even though it is the height of summer. His grip around the back of my neck as the battered barn door is prised open. "Gettout!" he yells, as I scramble to my feet. I didn't ask to be here. I don't want to stay.

I'm thrown into the back of his Range Rover, and am surprised to see a boy of around the same age. I imagine I would be seeing girls. Girls, women, teenagers. Dark hair, even darker eyes, a look of resignation drawn over their faces rather than any initial fear they may have once had. Some of them are Pakistani, Indian, like me. Underweight, filthy. The white boy eyes me, plump compared to my haggard frame of barely concealed bones.

I begin to wonder what I must look like. "Speak English?" I ask, not expecting a response.

He nods, eyes boring into my face. He is accompanied by something. The smell of toilets, the sour odour of a dilapidated stairwell of a council block is leaking from his pores. He's pissed himself at some point of the journey. A glance at his navy joggers show a half-dried damp patch. One of his shoes is stained with it too. The smell catches at the back of my throat, astringent, and it's all I can do to prevent myself from dry heaving.

"It'll be ok," I try saying, but my comment has an unusual lilt at the end, making it sound more like a question.

"No," he states. His accent is not British, certainly not Sheffield. He finally looks away from me, down to his feet. I know he's wondering if I have taken in his urine-soaked trainer.

The Range Rover starts up and we are violently thrown forward, my head crashing into the wooden board which separates us from the front of the car. Our windows have been painted black, lest we try to look out or, God forbid, try to escape. I wonder if we're still in the Sheffield area. Perhaps we are on the Snakepass, heading towards Manchester; it's a rough enough ride that way and would provide very little surveillance from the authorities. I don't know what to say to the boy, so I simply stare out of the front of the vehicle, towards the windscreen, which provides the only light that floods into our space. I realise all of a sudden how tired I am, so inexplicably exhausted. I can't remember the last time I ate.

In an attempt to halt the cycle of negative thoughts that are threatening to flood my mind, I try earnestly to think of mum and dad, of home, but the memories are reluctant to materialise, and I give up, a sense of mental exhaustion coming over me. There is the involuntary, spontaneous vision of my piano. It waits for me to run my fingers over its ancient ivory keys; they are paused, patiently, for my hands. There *was* a piano. The notion of trying to remember anything is causing thought-fatigue, and a wave of nausea besieges my body as the car travels at unbelievable speed over bumps in the road. I begin, then stop trying, to think of my sister, because whatever I do, there is no real sister in my head, only a blur, the darkened silhouette of who she may or may not have been.

When I open my eyes I feel the engine has cut out, and I hear the whiny screech of the brakes. A glance at the boy opposite tells me he is fast asleep, head lolling, mouth slightly open, snoring quietly. The driver turns to look at me and shouts, "Get ready, girl! This is you. No talking." His accent is hard to place, perhaps Eastern Bloc. Could be Poland, vodka at the ready, fur hat of some pathetic rodent's pelt.

I scramble to my feet, but he is already at the rear of the Range Rover, door swung open with such force it feels like it'll be torn off its hinges. I feel his calloused hand's grip at the back of my neck and I am immediately paralysed, with pain or with fear, I'm unsure which. My headscarf has been pulled back, exposing my hair. I see a man appear out of a side door of the slightly dilapidated stone house ahead of us, he runs towards us with his head looking down, but he is mouthing the words "Quiet, be quiet!" at me and the other man. He pulls his hood over his face. I cannot speak anyway.

I find myself being man-handled towards the back of the house, my legs are lethargic dead weights in my too-baggy jeans. The wait for the second man to unlock the padlock on the door feels like an eternity. I'm not certain my legs can hold me up much longer. The stench of stale cigarettes from the man's paw, still clenching the back of my neck, is close; too close and I can feel myself about to gag. As a mouthful of acidic bile rises to my tongue, I notice there are no buildings beyond this cottage, only a vast expanse of green land, burnt sunflower-yellow at the edges from the intensity of the previous summer's sun. Once the wooden door of the building is wrenched open, my face is hit with a draft and the stench of all-encompassing damp. I wonder, matter-of-factly, whether they are about to dump me here.

A clumsy shove to my back sends me flying forward to my knees. I have been winded. It's nearly impossible to catch my breath. The back of my neck is burning, a rising heat from the sudden release of the man's rough fingers. Before I can raise myself to my feet, the door is slammed ceremoniously behind me, and the man, and the men are gone. A quick glance at my wrists tells me that I am not tied up, not yet. The pain from the previous occupation last week is yet to fade away; reddish and purple-hued weals have created a landscape of knotted tree roots across my feeble veins. I bite my lip and taste blood.

Chapter One

Yalina

March 2007
Harrow, Middlesex

I'm temporarily interrupted from my thoughts as the early
morning cleaner tiptoes into my room, a green figure barely
differentiated from the matt lime-greenness of the walls
which surround me. She doesn't look up. I find myself
staring at her, waiting for a greeting, a nod, anything. She's
seen too many like me, too many wake-ups on the ward, too
many post-operation hazes. The disinfectant sluicing the
floor from her mop creates a small back-wash which laps
against the metal legs of my bed. Except it's not *my* bed. It is
the property of NHS Middlesex Hospital Trust. But I don't
want to think of that now; my head feels muddled, lop-sided
at best. The lack of acknowledgement from the cleaner is the
distraction that I am focusing on as I try to recall the previous
day, the source of the greyness in my mind. Slowly launching
my body weight up onto my elbows, I glance at the yellowed
clock on the wall opposite. As I do so, a man and a woman
enter through the doorway to my left which is held open
conveniently by the cleaner's metal bucket. I catch myself
wondering why such a thing is produced in a material that is
doomed to rust, but my view is interrupted, drawn to the
couple. One of them pulls a chair to my bedside, the woman
jutting her head forward a little to gaze into my eyes. She is
familiar. Her stare into my face annoys me.

The man carefully sticks out his arm to guide her into the

chair at my right side. "Faiza!" He rolls his eyes, glancing at me by way of concern, or waiting for me to laugh. "Give her some room!" His sense of friendliness seems to vanish as he grabs his wife's wrist and yanks her down into the chair.

I stare at him but am suddenly aware of being exposed. I feel for the top of my head; at least it is covered by fabric. My father would be less pleased to see me, should it not be present.

"She's just concerned," he offers, yet I see his furtive glance at her, sideways. When he returns his face to me he is still glowering.

The woman is yet to speak, reaching inside her handbag for something. Her sarong is of familiar colours; reds and purples.

"Say hello," orders the man, black wiry hair, slightly fuzzy grey at the temples. His age is the wrong side of sixty. The woman and I glance up, neither of us sure who he is addressing, so we both speak at the same time, and both withdraw at once, politely laughing.

"You do look much improved from yesterday!" exclaims the woman. "All this fuss."

Fuss is the last thing I'm encouraging from anyone. I look to the man for help. He is familiar too. *Women shouldn't draw attention to themselves.*

"Is your brain still addled?" continues the woman. More of her face is covered than mine.

I nod. It is enough to satisfy her curiosity.

"You look fine to me. Doesn't she, mum?" says the man, expressionless.

Mum. Ok. I smile sweetly at the man and decide to play along with this little scenario.

"Dad, how long have I been in here?"

The man doesn't baulk at the question.

"Only two days now. Feels longer does it?"

"Yup," I manage to croak. My voice is groggy, my speech reluctant. I see the woman lean towards her partner. She mumbles something indecipherable. I realise I don't actually care what she's saying. I suddenly feel conned that whatever medication I have been fed in here is affecting my memory, and apparently my will to care. My *parents* sit for several more minutes, which could be hours, and I nod in all the right places. Karen Eave's son Michael has passed his driving test after four attempts. Mrs Patel next door hasn't been looking after her dog very well and the RSPCA are threatening to have it taken it away. I want these people to leave, I want them to go home. After what seems like a day, the man stands and scrapes back his hospital chair, grasps the woman's hand and hoists her to a standing position, almost forcefully. I pretend not to be alarmed, and stifle my yawn.

"So we'll catch up with you again tomorrow," says the woman. "But how is the ...." She pauses here, before delicately choosing which words to pick. "...scar?"

I move my hand slowly across my chest to gesture where the pain is. I see the woman glance at the man with concern. I *think* it's concern. It's pretty difficult to tell with people you've only really just met. "Hurts," I offer. "Bruised."

"Well, it will be for some time," says the woman. "You mustn't exert yourself. Don't try to lean forward to turn on the tv or anything. Once you're home you must lie low for a long time. Perhaps six months."

My eyes jerk wider at this. "Six months? What are you saying?"

The man is holding the woman's hand. It's quite a grip. "She's saying you need to look after yourself. Take the tablets. Rest. Let the wound heal."

Her eyes are glazing over as she studies me, staring into my face. "We'll come see you tomorrow," she warbles. That will be ok? Lil?"

My heart suddenly slips into my throat and again I struggle to articulate the words on my tongue. Visions of white flowers enter my mind, their pointed, gaping mouths, blood-pink at the edges. The funeral flower.

***

The 90s dado rail painted an off-white colour is not the only dated thing to adorn my bedroom; the peeling posters of

9

whatever baby-faced man was in the Top 40 at the time cover my walls and stare at me beseechingly from their A3 sized glossy paper. It's not as strange as I thought it would be, living here. The dank smell is not too off-putting, and my sheets are clean at least. I'm in a time warp. Nothing has changed. I open my wardrobe door and am amused by the clothes still hanging inside. My prom dress, peach coloured and puffy, the tulle sad and reminiscent of 1997. I try to envisage a time ten years ago when I would have even been allowed to attend prom. *As long as you keep far away from any boys.* I can just hear the voice now. *Remember your reputation. And ours.*

My baggy jeans, complete with a wide leather belt. *What was I thinking?* There is a pain in my chest, physical or emotional, I'm not sure, but it's there all the same and makes me gasp at the suddenness of it. I won't look at the scarring; it's hidden under swathes of bandages and to look at it would be to accept that I have been cut open. It's a concept that doesn't sit easily with me. I hide the idea under the wraps of thoughts and memories in my mind. It occurs to me all at once that my brother has not made contact to check how I am. *My brother.* The effect of the hospital medication is playing tricks on my mind; once again I am reminded of how I had always longed for a brother as a child, rather than my sister Raim. It has its benefits though, this medication. I can barely remember Raim's face, or the reasons for my apathy towards her. She is merely a dark shadow lingering in the corners of my mind at this point. Perhaps that's what happens after serious surgery. Mum has told me that Raim would come round soon to see me. I don't care. To shake my emerging guilt away, I let the wardrobe doors clip shut and spend the next hour seeking out further historical delights from my childhood room. Shelves containing folders of GCSE and A-level coursework, novels, Enid Blyton stories from the 70s. Smuggled-in Judy Blume books, no doubt hidden from my father, perhaps my mother too. A dilapidated version of the Koran, well-read over the years. *Quran.* My room, a space littered with muted colours; beiges, greens, a landscape of wasted things. My eyes trip upon an upright black and white object, a keyboard. Grabbing it with one hand, I dust it down with the sleeve of my hoodie and turn it on. Instinctively my hands run over the keys, and I find myself playing a melody I'm barely aware of, a lump forming in my throat. There is a sudden thump at the door; *mum*, her steely knuckles, her thick ankles, I can sense the weight of her boxy, rotund body against the wood.

"Yalina, can I come in? What were you playing just then?" The door opens without consent. "Lil?"

She is wringing her hands in a kind of pathetic, waiting-for-a-reaction kind of way.

I say *"Yes?"* almost rudely, and look down at the floor.

"It's great to hear you playing that keyboard, love. I'm sure Dad bought that for you when you were around ten years old. You never did show much interest in it."

"Great," I respond. It wasn't meant to sound quite so sarcastic. I can see the expression on my mother's face suddenly drop and mould itself into something else.

"Sod you, then!" she growls as I'm left with the slam of the door reverberating in my head. I hear her mutter something about my father. I exhale and let my body slide down on the bed, my single bed. It was used for years since about the age of twelve. There is a space on the other side of my room where there had been another single bed, the grooves in the greeny carpet are testament to this. I realise that my sister must have shared this room with me at some point. True, she is my elder by six years, so perhaps would have moved out of the family home years before I was ready to do similar, yet I don't recall a time when her body would have flounced into the space of the corner of the room upon her mattress, perhaps stroppily, perhaps laughing. I wonder who her friends might have been. Were they my friends too? Did my father obsess too about menfolk going near her? There is nothing entering my mind, no fizzles of remembrance, no words halting on my tongue. Maybe you just forget the everyday stuff.

***

Raim is an ordinary-looking kind of a sister. I don't know what I was expecting. Maybe someone less...*matronly*. She is bold in a very straight-to-the-point kind of a way.

"Are you taking your tablets?" Her first greeting to me is an accusatory one.

I nod. I notice that even the clothes she is wearing look like a nurse's. I should know, I've seen enough over the past few days. Blue, shapeless dress. She always did want to be a doctor. Even her headscarf looks like she is some form of medical staff.

"Why are you looking at me like that?" she queries.

I pull a I-don't-know type of expression, hoping she will understand my face so I won't have to speak.

She takes a step closer to me. She may as well be holding a magnifying glass up to my face or asking me to stick out my tongue and say "Aaaaaaaaaah."

"Why are you mute?"

I laugh unexpectedly; the word *mute* makes my mind conjure up visions of a clown with a white painted face, a black tear embossed on his cheek.

"I'm not. It hurts to talk." It's a lie.

Raim frowns. "Well, it shouldn't. Surgery wasn't oral."

This again makes me laugh, sordidly, but my chest hurts more than the laughter was worth. I grab at my padded wound with my left hand. I can almost feel the stitches being pulled taut. She *thinks* she's a doctor, but she isn't. *Mum* and *Dad*'s dream.

"Easy, easy. Don't laugh so hard," says my sister. "And don't wrench the scar!" She finally sits on the chair next to my bed, and I feel slightly less like a bug under a microscope.

"So, what are you thinking?" asks Raim.

I'm not sure how to respond.

"Will you return to your normal job after all this?"

I can hear clogs turning in my head. *My normal job*.

"Probably."

12

"You not so sure?"

Damn right, I'm not so sure.

She glances around my jaded bedroom. I can see a smirk forming on her thin cat-like lips.

"What?" I ask. She's pissing me off.

"Decided to have an ickle play on the ol' keyboard? What have you been playing?"

I stare at the door, wishing her away.

"Play me a little tune," she says, staring at me.

I shake my head no.

"Go on."

"Nah, it's not great for me to sit up so straight."

She nods whole-heartedly in agreement.

I think of asking her about my friends, but I don't want to give her the opportunity to feel superior to me.

My sister closes the door behind her so quietly that I can barely hear it click shut.

Chapter Two

Yalina

June 2007
Harrow, Middlesex

It comes as no real surprise to me. His name is Ali. I found him on social media and he's been talking back and forth with me. I haven't even bothered to argue with *Mum and Dad* about why he hasn't been in touch; they aren't at all open to talking about anything. My heart lurched as I realised that I had been right ever since my operation, that I was closer to my brother than anyone else. He lives in South Yorkshire; Sheffield. It makes me think of a vast expanse of factories; grey and steely, churning the skies up with its smog and dust and debris. I've made obligatory jokes about the cutlery factories up there; does he buy a lot of steel goods? He's been replying *yes*, humouring me. An all-encompassing weight has lifted from my chest, where my insides were so compressed, so heavy. Damaged.

He explains that Mum and Dad *have it in for him*, something about money they lent him not being returned. I find, to my surprise, that I immediately have his back. He explains that they are not the sort of parents anyone wants. I believe him. My own memories are so patchy they are simply unreliable. He tells me that he has been looking after a piano for me, after I tell him that Mum and Dad have left me with only a tiny, shitty keyboard and none of my music books. He states *that's Mum for you,* and I am warm with relief that I have found someone else on this damned planet who understands me, recognises what I'm going through. Warm is an understatement. Correction: *Elated.* We arrange to meet up; his work commitments mean he can't possibly get time off in the next six weeks, but I am impatient. I book the train ticket online for the day after tomorrow. He'll collect me from Sheffield station. The pains in my chest seem to be exacerbated by my sudden excitement, but I try to quiet the complaining from inside. I've been asleep the other two times my sister has come to visit me. Well, asleep as far as my eyes being closed and my ears not hearing the words of a stranger being sprinkled over me like wasted confetti. I've been resting for thirteen weeks. You would think that would be enough. Thirteen weeks of kicking around in this bedroom; this house, with two people I feel no attachment to, despite their continuous checking on me and delivering meals to my room on a tray with their painted-on smiles. Of course I will not tell them that I am about to visit Ali. They have done their bit for me. They agreed to have me cut open, and they've done their best to ensure I am repaired and renewed. Three months on and I still have only foggy memories of signing the consent forms in the hospital to declare enthusiastically *yes, I'd like my ribs broken and reset,* and apparently it is normal to not remember such things. It's due to the anaesthetic beginning its planned journey through the weaves of your veins, contaminating you ruthlessly with its sleepiness. The gift of unconsciousness.

The ticket in its envelope arrives with a plop on the *welcome* mat. My mother catches sight of it first and covers the ground up the flight of stairs in less time than it would take a dog sniffing out a hare. I know she is on Dad's orders.

"For you," she states as she once again enters my room without knocking. I struggle up to my feet and almost snatch the letter from her heavily-hennaed fingers. I notice she is jittering slightly. Her owl-like head tilts to one side as she waits for me to open the envelope, her eyes and jutting nose peering out from her hijab.

"I'm not opening anything in front of you." It is a statement;

not up for negotiation.

I see her eyes brim with tears and look away. *Why are mothers so bloody emotional?* As she reluctantly leaves my room, I stash the train ticket, my unearthed secret, into the middle drawer of my dresser. Tomorrow I will begin my new life. Tomorrow will be the start of new things. I will be investing in my next fifty or so years by rebranding my life.

Thursday seems like it is taking an age to arrive. I am aching to leave. Ali will meet me at the station at 7:10pm. I am packing as much as I can into the suitcase I discovered on the top shelf of the wardrobe. It smells new, of vacuumed cars, rented automobiles on holidays. Folding my clothes into neat piles, I am struck by just how small my clothes are once organised. Diminutive, even. They whisper to me *you barely exist.* I cram a bottle of shampoo, conditioner, phone charger and some make-up into the washbag I used in the hospital. The drugs given to me spill out onto the bathroom work surface. Just seeing them again makes me feel a wave of nausea. I have been throwing the letters away from the hospital. I don't need a check-up. This is because I am healing. I'll be healing even more from Thursday.

Chapter Three

Yalina

June 2007
Harrow Station, Middlesex

I've said I'm going to see a friend from university for a couple of weeks. *Mum* tried to make me stay, but her words were jumping from her mouth and over my head. I expect she'll discover the torn up letters from the hospital in my bedroom bin, too. Let her. I know she won't even have told her husband, not yet.

The thought of seeing my brother is what is keeping the butterflies dancing in my stomach and giving my hands the slight shakes as I haul my miniature suitcase up into the luggage compartment of the carriage. He says we lost touch when I went to uni. I was rubbish at writing to him, he was slack in calling me and getting sick of my friends not passing on his messages. I can hear the melancholy in his voice when he talks of our parents not wanting to know him when he couldn't repay their money. My stomach twists at this part. I am sure, when I am a parent, that I will not let money issues keep me from my children. The wistful tone to his voice makes me dislike them further, the woman and that man. There's something about them that doesn't sit well with me. Particularly the man, and the hold on his wife.

My head is pressed against the grimy window, my feet tucked under the seat I sit on, and I have a temporary panic as the train flies through the fields of Hertfordshire. *What if he isn't what I've made him out to be? What if Raim had been warning me of leaving home too soon?* I realise these thoughts are natural and allow myself to relax a little, my head lolling with the speed of the train. A tall man, with glasses and a tablet device, sits opposite me, and I find that I'm trying to make myself smaller. He flips open the lid of his tablet and begins typing. What if he is writing something about me? Perhaps his webcam is filming me. He catches me looking at him and I hurriedly look away, out the window at nothing, just green and grey blurring before my eyes. I can hear the *tap, tap, tap* of his keyboard and I slowly glance back again. Would I know if I had ever seen this person before? I look at the twitch of his mouth, the indentation lines from his nose down to the corners of his lips. Laughter lines. It is difficult to imagine the man laughing. I squint, try to get a look at his eyes. Grey-ish. Perhaps grey-greeny. It's hard to tell with the thick-lensed glasses he's wearing, and the jig-jig of the carriage as it hits a particularly turbulent point on the rails. I glance around at the other people on the train; a woman and a young child; the woman probably mid-thirties, the child of six or seven. There is a group of men in their forties, probably, each sporting a red nylon football top and holding a can of lager. *Liverpool?* One of them is roaring with laughter about something his mate has said; I don't care to listen to their conversation, and instead zone out into my own empty brain. Something is bugging me about these people...or is it my reaction to these people? I feel as neutral about this slice of society as I do about my own family. *How is someone supposed to feel?* With a weighted heart, I realise the problem may be with me. I have left my family to go and find someone who I can't even recall properly in my head. I destroy this debilitating thought by noting that at least there is the warm, glowy feeling inside me when I think of my brother. I know he has been a friend to me in the past. My sister, though? I fail to recall anything solid. It's like reaching your hand out into a cloud of bubbles just to feel your hand swiping through, not being able to grasp a thing.

The train creaks to a halt, and I'm already here in Sheffield. I wish the journey could have taken just a little longer. As I step off the carriage, blocked by a pushchair and an irate mother, I can feel eyes on me and I am weighed down by a sudden feeling of self-consciousness. I have not given a thought to my own appearance over the past few weeks and a streak of embarrassment shoots right through my limbs as I consider the idea that my brother will be disappointed. I head towards a pasty shop and queue up behind the dawdling line of commuters, waiting to be fed. In my purse there is only a five-pound note and a few paltry coins, and I feel my heart sink as I regret not taking the hundred pounds Dad had left on the table for me. He said I would be back at work by mid-June, but he was wrong about that. Cleaning out animal cages for minimum wage? My toes curl as I think of the things that used to please me; small pets, mammals, taking other people's dogs for walks. I would rather lie in my bed. Mum, when she thought I couldn't hear a thing, had been whispering the taboo word *depression* into Dad's ear. *She's depressed, Mo.* These words would be met with silence, perhaps a shrug of his shoulders, or a disagreeable shake of the head. *She sees nobody, Mo. There are no friends any more. She needs to be seen.*

I find myself at the front of the queue and am flustered trying to gather up my coins, the whisper of my mother's words curling their way around my ears, like serpents waiting to suffocate me. I feel the eyes of the impatient queue boring into me and the heat rises to my cheeks and my chest, prickling me.

She needs to be seen.

Eventually I drop my fiver on to the desk and shuffle away as fast as I can.

"Madam! Your change!"

The voice repeats itself but I am running, dragging my suitcase at my side, ignoring all eyes on me, eyes boring a hole into the side of my body. I run as far as I can manage until I feel so bruised, so raw in my chest that I have to stop and look for a bench, anything where I can sit. Sit and hide.

An elderly lady rises from the bench I have stopped at, and I fling the suitcase to the floor, not caring that it has capsized and its wheels are spinning, turning. She mutters something under her breath as she leaves and I fix her with my best stare. As I sit, the heat is still pounding through the capillaries of my face, and the serpents are doing their best now to restrict my breathing. The oxygen I take for granted is failing me now, and I struggle to swallow down the air I need to breathe.

I hear a woman and her male friend discussing paper of some sort, and suddenly a white bag is thrusted under my chin, kind hands offering paper presents. "Breathe, love. Breathe into this."

The accent strikes me as something from a comedy act.

"That's it, love. Slowly. In. Out."

My chest is searing from the pain of trying to grab at air. The stitches are pulled tight, at their limit. I'm coming undone.

"Slowly! Slow down. In. Out."

I feel my breathing slow with the guidance of the strangers' words, and my shoulders drop. There is a small crowd standing around our bench, but as they catch my eye, they turn, and walk away. The woman next to me is patting my shoulder, throwing more Yorkshire words my way, but they are dropped into the dark pits of my mind; gathering with the unread thoughts, unread letters. She is proud of me. I did very well. Her male friend is nodding with enthusiasm. I offer her the paper bag back but she is laughing and pointing to a bin. I do not wish to stand up though. I do not want any weight upon my legs. I want to feel light-headed for as long as I can. My mind slips back to my newly purchased pasty and I realise it has long since hit the floor, a muddle of filthy looking pigeons gratefully pecking away at its body.

"Do you need to catch another train?"

It is the man speaking this time. I am struggling to regain my thoughts, my composure. I am aware of sweat making its trail down the sides of my face, fake tears. My back and my chest are sodden. Do I need to catch another train? It takes a few moments for me to remember why I am here.

"No. No, I'm meeting someone. Here."

It sounds like I'm making it up. The woman rises to her feet, and she grabs the man's hand, hoisting him up, offering him his walking stick which has been resting upon his scrawny bird legs. They bid me farewell and wish me all the best. I nod, say thanks for the help, and they are gone. My suitcase is still upside down where I dropped it but the wheels have ceased their spinning. I realise I have no idea how much time has passed; it feels like hours, but could equally be only two minutes. Pulling my phone out of my pocket, I realise I was meant to meet my brother five minutes ago, and I try to stand. My legs feel fizzy, sparkling water cooped up in a bottle, waiting to implode. My eyes reach the stand where I'm meant to be meeting him, the newspaper stand, bowing under the weight of the trees it is holding with its metallic skeleton hands. There is only a mother and her three children, browsing the magazines, the little girl fingering every page of a pink-coloured comic. The owner of the stand glances disapprovingly at the girl, at her mother who is paying no attention.

He's not there yet. I don't know if I'm worried or relieved. My phone lights up and I realise it has been buzzing. I just miss the call. When the number pings up on the screen I feel disappointment as I recognise my home phone number, and realise it is only one of my parents calling me. An envelope symbol appears in the corner of the screen. I feel no guilt in ignoring it, and put my phone away in my pocket. I do not need to hear that voice right now, its whispers and betrayals leaking venom into my ears.

It's been an hour. I am slumped upon another bench, this one less comfortable than the first, yet right under the gaze of the newspaper man. He looks as shifty as I must do. I have become obsessed with staring at my phone. I have called Ali twice now, only to hear it ring off. No answerphone. My head drops as I realise I have been stood up, tears pricking at my eyes. I am the biggest fool. My suitcase appears bigger than it was, bursting with my clothes, my hopes, my stupid, stupid ideas. I use the back of my hand to dispose of the tears which are streaking down my cheeks without permission, and I wonder what a mess I must look. My backside is numb from sitting. The clock over the turnstiles hits 8:30pm; I am grateful it is still light, and I stand to drag my suitcase towards the monitors informing when the next train back to London will be. As I clutch at the leather handle, I notice a man walking towards me, unshaven, tired looking. "*Alright?*"

I nod, but hesitantly. I don't know if this is Ali. This does not quite match the mottled patchwork visions of my brother, nor the image on his online account. This man's skin is too white. *People always stick up pictures of themselves from ten years ago.*

"Alright. Coming with me, then? Everything is cool."

I don't offer my hand, or any words. He has a coloured tattoo creeping up his neck from the collar of his t-shirt. I wish he'd say what his name was.

"My car is just out the front."

His smile shows me the many gaps between his ochre-hued teeth, but somehow he now looks softer. He leads me to his car, parked confidently on double-yellows just outside the main station entrance, and chats about my accent, laughing; *posh girl.* I think about swerving away from the man. Making a run for it. But clearly he is here for me; we arranged it.

I wonder about his own accent, it doesn't sound like those that had been surrounding me like an echo at the station. *Of course not, he is a fellow southerner like me.* His car smells of too-strong air freshener when I get in, and the filth of the car makes me hold my breath for as long as I can muster.

"So it's not much of a drive from here."

He drags out the vowel sound in *here* and I see him wink in the mirror at me. Is he taking the piss out of me?

Before he starts the engine, he grabs for a lighter from the little well of coins and parking tickets, and lights up a cigarette, only opening his window a fraction. I try not to cough, but my throat involuntarily splutters out whatever chemicals it has taken in.

"Not a fan of the smoking, then?"

He is laughing, humouring me.

I get in his car and we are zig-zagging through the traffic, switching from lane to lane, in a fight to get away.

Glancing at the phone in my hand, I see there is a message flashing in the top left corner. It's been there for fifteen minutes, according to the time it was sent. I don't have a code to enter into the phone; it's quicker to get to stuff that way. I click on the message, hands sweaty.

"Lil, sorry, it's me. Something's gone wrong with the car. Are you ok to wait an hour? Apologies. Al. x"

The sweatiness in my hands has spread to the rest of my body, and my feet are pounding, marching in the footwell of the passenger seat. The man doesn't look at me, but I can tell he senses my fear.

Chapter Four

Yalina

June 2007
Somewhere near Sheffield

I wake up from broken sleep and feel shooting pains in my neck, my chest, and a mouthful of my own hair has twisted its way around my dry tongue. A glance to my right tells me that he has pulled over, in a layby of sorts. I don't know whether to speak to him or not, so I refrain. I consider the dream I just seemingly fought my way through; its shards of light and blisters of water still muddying the haze of my sight. There is a cat, long and sleek, its hair like that of a fox from the countryside, not a city fox; dirty, bedraggled, eager to steal. This cat knows things, it approaches me with its fuzzy brush tail and beseeching eyes and I rise to follow it. I believe it to be a she. As I tread her path, I notice the air beneath my feet and the calm realisation that I am floating, not high in the air, but a few inches off the ground. The cat turns every now and then to ensure that I am behind, and I smile. Eventually the path leads to the edge of a darkened forest, where the cat's pace picks up and she nips at my jeans with her mouth. To begin with, I cannot make anything out. Ashes, beeches, an oak. In a small clearing between the trees there is a woman. She looks down at the ground as if she cannot sense our treading on twigs and leaves which make such an obvious sound. Her face is smeared with dirt that must be days old, her clothes muddied with whatever she has been lying on in the forest. They look like they may have been brightly patterned, African clothes. When I look around

I see that the animal has vanished. I glance back to the woman, scared at first to speak to her. *My baby,* she is saying. *My baby has gone.* I hold my arms out to her as I crouch down on the forest floor, but she doesn't see me. My feet are warm, and I see I have crouched in what looks like a pool of blood; I notice her legs, her body, are bloody below the waist. Her eyes meet mine for the first time. *Give me my baby back* she mouths at me. There is no voice. My eyes search desperately for the cat, finding nothing. The woman is staring at something on the ground, and I see her hand is clutching at a bloodied rope. My eyes follow the rope to where it is attached on the ground, my eyes close as I feel myself falling, my legs giving way under me. I grab for my ribs, protecting them as I inevitably hit the ground, gnarled tree roots, with a force I wasn't expecting. When I look up again, towards the woman, I can see bruising around her eyes, more bruises peeking out from the top of her shirt, a landscape of purples, greens and blues. She is turning and walking away, flicking at her shirt as if attempting to be rid of me. The cord and the puddle it is attached to remain on the ground, a mass of darkness.

I force myself to stare at the road ahead as the man puts away his phone and pulls out of the layby. Whatever was going on in my mind a minute ago is lost, locked away.

"Spaced out, huh?" says my driver. I don't know how to respond, so I simply raise my eyebrows. He doesn't seem too put out by my lack of speech, and as I continue to gaze out of the mud-speckled window I notice that darkness is falling slowly. A fear in my stomach threatens to rise up my throat and scream *Where are we going?* but I silence this voice of sensibility.

Grasping at a brief moment of bravery, I find myself asking, "Where is Ali?" There are moments of silence where I can hear only the gears shifting as we hurtle around the countryside lanes, my body pulled left, then right.

The man doesn't answer. I am wondering if Ali has sent him to collect me.

I am too cautious to let myself fall asleep again, lest I miss where we are supposed to be ending up. A quick glance at my phone tells me it's nearly 9:30pm, and there is another envelope symbol flashing again in the corner of the screen. I can tell from my missed calls notifications that it is either my mother or father who has been trying to call me.

"So we nearly there?" I hear my voice testing, my fingers gripping at my seatbelt. I am wondering, manically, whether to open the door and jump.

"Yup," says the man, and within seconds he has turned off the beaten track we are driving on, onto a crunchy driveway with what appears to be farm buildings to each side; it's difficult to tell in the almost-dark. He brakes with a sudden force and immediately he's out of the car, his door slamming, and mine thrown open. His hand is gripped around my arm and I am being pulled along.

I try to kick out at him, to break his grip on me. My legs are weak and shaky, and I miss my target.

The man doesn't flinch at my attempt to break free. His teeth are glinting at me in the fading light as he is dragging me into what looks like an animal barn. I am still flailing, arms trying to swing like pendulums in order to escape, but his grip is iron-strong.

My suitcase is in his hands, my only possession, and as I look up I see the man empty the contents on to the barn floor, grabbing at my laptop and headphones, my leather jacket. He already snatched my phone when we pulled up in his car. He folds my items under his arm and marches out of the barn door, closing it abruptly behind him. The lock rattles the whole of the wooden structure. I hear the engine of his car fire up, the sound of the stones of the road as he reverses and disappears. I stare at the door for what feels like hours, my mind whirring, my heart beating in my ears. There are stars spinning in front of my eyes, Catherine Wheels.

"The door is not going to open, no matter how long you stare at it," breathes a voice in my ear. A female voice. I don't even turn my head. My muscles are locked.

"Such clean, pretty hair!" the voice continues. "You are so

clean!"

My eyes shift sideways to catch the profile of the girl speaking to me.

"You're scared. I get it. We all scared at beginning."

The girl looks younger than me; eighteen or nineteen years old. She has sallow skin and a putrid smell to her breath. Her clothes, sparse, look as though she hasn't washed in a while. Still, I can find no words, and the draft that envelopes us makes me aware of my silence.

The girl continues. "It's the not knowing, that drives you... you know..." She eventually finds the word. "Insane." She seems very satisfied at her ability to pluck the word from the air, and she rests her right hand on my arm, over familiarly.

"I'm Petrova," she announces, seemingly not bothered about our one-way conversation. "They brought me here two nights ago. I've seen a lot of work at the car-wash. That was up near Donnie though. The beds there were so bad."

I wince with the cold that is circling my legs, notice the eastern-European accent which encases the words dropping from her mouth.

"What were you promised?"

Moments pass before I realise she has asked me a question, and is anticipating a response.

I clear my throat as my eyes assess the contents of my belongings, strewn across the barn floor, a dingy lightbulb casting its hue over what is left of my worldly belongings.

"My brother," I croak.

The girl sits back on her haunches, and I feel her assessing me, looking over me.

"I do not know whether to laugh at that," she finally comments.

I am overcome with the sudden urge to cry. I feel a lump threatening in my throat, and I swallow it down like a reluctant pill.

"Do you know Ali?" I finally ask.

The girl is standing now, poking at my remaining clothes on the floor with the toe of her trainer.

"Hey, do you mind?" I hear myself saying. "Those are

mine!"

Petrova looks up. She goes back to eyeing my black, now crumpled denim jacket on the floor.

"You'll learn that we do share everything after a while," she voices, almost sadly. I think that she is going to burst into tears, but she doesn't, instead, does a strange kind of waltz to the furthest corner of the barn, where the dim light fails to reach. She motions with her hand for me to come over, but I don't.

"You do not want to see where we sleep," she queries, although it appears to be a statement.

I shake my head, feeling my own tears breaking their way down my cheeks. Petrova notices and suddenly her arm is around me.

"It is not so bad," she breathes into my ear. "We are happy we have work, no?"

The sheer desperation of the girl's statement gets to me in such a way that I let the tears of fury mark their way down my face.

In the corner of the barn by the door I was forced through, a solitary mouse momentarily looks up at the lightbulb, frozen, then blinks at me before disappearing, its freedom there for the taking.

When I open my eyes I realise it is morning, and I find myself curled up, shivering on a filthy mattress next to the girl's sleeping body. Although it is June, the cool air serves as a reminder that I am not at home in my safe room. I am somewhere that scares me. My dry mouth is like cardboard, and I pull myself up to a seating position where my eyes can scour the barn for anything I can drink. There is only a transparent bottle of some purple-ish drink near the girl's head, so I kneel over and help myself, careful not to finish the whole bottle or to make a sound, or drip anything upon the girl. I remember from the night before that she had said her name was Petrova, yet the passport stashed by her shoes on the floor states the name of Lubna, born 1988. I pretend I have not been glancing at it as she twists in her sleep and opens her eyes, staring at me, her face bearing no expression.

"Morning," she mouths at me, with no sound.

"Morning," I say back, embarrassed that I clearly have stolen her drink, and am being caught red-handed. The girl doesn't seem to notice, or care. She sits up, glances at her passport on the floor and then back at me.

"So they call me Petrova for safety," she says, by way of explanation. "We don't use real names. He's taking this back off me tomorrow."

I sit back on my mattress, put the bottle on the floor. "Who's we?" I venture.

She gazes at me for a while, rubbing her eyes, then is straining her neck towards the tiny crack of light sneaking in from a slight slit in the barn's roof.

"Them. The people. The bosses. You know."

I don't know. I don't know what she is talking about, and my chilliness is replaced by a sudden searing heat that is travelling up my spine; panic.

"I'm here to meet my brother," I offer again, remembering that I had already mentioned him to the girl the night before. "Ali." Hearing my own words here make me suddenly feel more confident, makes it more real.

The girl's eyes narrow. "There is no Ali which I know of," she states in her perhaps-Polish accent. "Although we don't always know some of their names. The men at the carwash, they are Jonno and Keith."

I wonder if the man who dumped me here was one of them. I don't know why she has mentioned a carwash again. "The carwash?" I repeat.

She nods. "Where we worked before. In Donnie. Doncaster," she offers, by way of explanation again. "Me and others. But others have gone now. I don't know where."

A silence whips itself around our bodies, and I stand for the first time since I arrived here, noting the sounds of a cockerel outside, and sheep, perhaps in a field nearby.

"I think there has been some kind of mistake," I try telling her gently.

She tips her head towards me. "A mistake? You don't want

29

job?"

"That's right. I don't want job," I say, realising immediately that my mocking of her accent won't help the situation. If she is offended, she fails to show it. As I am standing, looking at her, I see that she is so tiny, so thin; jaded. I want to ask her age but for some reason I cannot find the courage.

"We all want job, no?" she queries. "Just not other stuff that comes with."

I sigh, try not to lose my patience. My skin feels dirty. I have been sweating all night and am now wearing a thin, sticky veil of dried perspiration. I pull my head covering over to touch my hairline.

"Is there a shower?" I ask, and am met with only a shake of the head.

"Why are we here?" I finally explode. "I don't understand what is going on? Why are we locked in here?"

But the girl is lying back down on her mattress, facing the wall, her hands twisting together.

"For the work," she offers, and then she is asleep.

Chapter Five

Yalina

June 2007
Somewhere near Sheffield

Petrova (she likes to stick to her newly given name) is Romanian. She doesn't want to talk about how she got here. Instead, she seems to enjoy reminiscing about my own childhood. We've been in this barn for two days now. I've counted two sun-ups and two dyings of the light. I could hardly call it a sunrise or a sunset, besides, there's very little to see from the tiny gap in the sides of the barn door; an apologetic slither of light forcing its way through. And an expanse of grey light hovering over a filthy plastic window grid in the dilapidated ceiling.

"Tell me again!" laughs my new acquaintance. She wants to hear about my upbringing in the countryside of Hampshire. I'm not sure why. We're rural enough where we are right now. It's a lie, anyway, the Hampshire thing.

"Say it!" She is like a child, her eyes wide and naive, despite what she has possibly been through.

I steel myself. "So, there's my mum and my dad, plus a brother and sister. We live in a large white detached house with a very large garden. We live next to a farm."

Petrova is almost squealing with delight; my sideways glance at her tells me she is sitting on her knees, almost in prayer, her hands clasped together.

"Do you think they'll come soon?" I query. She doesn't respond, instead remains gazing at me, waiting.

I clear my throat to continue. "And we have two dogs,

31

chocolate retrievers. They're brothers. We've had them since they were eight weeks old." I pause, knowing Petrova loves this part. She is still gazing straight at me, nodding furiously.

"And we rescued them as their mum couldn't feed them. We had to feed them ourselves with tiny newborn bottles and special puppy milk."

"Keep going!"

"Well my sister, she is called Marie, and my brother is called Henry. My mother is a librarian at the local school. My father is a doctor. We're all pretty much best friends. As a five-year-old I took up ballet at dance school in London; my mum would drive me up every Monday, Wednesday and Friday after school to attend. This worked out well for me as when I was sixteen I was accepted into the National Ballet."

This time I can barely face glancing her way. The story is bullshit, she must realise this. It's all I can do to keep myself sane.

I stand up from my wilting mattress on the floor and again attack the wafer biscuit packet with some force. "Is this seriously all there is to eat?"

Considering her frail limbs, and sucked-in cheeks, I don't wait to hear her answer, instead, suddenly choking back tears, I shriek, "What is this? Where the fuck are we? Why isn't anyone coming?"

Petrova rushes to my side, her filthy hand on my shoulder. I shake her off as best I can. I can feel the heat rushing through my veins, an anger impossible to describe. "Why are you just so accepting of this?" I cry. She stands back to look at me, her hand now limp at her side. "Why aren't you trying to get out? What's wrong with you?"

She pauses, then feebly offers me her wrist. There are purpley red marks, I can only assume where swathes of rope have fastened her in previous sittings. The feeling of shame dampens my anger and I try to reach out to her. She bats me away.

"I do try!" She is almost screaming. "But this is what happens!" She lifts her hair to expose a circle of black pain behind her ear. I can almost make out knuckle marks. It's an odd place to be hit. I can't stand to be here a minute longer and make a grab for the rake I can see lying in the darkest corner of the room. I charge at the slightly battered wooden doors. Nothing. No movement. I stand further back and try again, this time the force of my weight making the door gape a little and let a fraction more sunlight flow in through the crack. My hands are sore from the sudden gripping and forcing. I see Petrova standing in the centre of the barn, arms flat by her sides, her eyes watching me. She says nothing but is shaking her head from side to side, like a broken doll. I can feel rage creating itself from the pit of my stomach, gradually climbing up the walls of my body until I find myself lurching towards the doors for a third time. The wood bends and tears under the force, splintering, and finally giving way as my body falls forward, rake still gripped in my hands. The pain as I land on the ground, splintering through the torn door is like a heat, a ball of fire pressed against my skin. I see Petrova standing, staring, still not saying a word. Despite the obvious break in the still-padlocked doors, she doesn't move.

"Come on!" I shriek.

She is rooted to the spot. I stand, kicking the rake away and wipe myself down, tiny wooden splinters in my shoulders, my forearms, my knuckles.

I turn to see her staring at the gap between the broken door, mouth slightly open.

"Sod you then!" I begin to walk away from the barn. I realise I sound like my mother. Petrova's back is now turned; she's walking away to the rear area of the barn; our sleeping hole. *Institutionalised.* I curse the sun and its obvious glare on me as I pause to decide which way to walk. I need to get to the city. I should have done this at night. Memory tells me to turn right at the end of the stony driveway, and after tripping on brambles, I make my way onto the road. There is no traffic and no footpath either and I remind myself to walk towards the way the traffic would face me. Tiny palpitations of pain are searing into my limbs, my arms, the backs of my hands as I try to ignore the reminders of what I had to do to escape. I wonder what the bastard has done with my phone.

The sun is starting to lower slightly in the sky as I find myself spotting the city over the tops of vast hills of purple and white heather. God knows if we came this way originally. My feet throb from the walk, at least five miles so far by my weak skills of calculation, but I feel energised as I glimpse the steel city scattered under my feet, the gentle light of early evening softening the landscape. A quick frisk of my back pockets reveals a fiver and a couple of pound coins, and my heart drops as I realise I'll have to beg if I want to make it on a train home. *Home.* The place I rejected after my operation but would drop down to my knees to see again now. The faces of my *parents* flicker before my eyes, and the need to feel safe again overrides any feeling of particular warmth I have for them. I pick up my pace and ignore the soreness of my heels against the back of my worn-down leather shoes. Thoughts of Ali leap into my mind; he's probably been trying my phone, with little success. He must have turned up at the station that day, a little after I left there. Perhaps he would have left a note with someone, or an email address. He must think I'm a shit of a sister. Catching my eye is a silvery sign of metal at the side of the road bearing the words *Sheffield City Centre* and also *Train Station: 1 mile*, one below the other.

There is a flip of excitement in my otherwise-empty stomach and I realise that I am safe, that life will be normal again. The only thing to worry about is having to ask someone for money for the journey. I briefly think of calling Raim, but realise with shame that I do not know her phone number. I don't even know Ali's number. Well, perhaps the last three or four digits, but who is that going to help? A searing pain in my chest reminds me that I am meant to have been resting these past few days, complete bed rest. I haven't been showering so there's been no reason to look at the dressing that mottles the place near where my heart has been murmuring sadly. I continue to follow the footpath that travels down from the very outside of the city down a continuous hill. Houses and buildings of an infant school are beginning to build up around me now; corner shops and parks. I had never realised a city could be so green. Meersbrook Park. It's summer, there are people rolling up their sunbathing towels, packing up toys, kids running around in an attempt to evade going home. I see white children, white teenage girls, free to do as they please, and a stab of jealousy cuts me in half. I picture their relaxed white fathers at home, not pacing the floors wondering where their daughter is, and who she is no doubt flirting with. I try not to think of the city as a beautiful place, I need to concentrate on getting home. I pause outside one of the corner shops, considering whether to go in and buy a drink with the meagre change that I possess. I step through the single-width door; a man shoulders me as he's leaving, scratching at the Lotto card in his hand. "Careful!" he says at me, eyes peering up from the card he's holding.

"Ali!" He has the same glinting dark eyes as my brother on his Facebook profile.

The man shakes his head and laughs, the woman behind the till peering at me on tiptoes as I fumble around for my change. I feel the warmth of embarrassment enveloping my face and wait a few seconds by the door of the shop before leaving, lest the man who laughed at me is still lingering nearby.

The walk is further than I had anticipated, but I can feel the excitement twisted around the weariness in my being. I must have walked six, seven miles. The semi-conscious dream I had when I was in the stranger's car finds its way into my mind again, and I brush it quickly away. I don't need to be thinking about abandoned women in forests right now. I wonder if he had drugged me. This thought only lasts a fraction of a second as I realise I wasn't given anything to drink or eat. My mind creates a slither of pride at having escaped from this stranger who tried his luck with me at the station, immediately followed by a twinge of sadness at the world I had encountered for forty-eight hours. That girl, Lubna, according to her passport, must have been through an incomprehensible amount of hell to be too scared to leave. It occurs to me that I should contact the police once I am safe on my train. I should not leave her there, subject to whatever is coming her way. It is my responsibility to ensure she is safe. To protect a fellow woman. I duck my head as I take a shortcut through a gap in the railings of the train car park and pause as I'm made aware of a shadow looming over me, a hand forced brutishly over my mouth and another hand yanked tightly around the rest of my body. "Not this time, girlie!" exclaims an English-sounding voice. I gasp for air, and then there is only darkness.

Chapter Six

Yalina

August 2007
Somewhere near Sheffield

It's the soft singing voice which awakens me, and the warmth of the summer air that circles my feet as a door to the outside is opened. I'm used to the singing. She's waiting for me to rise so I can be an accompaniment to her melody. I sit up and smile at her, but I don't feel like playing right now. My wrists are sore from being manhandled two nights before, but I pull my sleeves over the areas of pain and try to think positively. Her voice is reaching the higher notes- almost straining. She's glancing at me from the table but I'm pretending to be interested in placing the sheets back on the bed carefully, smoothing them out with my hand. She reminds me of Petrova, but her voice is more meek, less confident. I'm pretty sure that Rebecca isn't her real name. She's pointing at the piano but I shake my head, stretching my arms over my head in a pointed way, trying to tell her it's too early. This house is generous in size and style. The floor-to-ceiling windows and broad fireplaces in every room tell of a wealthy family who perhaps hit hard times, or moved on to somewhere more grandiose. There are dirt marks on the walls, though, evidence of struggle, and no beds. Only mattresses. Well, there are beds, but they're for *performances*. We hate to use the performance beds. I'm lucky, my mattress has sheets. I asked for them as one of my favours. I don't think Rebecca cares about sheets. She will when it's winter. I sit up at the table with her and we share the toast she has buttered. She has weals of purple marks up her right arm. I don't ask about them. Nobody asks about anyone's marks or bruises. We scan through the newspaper which has been left on the table. Nothing of real interest. Sometimes I think I will read about my parents, hunting me down. But I am a twenty-four-year-old woman. They will have thought I simply walked out. I sometimes wonder if there will be anything about Ali, about his hunt for a sister.

I can't stop myself from thinking about him at times. I fantasise that he will break down the door to this Yorkshire house, police flanking his sides. They will be armed, and they will take Jonno and Keith from their rooms on the top floor. It will be a 5am raid, and us girls will stare at each other, not sure what to do, not knowing whether to rejoice yet.

There is a cat that makes her way into the house most days. She's a gingery coloured thing, with white patches and white paws. We call her Luna. Rebecca is the most enamoured with her, patting her lap until the animal steps on to her tiny thighs and makes a temporary home there. I'm not that bothered about making friends with Luna, I'm not sure why. Perhaps I'm sick of being touched. I used to look after cats all the time. It was a job that involved rehoming the animals, mostly, but of course I would get overly attached and be most reluctant to let the families through the door to take a look at what we were giving away. It wasn't just cats either; there were tortoises, rabbits, dogs, guinea pigs, everything. My job was to care for them and introduce the families, as well as checking out the potential families' homes. More often than not, I would find fault with many of these abodes. Too small, too close to a busy road, or small children present who would manhandle the animal in question. After a while I was relegated to just looking after the animals. Suited me fine. I was getting in the way of the animals being adopted, they said.

Eventually I give in to Rebecca's nagging, and I am up at the piano, the music papers curling with age in their rack, my eyes devouring the notes. I start with the D sharp chord, then work my way through the notes on the page. They are starting to come more quickly these days. The music I am playing are the songs of Gloria Estefan, 90s *phenomenon*. This is the only music book there is in the house. It doesn't stop me. I'm interested in any music I can create in this place. I feel a slight grudge at Rebecca sitting so close to me and squashing my hip on the stool made-for-one, but I say nothing. Her voice is becoming more shrill with each note. Sometimes I wish for her to stop, to let my hands do all of the work. But I continue to play and nod along with her voice. She turns the pages before I am ready, and I let her.

The work that brings us favours is not work. It is a period of time where we focus on something on the wallpaper, or the ceiling, or the tiny fly caught in a spider's web up there in the corner of the room, just above the curtain rail. If you learn not to fight, if you learn to breathe calmly, and make the right noises, it will be over far sooner. You can take the time to learn a lot about a person's hair colour, if you so wish. You can learn that body hair can take many different shades, so different from the hair on the head or the stubble on the chin. The stubble. Out of all of the parts of the process I object to, it is the scrape-scraping of the stubble on your face. Well, that, followed closely by the bad breath. Old smoke. The best part of this old house is the sound-proofing. I don't know if it's intentional. One of the girls went upstairs with Jonno and the group of men that came round, and I've heard barely a thing since. Jonno and Keith are very careful about who they let through the door, and at what time of day. The men don't come around 'til after 9:30pm. The darkness has to arrive first. Even in this rural location, with nothing but the fields of burnt yellow and brown as our neighbours, and the relentless sun as our witness, you can never be too careful. The men often arrive wearing hoodies, despite the temperatures. We rarely see faces. Until the act, or the *performance*. Then we try our best not to see. It's agreed between us in an unspoken vow, between us girls. You hear thuds, the odd voice. It's the silent parts that create a knot in your stomach, and make your hands shake. The minutes between the thuds seem to last forever. When it's happening to you it can seem like it lasts an eternity. I don't know what is worse, the pain of that, or guessing what can be happening to another girl in the next room.

***

Abruptly, the doorbell rings; a shrill, screechy sound that makes each of us jump. The doorbell never rings. Punters are encouraged to knock at the back door when they arrive. Voices are stirring upstairs, the shower turns off, I hear heavy feet on the landing. It is surprising how quickly a bright mood can be pulled down at speed to an empty place within you. The music sheets are put deftly away behind the piano lid, and Rebecca slides silently off the stool and back to the table. I don't follow for a few moments. I want to stand my ground, but Rebecca squeals at me as a warning, so I walk, slowly, to the table, to appease her. As we hear Keith close the front door to the visitor, I see each of the girls, who are sitting in this room, shrink into themselves. They keep their eyes lowered, but I don't. It's the waiting that's the worst part for them.

I like to stare the men out.

Someone had left their jacket at the nail bar. Keith comes away from the front door, aforementioned jacket slung over his arm. He is pacing the room. I notice the beautiful shafts of light streaming through the huge windows. It makes me picture old religious paintings, with disciples staring at the holy trinity, skyward. I refuse to meet his eye. Keith knows it cannot have been me; I have yet to work a day at that place. He walks towards a girl from upstairs who is perched upon the old sofa, shakes her hard by the shoulders, her head lolling back and forth; a ragdoll.

"Leave her alone!" The scream of my voice is ringing in

my head, the sting of heat that bounces off my right cheek brand new, smouldering. You would think that each time it would burn a little less, but it doesn't. It doesn't deter me, either.

"Keep out of this!" Keith is snarling, the veins in his cerise neck prominent. I wonder what the mess would be like if those veins burst.

Rebecca and I glance at each other, unsure of what happens next. She's rubbing her neck. We don't know who it was, who would take a jacket with them in the chilly early morning only to lug it back with them in the heat of the evening. I wonder if it was the new girl on the middle floor, the young one with the auburn hair and red polka dot top and red trousers. No. She hasn't even started work at the nail bar yet, either. Still, I motion with my finger and point up towards the ceiling. Keith glances up where I point, despite not being able to see through the plaster above. He is already stomping towards the staircase.

"Her?" he grunts. He probably doesn't know her name. We don't need names here, not really.

I feel guilt drop like a heavy load into my stomach as Keith paces up the stairs two at a time and bursts through a door which hits the wall. I avoid the look that Rebecca is giving me. We cover our ears and we can't hear. The girl comes downstairs an hour later. Jonno is down too, cheerily whistling after ending a phone call. It was *just another worker* from the ring who brought the coat to the door. Not a shop owner or a customer. Our address is still secret. Too late for the girl, though. Her hair hangs over her right eye, barely concealing the darkness that surrounds it. When I ask her name, she just shrugs, lets her hair flop down back over her eye after showing another girl down here. Maybe she knows I got her into trouble. There are no apologies. Jonno just asks if she wants any bread before the men come round. He doesn't tend to ask if we want food. She doesn't respond. He doesn't realise she is ignoring him. He thinks she speaks no English. Luckily for her, she probably doesn't realise the implication of *before the men come round.* She will later.

Chapter Seven

Richard

February 2006
Islington, London

I did try, I know that. Perhaps he knew that his father wasn't cut out for it. (*Parenting*: A verb. A verb is *a doing word*. I guess I didn't do too much do-ing.) Of course his mother was born to be a parent, right from the word go. She didn't hesitate in rushing to pick him up from his cot in the depth of the night, rubbing the back of his sweet fuzzy little head into her shoulder. It would probably have been hours until I realised he had been crying, finding his little hands clawing at me from the centre of our super king size bed. Suzie had been determined to get this bed, right before our son's birth. She had claimed we would need it when the *baby wouldn't sleep*. And she had been right. I would wake most nights to find the child sitting up, 4:16am according to our flashing digital alarm clock, with strands of my hair wrapped around his damp little fingers. Suzie would find it endearing, and smile at the boy, almost encouraging him to tug harder on my hair. The child could do no wrong. And it's fair to say, he never did. Our divorce came through in a matter of weeks, and at thirteen years old, it didn't seem to have affected him too much. He was a strong boy; kind, generous, and not given to episodes of emotional drama. I didn't miss watching the football. The parents' evenings were far more interesting to me, a Classics and Ancient History don who gained his undergraduate degree in the aforementioned subjects at Oxford, no less. I'm not meaning to boast, but I just wanted to set the scene. Our son, you see, was an academic genius.

We first noticed the snippets of genius from when he could speak, and how he didn't seem too enamoured with the ordinary age-appropriate toys we would provide for him. Cuddly toys? Nope. A miniature kitchen where he could pretend to bake and fry to his heart's content? No. He did love the building blocks, though, and would create the most ludicrous towers; seventeen, eighteen blocks high. Once the final block had been placed with extreme care at the top of the tower he would glance at us and squeal with delight as his right arm would swing round from nowhere and smash the building to the floor. My wife called it normal. I thought it was slightly sadistic. At eight years old he could tell us the positioning of every planet in the solar system, not to mention the size and weight of each of these planets. If we were to zone out of any of his detailed lectures on the planets or indeed their sizes or weights, he would grab whoever's jaw it was who wasn't listening and pull it round to his direction. "Listen! Or you won't learn!" he would scream. Occasionally I would wonder if it would be appropriate to do the same thing to him when he was refusing to eat, or get in the bath.

After the divorce I found myself a one-bed flat to inhabit; my wife, naturally keeping the three bedroom apartment on Litmus Drive. Islington isn't the cheapest place to live, granted, but I had enough money left over from the child maintenance and mortgage payments to Suzie to make sure I had a roof over my head in a road not too far from my young son and daughter. Did I mention we have a daughter too? Zoe. The light of my life, a younger sister for George. I suppose I had always felt sorry for Zoe. It's never easy to live your life in the shadow of your older sibling, much less if that sibling was praised and hurrahed by all who met him from nearly the moment of his birth. Zoe's a good kid. Amiable, malleable, easy to do. What you see is what you get. I would look forward to Saturday mornings, ringing on the doorbell of the apartment that I paid for, and didn't live in. Suzie answering the door, always flustered, seemingly angry at my two or three minutes of tardiness.

"Why can't you ever be on time?" she would moan,

cheeks mottled red, lipstick newly applied.

George would be standing behind her, a shadow, his eyes glowering at me. They were a pair of angry receptionists at the door.

It would take only a minute or two for Zoe to appear, all smiles, her arms reaching out for me. "Daddy!"

I believe if it were not for my little girl and her exuberance at seeing her father, I may have dropped out of the weekend visits completely. She had these long, dark curly eyelashes that got to me. "They're like a giraffe's!" I would exclaim, knowing this would have her in fits of giggles, and thus adding to my feeling of popularity on the doorstep. A kind of *See, someone likes me* protest at my ex-wife and son who would still be standing, gawping. Another of Zoe's favourites from me was my "I'm going to squeeze the pips out of you!" as I wrapped my arms around her, mockingly too tight. This would also be met with a roll of the eyes, by either Suzie or the mini replica human now standing beside her.

Most of these weekends would be spent with both George and Zoe trailing round either London Zoo or the local park; Zoe swinging around every pole or swinging sign she would come across, George engrossed in whatever book he was reading. Neither of them would really converse with me. With George, I didn't know if it was his newly teenage status, or the fact he found me dull, or that his mind was simply on another level. The teachers would claim that he was a world apart from the other children in the class. I would participate in our father-son relationship every other weekend, don't forget Wednesday evenings too, with a round of dominoes (*Dad - you can't even stack dominoes without getting it wrong*) or a half-hearted game of Scrabble. Zoe would be there, sticking up for my mistakes, my misgivings. When it was time to drop the kids back to the ex-wife, the door couldn't be swung open quickly enough, the accusatory questions firing at me like hot bolts of ammunition.

Chapter Eight

Yalina

Mid-October 2007
Somewhere near Sheffield

It's so strange how the music makes me relax, especially when the men are out of the house. I love the late afternoons. I don't know what I'd do without this piano. There can be voices shouting in the background, a girl crying somewhere upstairs, and I can't hear it. I don't recognise the person I've become. Perhaps I have matured all these weeks I've been held captive. All I know is that the music is what helps me to get by. Only tried escaping the once, after getting caught at the station. They don't believe in sending people to hospital to get mended here, so my ribs had to fix themselves. I will escape again. It's just a matter of time. Rebecca's eyes close in a slightly amusing manner as I play Gloria Estefan's *I Can't Stay Away From You* on the jaded and clunky piano. It can't have been tuned in years. I tell Rebecca that I am going to ask Jonno or Keith to get it tuned for me, but she looks at me, aghast.

"You serious?"

"Yeah. As one of my favours."

She rolls her eyes, and I'm immediately pissed off. "You're crazy. They're not going to pay for you to have a favour, you know." She is toying with the music paper, curling and recurling the corner of it. I don't need the music for these songs any more, I know them by heart. I feel a stab of annoyance that she is so willing to yield to the men.

"Well, I do enough for them."

Rebecca stands up from the piano, tries to push the stool away but my weight is making it remain held to the ground.

"You know they never like us to ask for much. You'd be asking for trouble."

I know she is right, but I hold her gaze, steadfast. I just don't care. "The least I can ask for is some bloody new music then."

She has hoisted her legs over the stool in order to leave, is making her way across the living room. "Is there anything to eat?" she ventures.

"Is there ever?" My voice sounds tired, bored. I notice there is a stain of red showing from the underside of Rebecca's skirt.

She must feel me looking at her, as she turns and stares at me. "What?"

I know she wants to tell me something.

She drops her eyes to the floor. "They're making me work at the nail bar. From tomorrow." Her last couple of words drop off so quietly, I can barely hear her. But I grasped the rest of what she said, and my face feels drained of all its colour.

"No?" I say, my tone flat; pathetic. I don't know what else to say.

"It was going to happen, sooner or later. We both know that."

I stand to put my arm around her, but she pulls away. Really, I am knocking away the anger that is trying to consume me.

"I thought they made out that we were safe from all of that." My voice is unconvincing.

"Yeah, well, they never said that *exactly*."

I realise I am thinking selfishly. I am imagining myself in this big house during the daytime, practically alone, nobody to make music with. I am not thinking of Rebecca, dragged into the *bar*, made to work up to thirteen hour days. "So you get to stop the night-work?"

"No. Still doing that too."

I pause. "But that's not fair! We only do one or the other. They said if we did the work at night, we don't have to work in the day. At those places."

She motions for me to sit next to her on the dated sofa. I plonk my body right next to the arm of the chair and say nothing.

"They like you," she says simply. "They don't seem to want to get you to do the work."

I give a snort. "Apart from the worst stuff, obviously. And they won't even give us proper contraception."

"Still better than working from dawn 'til dusk." She ignores my contraception comment. "With those chemicals. The girls have told me about the God-awful headaches they get. And the bosses there who think nothing of lamping you if you so dare to try to ask for a break. They're not even in Sheffield. We have to be driven to Leeds in the early hours. Every day."

I let her comments spiral around the room, like dust in the sunshine. You would think we would be trying to think of ways to escape, a way to get out of this scenario. Maybe there is nothing better for Rebecca, eighteen years old, fresh out of the care system. It irks me that all I can think about is the music. I try to picture the friends I would have had before, but still, my mind dredges up nothing. I can barely remember my sister, she is the dream that I woke up from before I encountered the good stuff. With a twist in my stomach, I realise the light is beginning to fade, and it will be night-time soon. The men will come. I will *know my place.* Those words always seem like an echo, a line that has been marched out to me before. I will get to perform on the bed upstairs, middle floor. They will expect me to do as they request, I will stare at Jonno and Keith with my best pleading eyes, *no, not more than one man at a time.* They can sometimes make as much money with me seeing the men separately, one after the other. It makes it less of a human car crash in my mind.

There are only two men tonight. Romanian accents. Well, Eastern bloc. They remind me of the men in the van. Their hoods are up as we traipse into the living room. Jonno gave them the choice of me, Rebecca, or one of the newer girls upstairs. I can't remember how many new girls there are up there on the middle floor. Perhaps two or three. We have to parade ourselves tonight so the men can see what they would prefer. I am wearing something the men have given me, a silk pink negligee, worn by however many women before me. It has lace around the edges. They have made us wear high heels too, and I see us like an outsider would, tottering around the room ridiculously, a toddler in her mother's shoes. We only wear the heels once a week, perhaps for the most special of clients. Sometimes we argue over who gets to wear the prettiest heels, the ones with the delicate straps. God knows I would never have been permitted to look at a pair of shoes like that at home. The men are eyeing us up and down. I wonder if, perhaps tonight, I will not get chosen. But one of the men is smiling at me, taking in my figure, my legs, my chest. I can look away all I want but he still desires me. He points, hand over his mouth. He nudges the man next to him; friends in this together. His friend seems preoccupied with the view of Rebecca. It is the third girl from upstairs who drew the short straw, so to speak. But she is free. She grins at Rebecca and me and gets to return to the sanctuary of her bedroom upstairs.

I insist on a condom, and he obliges. Jonno has pre-warned him. The whole act takes less than fifteen minutes, and I notice my neck is in pain from craning my face away from him. He appears almost embarrassed afterwards, as he cleans himself up. I notice spiders' webs around the corners of the window frame, illuminated by the single hanging light bulb in the centre of the ceiling. There are no light shades in this house.

"Ok?" he grunts at me, zipping himself up. I don't know if this question is simply to alleviate his guilt.

I nod.

"You were definitely the best one," he comments. "I like

48

an older woman. Especially a brown one."

I roll over on to my side, eyes on the door. "I think we're done now."

He grunts something and exits through the door. I can hear sounds from the next room. The new girls are arguing about something. I strain to hear but cannot decipher what they are squabbling over. It sounds like two girls against one. Their language is not English. Perhaps they are Russian, or Romanian themselves. I do not know how they got into this trade, perhaps they know the man who just saw to me. They could be family.

This job makes your brain like wallpaper paste.

***

The next afternoon, I find some paper in one of the cupboards towards the back of the dining room, and I find myself drafting a letter to the people at home in Harrow. It feels fake to call them my *parents*. I am not happy here, but I am settled in a kind of messed-up way. I suppose like a dog still loves its abusive owner. *What do they call it? Stockholm Syndrome*. Not that I even like the men who are holding me here. But, I know my routine, and I know I am one of the luckier ones in this business. Sometimes I wonder if it's solely because I'm Pakistani, or English-speaking, or because I'm one of the older girls. Perhaps Jonno and Keith are trying to keep me sweet because they fear I will be the one who turns them in.

The paper is lined and on an A4 blue pad, and I don't know what to do about my address in the top right-hand corner, so I simply write *The North*. I date the letter, think of how to address it. I decided on using the monikers *Mum and Dad* to stay polite and friendly. The main reason I am writing to them may seem bizarre, but it's what I have to do. I need some sheet music. It's all I can think of. I don't want to keep playing Gloria Estefan's Greatest Hits. I think Rebecca is getting sick of it, too. In the same way that I can't remember my family very well from before, I cannot place the music I

49

used to play. I find, however, that whatever sheet music is placed before me, I can create the notes. There doesn't seem to be a limit to what I can stretch myself to. Perhaps the stress-dealing section of my brain has kicked in and is making my mind more open to new tasks. I don't know.

I begin to write the letter, starting by saying how well I am, and that I am thinking of them constantly. What bullshit. I tear the page up and crush it into a ball, throwing it to the far side of the dining room. A hard, angry lump is building up in my throat, but I'm not about to cry. It is anger. Rage. I sit up at the table and try again with the letter. Even writing the words *Dear Mum and Dad* feels so contrived. I just want the music. I'm not bothered how they are and I'm not bothered about letting them know that I'm sort of ok. As I stare into space, there is the sound of the door to the basement opening from near the entrance of the dining room, and Jonno steps out. He ducks his head when he sees me, heads towards the kitchen.

***

The girls upstairs still squabble a lot. The one who looks about sixteen with the reddish hair and matching red polka-dot clothes is called Ruby. Well, that's what they call her. I think she gives them lip. Good on her, I say. I'm many years her senior and I like to think of myself as rebellious, but I'm not yet at Ruby's level. I've heard Keith storm into her room, the muddle of words disappearing into a fug of smoke and the heaviness of the curtains. There are sometimes bubbles of silence, followed by the other girls shouting, perhaps sticking up for Ruby. There are two other girls, their names I have yet to discover. Ruby rarely comes downstairs, but when she does, she is hungry. Today, I watch her from my piano stool, gently padding her way into the kitchen. She picks at the bread, *is it stale?* If she can feel my eyes on her, she doesn't show it. She stands on tiptoes, fingers touching all of the mismatched coloured plates in one of the 70s-style cupboards. Deciding on one, she deftly lifts it from its shelf and blows away the dust. I wonder where she has come from, and how. A lorry? A fake passport? I feel lucky again to have not endured such a journey from outside the country. There is three-day old curry remains in the fridge which she sniffs and then, with a fork, piles on to her carefully chosen plate. Finally she catches my eye.

"Afternoon!" I say, in a too-cheerful and too-British-sounding accent.

"Hi, yes," she responds. She is looking for something else in the kitchen.

"Glasses are all dirty in the sink," I say. She glances to the overflowing metal sink, her hand pausing in the air when she sees the clutter of bowls and glasses piled up there.

"I don't think I will," she says, walking out of the kitchen and to the dining table. I watch her stick her fork into the cold curry, lift the fork to her mouth.

"I'm sorry about the food. Or lack of," I say. It is not my responsibility to keep the fridge stocked. But because I am older, or I have been here longer, I feel that it is.

The girl shrugs, chewing slowly on her mouthful. We both feel safe, knowing the men aren't in the house.

"Ruby, isn't it?" I query.

The food is still going round and round in her mouth, a cement mixer. She is nodding as she chews, attempting to indicate either a *yes* or that she is trying to finish her mouthful.

"Yes," she manages, and she skims her fork around in the dry-looking rice. "This your food?" she queries.

I don't know if she is asking that because the food is curry, and I am brown. I shrug.

"You've not been here long, have you?"

She rests her fork on the side of her plate and looks at me for what is more time than is comfortable. "Four weeks now. You?"

"June," I say.

"You're British."

"I am," I respond. I don't know why people are always so surprised to discover this. "So is Rebecca. I'm a bit older

51

than you." I don't know what point I am trying to prove.

She scoops up more curry but pauses. "Four weeks is too long. I wasn't promised this. I was promised something else."

Her words make me think of Petrova. *What were you promised?*

I sigh. "Get used to it. It's not going to change."

She raises her eyebrow at me. "It will. And I am not so young. I am eighteen. I can get away."

I was going to ask her *How exactly?* But I manage to hold my tongue. "Well if you figure out how, can you let me know?"

She laughs and then points to the nearest window. "These windows on the ground floor. They are not all bolted." She walks over to the kitchen window, leans over, twiddles the loose bolt.

I nod, but she is not understanding.

"One night, I am simply going to leave from one of the windows down here."

She really is braver than me. Or more stupid.

She continues. "Jonno caught me tying bedsheets together the other night, the girls had helped me. We were all going to leave from the window upstairs. He caught us."

She lifts her hair to show a greeny-yellow-hued bruise. I nod.

"That man, he hates me," she adds.

Last time I tried to make a runner was from that barn after only a couple of nights.

Ruby coughs. "Do you want alcohol?" She is furrowing her brow at me. I am wondering how she got alcohol into her room.

"Rebecca," she explains to me, even though I haven't asked.

Rebecca? Surely she would have got a beating if the men had found out she'd been trading alcohol with the other girls.

"Sure," I reply. "What have you got?"

I feel a sinking feeling inside of me, but also a stab of excitement at the same time. I probably shouldn't try drink.

"Lager. Vodka."

"Yes please." I sound too keen.

She sits up straight in the rickety wooden chair. "Which?" she asks.

I sit up too, mirroring her actions. "Can I see what you've got?"

She nods. "Come," she says, and I am following her out of the room and up the stairs to the middle floor.

Her room is huge, shared with the two other girls, who I learn are *Lauren* and *Emily*. *Couldn't they could have come up with more Eastern-European names?* There are scattered clothes all over the red swirly-carpeted floor. One of the girls, I don't know which, is painting her toenails an alarming scarlet colour on a messy-sheeted mattress on the floor. The other girl is *working*, she tells me.

Ruby tiptoes up to her own mattress, turns with her finger held up to her mouth in a *shush* gesture. She pulls out a cardboard box from the end of the mattress, full of lager cans and one large bottle of vodka. All are cheap supermarket brands. She must see disappointment in my face, as she tips her head to one side and mutters, "Beggars can't be choosers."

I put on a fake, hopefully-convincing happy face. "No, they're great. Can I have a couple of lagers, please?"

Ruby pulls out three cans and shoves them under a cardigan she has grabbed from her floor. "Keep them hidden," she says, handing me the concealed drinks. "Drink before the sex. Makes it easier."

I nod. She offers me a swig of vodka straight from the bottle. My hands are full, so she tips the bottle into my mouth. The liquid is warm, and tastes even hotter as it snakes its way down my throat. I don't tell her that I have never tasted alcohol before.

"Shit, that's strong!"

"It's how we like it, back home," she says, and she looks at the other girl for reassurance.

"This is true," adds the other girl, temporarily looking up from her toenail art, bored.

"Anyway, thanks for these," I say, as I begin to walk

backwards towards the door, gesturing with my chin towards my new haul.

"Not a problem," says Ruby. "And I would like my cardigan back."

I leave the girls' room and stop to see a flick of Rebecca's hair disappear around the corner of the landing, and up the stairs to where the men's rooms are. I pause, waiting to see if she will reappear. She doesn't. I make my way downstairs.

***

It was *a real arse of a day*, according to Rebecca. Her hands smart and so does her neck from craning over other women's fingers. And toes. *Stupid rich bitches*, she calls them. She has the obligatory headache from the chemicals of the varnish remover. And now she has to *go sleep with some men* as soon as 9:30pm hits. It's 8:15pm already. She is visibly exhausted, her breath acidic; the tell-tale signs of dehydration. I have not mentioned her lingering outside Ruby's room last night.

Do you get given drinks of water?
No. Not really.

I am seething. She is eighteen but in many ways so much younger. I feel almost maternal towards her, despite her childish mannerisms; it is up to me to protect her here. Nobody else will. Some nights I lie on that depleted mattress and think of a way to alert someone, anyone. It doesn't have to be the police. A dog walker, a postman. Maybe I could hammer on my window; it faces the road. They were pretty trusting, putting us in a downstairs room, at the front even if the window *is* bolted. Trusting, or very stupid. It wouldn't take much, to grab the attention of a passer-by. Except there are barely any passers-by. The house was surely chosen for its remote location, a no-through road in the middle of the Peaks. The needle in the haystack.

Sometimes I can't take what the men are trying to make us do. And why they are so demonstrably harsh with Rebecca.

I don't mean to, but my feet are charging up the stairs, two at a time, stopping abruptly on the middle floor, awaiting further instruction from my brain. My heart is hammering in my chest as I pause outside Ruby's door. I know he's in there. It takes me a few seconds to sum up the courage to knock. Keith opens the door a crack; his green almond-shaped eyes appear from a dusky gap. "Yeh?"

I swallow the excess saliva in my mouth.

"It's about Rebecca," I say, gulping. "I think she's too tired to work tonight. She's been at the nail bar all day."

I can only see his eyes but I can tell that he's grinning as they are scrunching up at the sides, wrinkles appearing in his mottled skin.

"You what?"

Oh God. "I…"

"Are you fucking joking me?"

The door swings open and I am taken aback at the amount of smoke in the room. He is standing there, a cigarette in his right hand. I can just about make out the diminutive figure of Ruby in the background, sunken into her mattress. Her eyes are dark slits through the fog.

"I just think…she needs a rest. She's only eighteen."

He grins that vile grin again, skin scrunching up at the sides.

"Yes, she fucking is!" He is laughing but I can tell he is angry. I've seen it before.

I can feel my hands starting to shake and I take a step backwards on to the landing. He grabs my shoulder and yanks me towards him into the smoky, stale room. Ruby is blinking at me, pleading, but then she stands, brushes past us and leaves the room.

"So what's your problem?" It is a statement, not a question.

"My problem," I pause, racking my brains for something. "Is that you men are taking the piss with us."

He leans forward and peers into my eyes. "She brings in more bloody money than the likes of you *ever will."* He is sneering now.

I feel like telling him that I never asked to be part of this business, to just let me go. But of course, he won't. He will be terrified that I will rat on him and the rest of the ring.

I can feel his hand shove me in the small of my back, and I am thrown upon the bed. I can smell the staleness of the sheets, can see the beigeness of the once-white linen. I should stop wearing skirts and dresses. They are too easy. His right hand is pinning me down at the back of my neck so the rancid cotton of the sheets is almost suffocating me. The other hand is pulling down his jeans. God, no. *Not this*. I grit my teeth and manage to foist myself on to my elbows to turn quickly, knocking him from his balance. He slaps me across the face and I pause, the sting freezing me. When I come to my senses I kick out at him. His face bulges over me, red, repugnant. He is reluctant to move. I wish he would put his trousers back on; I avert my eyes. He steps away, turns his body towards the door. I creep off the side of the bed, pulling my underpants up, brushing my skirt down.

He leans to one side so I can leave the room, but then grabs me by my collar. "It's not over yet," he promises, and he is smiling as he lets go. "Only for today."

I spit at him but he doesn't notice. My aim has missed, anyway.

Chapter Nine

Yalina

Late October 2007
Somewhere near Sheffield

He is sitting with me at the table as I slowly munch on my toast. Brown, stale, one slice. I will not look at him. I can feel his eyes on me; they flicker away as soon as I look up. I know what he wants.

He is trying to make small talk. It's not going to wash with me. I refuse to answer his questions.

"You like your music, dontcha?" he asks, tapping his cigarette on to the small bread plate to his left.

I don't respond.

"How about I get you whatever you want, music-wise. CDs, another instrument, just name it."

I am intrigued, he knows this, but I will not show it. "No thanks," I say.

"Seriously. What about a guitar? I used to love playing guitar as a kid."

"I thought this was about me?"

He nods, inhaling from his fag. He releases the drag of smoke over the rest of the kitchen. I try not to enjoy the smell. I don't know if I used to be a smoker.

"So what do you want, then?" He isn't looking at me. His eyes are focused on the bottom of the staircase. Of course, he is worried that Jonno will hear.

"Music."

Keith takes a long drag on his cigarette, closes his eyes.

"What type? Saying *music* is a bit broad."

"Sheet music. So I can play more on the piano. I'm sick of Gloria bloody Estefan. I want the classics; Brahms, some Beethoven. And some Beatles songs too."

He is laughing, stubbing out the cigarette on the little plate. I watch the ash flick around in the air above it. "You'd be lucky," he says. He stands and walks out of the room, returns with another music book. "This was in the shed," he says, frowning.

On closer inspection, I see it is a Rolling Stones book collection of sheet music. Surely he could have given it to me before? I will not show that I'm pleased with the music.

He gets his fag packet out of his top pocket, hand hovering over his abandoned lighter on the table. "That bloody piano."

I hold my breath. He looks at me. "If it was worth anything, we'd sell it. Waste of space. Make the most of the book." He stands and leaves me with the bread plate and the black ash. I see him glance out of the back window in the kitchen as if he is waiting for someone, but he gives up and goes back upstairs.

In my room on the ground floor I crawl onto Rebecca's mattress and enjoy the warm surge of the donated lager hitting the back of my throat. It's not as immediately comforting as the vodka, but it's not burning the top layer of my tongue, either. From Rebecca's bed there is the view out of the window. I keep drinking the lager and take a moment to gaze at the view; there are goats or sheep in the furthest field, and some empty fields with a woodland area to the left of them. The house we are in is detached, so it's not like we have any neighbours. The view is stunning, really. The October sun has turned the leaves outside a darker red than I think I have ever seen before. The once-yellow fields have been steam-rollered by the sun into a deep maize colour. Everything is changing, darkening, dying, yet waiting to start all over again. If I squint my eyes, I can see a figure with a stick walking through the wooded area, a smudge of a dog at their side. I wonder if they will look up at our house. They are too far away for me to see what they are focusing on and the trees are blurring my vision. I stand and walk to the window of my room, and I wave. They don't wave back. They are pulling at the dog on the lead, pulling it out of the woods; away. Lager in my hand, I take another swig and feel grateful for the fuzzy feeling that is taking over my body. I open the window and shout, "Wait!"

There is a crackle of activity upstairs; the sound of heavy feet on the landing. I pause, not breathing. The wind battles with the loose sash windows. The footsteps have stopped.

The figure returns to being a blur on the furthest side of the field, the dog just a dot.

Chapter Ten

Yalina

Mid-November 2007
Somewhere near Sheffield

I've learnt all ten songs in under a week. Rebecca has been singing and swaying by my side through *Paint it Black* and *Wild Horses,* when she's had a day off from the nail bar. The piano doesn't reach the music's potential alone; these Stones songs require drums. What I need is some classical music; some Brahms would do nicely, like I told Keith. What I know is that I can't ask him for more. He seems more intent on bullying Ruby recently, and far be it for me to end up as the focus of his rage. I stop washing-up and listen. There doesn't seem to be anyone else in the house, save one or both of Ruby's friends upstairs. It could be my mind playing tricks on me. They could all be waiting somewhere, breathing quietly, hands on knees as they squat, biding their time. I've got to call a stop to these thoughts. In my dreams at night, I don't know who I can trust. Each person in this house is an enemy.

Drying my hands on the back of my jeans, I pad through the kitchen, then the dining room and begin my ascent up the narrow staircase on the balls of my feet. The third and sixth steps creak in a way I've never noticed before. I can picture Jonno hiding behind the wall at the top of the stairs, a bat or similar in his hand. I would maybe not notice him at first, save for his white teeth against his olive skin. I bypass the first floor, hearing nothing, and make my way up to the top floor, following the vile swirly red carpet. My knees and ankles are clicking, and I'm sure my panting can be heard from the ground floor. I am outside the small piece of landing that separates one bedroom from the other. The carpet curls around the entrance to both doors. All I can hear is my own heartbeat pounding in my ears. I've never been in either room before. None of us would dare. I clear my throat. Nothing. "Jonno?" I call. Nothing. "Keith?" I hate saying their names. It makes them more real.

I touch the door to the left with my sweaty fingers, apply a little pressure. The door slowly opens, the friction from the carpet below making it feel like it's stuck. I pull my body cautiously through the gap, then stop and take a look around. Filthy. Clothes all over the floor, dust and cobwebs hanging from every surface. A spider eyes me directly from its home on the curtains, which hang limply in the grey light. I forget for a moment what I have come for, I am so mesmerised by the ordinariness of the room. I suppose I thought I would find a haul of illegal items; drugs, melted spoons and the like. I can't see anything of interest. There's a leather jacket hanging from the back of a chair which is perched in a corner. Socks and t-shirts are scattered like pieces of paper in an artist's workshop, wanted once but now abandoned. I try the top drawer of his dresser. Just odd receipts. The next drawer is practically empty and gets stuck halfway through pulling it. I try the third drawer. There is an empty brown envelope hiding a pile of things underneath. I flip it up, craning my neck to see. A passport, not burgundy like a UK passport. Several other different coloured passports underneath that one, including a classic-looking British one. As I flick through the back of each of the five passports I can feel anger bubbling in the back of my mind and making its way through my veins from my pumping heart, an angry sea ready to drown whatever is in its wake. The photos in each of the passports show me the drawn, pale faces of Ruby, and her two friends. One girl is short-haired, and still is. The other, more mousey brown and barely any eyebrows. The second to last passport - Petrova. So, he did take it from her. Her blonde hair is curled, as if she had spent the day preparing to have her photo taken; the passport her ticket to the England of her dreams. Perhaps she thought she would make it on the stage. I remember seeing her passport in the barn, at the beginning of my ordeal. I remember her birth name, Lubna. And a surname I couldn't possibly pronounce. Sadness seems to suddenly make my bones feel weary. I pocket the four coloured passports in the back of my jeans. The last passport, the British one, shows Rebecca at the back, perhaps thirteen years old in the photo. A child. *Clearly* a child. I slip that into my other back pocket without a second thought.

My eyes continue to scan the room until I find what I'm looking for. I glance at the digital alarm clock next to the bed; 5:35pm. I have little more than a couple of hours to do what I need to do, before Jonno and Keith return home with Rebecca and the other girls from the nail bar. I realise as I leave the room that I don't know which man it belongs to.

I thought I was feeling reckless, brave, in the moments after I had taken the laptop, but now my fingers have a shake to them and my breath is quicker than usual. It flickers like a moth's wings. *Come on. Don't bail out now.*

After the computer has turned on, sounding like a jet taking off, my face flushes as I am halted by the request for a password. *Shit.* I have to slow my breathing down in order to make my brain think imaginatively. I try *Sheffield.* Nope. I try his first name, for want of knowing his last name. Not that either. I hear myself give a small scream of frustration, causing the cat in the corner of my downstairs room to look up in disgust. She trots over to my sitting position on the mattress and makes herself comfy on top of the laptop keyboard, stretching out her front paws.

"Fucking cat!" I shout, in a volume that I hope cannot be carried beyond the four walls of my room. Christ knows how Keith can be so soft on his cat and so brutish with us girls. I stroke the length of the cat's back; she stands and exposes the keyboard for me, hairs sticking keenly to the tips of my fingers. I type *Luna* into the password box. The icon is swirling in circles and I'm in. Bingo!

Idiot man. Naming his password after his bastard cat.

I type the website name into the browser bar, and the blue screen with its icon welcomes me. I can see Keith's username is his email, but there is no password populating for his account. I try the cat's name again but this time it fails. Was worth a try. My heart begins to beat faster again as I realise what it would have meant for us girls, had I been able to log in to his account. Still, I realise I have power in my hands as I type my own username and password and see my own social media account spring up before me. There are several red notifications in the top-right hand corner. I toy with the idea of ignoring them, to save time, but I just can't. I click on the private messages first. Mum. *Lil. I know when you left, you did so under a cloud.* The message is dated June 21st. I don't have the time to read the rest of it and scroll down to the next message. Raim. I don't even open that one, and I scroll further, swallowing down the lump of guilt that is rising in my throat. What I'd do to have a sister right now. The third one makes a burst of adrenaline rush to my fingertips. Ali.

I click on his name.

Hi Lil. What's happening? We were meant to meet at the station that night, and now your phone sounds dead. Ali.

That's it. One message. Barely two sentences. Perhaps he'd decided I was bad news like our parents. I don't know what I was expecting. More pleading, more concern? The message's date is 2nd July. What excites me, though, is that there is a green circle next to his name. He is online. My hands are shaking so much with excitement that I can barely type.

Ali, it's me. I type. *I'm so sorry. Please listen. That evening you were due to meet me, I was picked up by what I think was a trafficking ring and dumped in a barn. They then moved me to this deserted house somewhere near Sheffield and I'm forced to have sex with men every night. Please can you look for me? I think we are five or six miles from the station. I don't know our address, but we are house no 2. No post ever gets delivered here. Can you look for me?* I press

Send and sit on my hands for what feels like hours, as my brother reads my message. I almost can't believe this is happening.

Impatiently, I begin to add more to my message.

The only thing that keeps me going is my music and the thought of meeting you. Please don't give up on me. If you don't alert the police because you can't locate my address, please can you send me some music on here? I'd like some classical music, sheet music. I've been playing the piano to keep me sane. Remember our mother didn't even tell me I like to play piano? Remember how she kept things secret from me?

I stop typing. I tiptoe out of my room to use the bathroom, giving Ali time to reply to my messages. A rushing sensation of fizziness takes over my body as I walk back to my room, the anticipation almost too much to take. I cannot sit down quickly enough. I make myself wait a few seconds longer, to preserve the feeling of ecstasy.

There are no messages from my brother, and the green light is gone.

Chapter Eleven

Yalina

Early December 2007
Somewhere near Sheffield

We knew we had been lucky so far. There are new women being herded into the house. Our house. There are seven of them, faces sallow, downwards glancing, no meat on their bones. They come in the wee small hours. Jonno will only let them travel by night. *Safety under the stars*, he likes to say, with a wink. In the morning, I wake and they are still there, three of them crammed onto the floor of the room Rebecca and I share. The others must be up in Ruby's room.

One of them is sharing Rebecca's mattress; Rebecca is forced up against the wall by the window, only her forehead visible under her filthy sheets. I am so angry I can't bring myself to even greet them. This is our territory; we were coping with how it was. A woman, perhaps seven or eight years older than me, is sitting up. She catches my eye and looks away. I think about the one toilet we have in the house, how overrun it will be. Our already meagre food supplies, dwindling. The anger burning in my belly makes me stare all the more at the woman, daring her to glance my way again.

I sit up and clear my throat. "Rebecca!"

Rebecca stirs a little but doesn't wake. I stand up from my mattress and pick my way across the new sleeping bodies, and past the woman who is probably looking at me. I find my friend's shoulder under the swathe of stolen sheets and shake her. "Rebecca, look."

Her eyes open, bleary, a look of slight confusion on her

face. "We're moving?" she asks. It is dark outside. A darkened December morning. It's probably about 6am. I can forgive her for thinking it is still the middle of the night. That she's being forced to move again.

"No!" I hiss. "There are newbies here. Look!"

She doesn't move for a while

"Oh." She sits up slowly as if she's in pain, eyeing the darkened room, only illuminated by a faint light coming from under the bedroom door.

"Where the hell did they come from?" I fire at her.

She doesn't know, she's just woken.

"I'm going to have it out with them," I tell her, meaning Keith and Jonno.

She shakes her head. "Not worth it," she says. She is looking at the three extra sleeping women in the room, one of them on the edge of her mattress. She sees the sitting-up woman too and averts her eyes. I wish she had more fight in her.

The room smells of unwashed bodies, sallow, dank; I imagine the reek permeating my own mattress, the one thing I can claim as my own. My anger is melting away, drip by drip, into a feeling of sadness, desperation.

The sitting-up woman glances at me, she is trying to say something. I reach over to turn on the light, a bare bulb, but she shakes her head *no* at me. "Please, where is toilet?" she asks, in an accent I cannot place at all. Her skin is jet black, beautiful, waxy. There is an air of mysteriousness to her. Immediately I want to know her life story.

I point with my finger to the door, but I am going to have to lead her to our tiny downstairs bathroom. She stands very slowly, and it is then that I see the bump protruding from her stomach; she goes to cover the mound with her right hand protectively. I feel a stab of shame at the anger I had felt for her minutes ago.

I prise open the door, and guide her through the dining room, and to the room at the very back of the house, alongside the utility room, its wooden door having seen better days. While she uses the bathroom, I wait outside. I

66

can hear the toilet flush, the tap run, and then she is opening the door.

Perhaps she is not as old as I thought. She is clasping her stomach again.

"When is your baby due?" I ask her, as if I am striking up a conversation with someone I had met in a doctor's surgery.

She shakes her head.

I lead her back to the bedroom, and as I open the door, am hit by the smell of the new bodies. I see Rebecca looking at me, hopelessly from across the room.

The other two women are awake now, looking at each other. One is mouthing something to the other one.

"Hello," I offer, as the pregnant woman sits down again on the carpet.

Neither speak.

Rebecca says to me, "They're called Gillian, Mary and Lucy." She is proud that she has managed to extract this information from them in the short period I was gone.

I have to stop myself from giving a snort of derision. Rebecca's eyes are on the pregnant woman. She glances back to me with a not-well-hidden look of angst.

"What is your name?" I ask the other two women on the floor.

"Lucy," says the skinniest one, who is taking up much of my friend's mattress.

The third woman, more of a girl, coughs. "Mary."

I feel slightly disappointed that it is not the pregnant woman whom our clever ringmasters have named Mary.

"So you must be Gillian," I say to the remaining woman, my eyes fixed on her bulbous belly.

She nods.

"When is your baby due?" asks Rebecca.

I flick my eyes to the ceiling. *Sheesh.*

She looks at the floor. The silence is painful. The skinny girl answers for her. "She doesn't know."

I nod, attempting to appear understanding. "You are all friends?" I say, trying to make the mood in the room turn itself around a little.

Skinny girl shakes her head. "We all only met last night. In the van."

I try to stop myself from sighing. At least the thought that they were a friendly trio, bound together by some form of camaraderie and shared experiences was making me feel less bad for them. But they are merely strangers to one another. Like the rest of us.

Rebecca is not helping the situation at all. "Do you know what you are here for?" she queries, almost winking at me. Perhaps she is not feeling so accommodating after all.

Skinny girl answers again. "Nail bar work," she states, very matter-of-fact.

I wonder about the chemicals they use and pregnant-woman. *Gillian.*

"Um, ok," says Rebecca, half rolling her eyes. I honestly don't think I've ever known her to be catty like this. "Nothing else?" she continues.

The girl who hasn't spoken bursts into tears and buries her head in her hands.

"She understands most English but she just doesn't speak," says the skinny girl, by way of explanation. "We haven't heard her say a thing yet."

Rebecca raises an eyebrow at me.

I'm not going to be the one who will tell them what is expected of them. Instead, I say, "What sort of jobs have you all been doing here in England?" and am met by a silence again.

The non-talking girl is still crying, her head bowed. Gillian reaches out her arm and strokes her shoulder.

"We've all been promised work in hotels and kitchens," says the girl, in a desperately quiet voice.

"Did they take your passports?" asks Rebecca in a voice too cheery for the conversation.

All three women nod. I suddenly remember the passports I stole from upstairs. I've got to hide them somewhere that has cast-iron security. Maybe somewhere outside. I find myself thinking of the fields out there, or the woodland. They would never go looking for them there. Leaving the passports in the house, anywhere in the damned house would be far too risky.

"Well, nail-bar work is a *proper job*," says Rebecca. God knows what has got into her.

One of the women smiles appreciatively, and I feel sick.

Silent girl is looking out of the window, eyes on the road. There is a car there, lights on, not moving. Nobody gets out of the car.

"There's other stuff too though," I add. "Other stuff they expect us to do."

I can feel the three new women staring at me.

"With men," Rebecca clarifies, too quickly.

Instead of looking alarmed, or melancholic, they merely nod. They already know. They've been here before. I see pregnant-woman is crying, silently, her hand rubbing her tummy in reassuring circles. The car turns around in the dead-end, and creeps away.

The passports are sweaty in my hand, and I turn them over, one by one. *The girls would be relieved if they knew I had them.* But I have told them nothing. I am more powerful like this; a secret saviour. Rebecca, Ruby and the others are working at the nail bar, including most of the new women. The men didn't waste any time there. Perhaps I should put the passports in an envelope, to protect them, if I can locate one. I walk over to the drawer where I had found the paper to write on. The pad I tried to write on for my parents' letter has gone. Removed. There are no envelopes to speak of, either. I'll just have to wrap them in newspaper, there's plenty at the back of the house. I make my way there and curse the mess on the floor of the tiny utility room. Shoes, the men's boots, boxes of crap, generally. I kick half of the mess to the side. Against the wall there's a battered box of old newspapers with a pale blue piece of paper half-screwed up on top. As I slip my one and only pair of shoes on, the photo on the notice immediately catches my eye. It's a picture of Rebecca. I pick up the piece of paper and smooth it flat.

"*Missing since June 28th. Rebecca Morley, fifteen years old. Last seen outside Sainsbury's in Wakefield. Of slight build and last seen wearing red hoodie with black jeans. Any sightings please contact local police on this number."*

I can feel the heat rising up my neck like a poison taking hold. They're looking for her. Fifteen-year-old Rebecca.

Chapter Twelve

Yalina

December 2007
Somewhere near Sheffield

The wind is sharper than I am expecting and it cuts at my skin like a razor wire. I am walking towards the woods, head down, hood pulled over. The wind continues to whip around my ears although they are covered. Thankfully, it is already dark at 5:10pm, and I am hidden by the vast darkness that stretches across the fields and towards the dales of Derbyshire in one direction, and the Peak District in another. The once-beautiful hues of the heather fields are muted in this season and in the darkness of the late afternoon. It's as if I made them up in my mind, they are now just a distant memory of warmer days.

The idiots left the kitchen window unbolted. I wonder how often they are this slack with their security. It was easy enough to manoeuvre myself up on to the kitchen sink and climb out of that top kitchen window.

My ballet-pump shoes which were once cream are now a dirty brown, not from these fields but from months of having worn nothing else on my feet. They won't provide us with shoes. As I'm walking to my planned destination I am hit with an unexpected stab of joy, the concept of freedom buzzing in my mind, and as the wind is whipping behind me it takes all my senses just to not run as far as I can. I could just leave. Now. I bury that idea in the back of my mind as I wander through the last thirty yards or so of the field before the woodland. The grasses are long and the effort makes my legs ache. I stop walking for a moment to listen. Nothing, just the wind, and the sound of distant traffic somewhere to my right. As I approach the trees, I notice they are not as sparse as I had anticipated; there are firs and other varieties I cannot name, chunky boughs blocking my way and roots determined to trip me. I feel more fearful the further I step, as the darkness is making it difficult to find my footing, and I can barely see more than a few inches in front of my face. I try not to remember the dream I had about the pregnant woman in the woods that I had experienced in the car that time. *Blackened trees, the even darker glob of human mess attached to the woman.* I stop about ten trees in, mindful of the fact that if I were to get lost this winter evening, I may not find my way out again. I feel disappointed for not bringing some type of instrument to help me dig into the soil, so I find myself fumbling around in the darkness for a twig, or a stick of any type. Finding nothing, I break off a small branch that is hanging close to my body, the sap leaking its way through my fingers and up to my wrist. It looks like blood in this light; sticky syrup blood.

I begin to dig, not too deep; that would not be necessary. The wrapped passports are in my hand now, and I find that I am shaking a little. I am unsure why. Yes, I am. It's excitement. It's the feeling of regaining control. I am doing this to save them.

I place the booklets unceremoniously into the little grave I have dug, and quickly pile over their newspaper covers with as much earth as is crumbled around the area. As a final gesture, I kick another clump of mud over the top, and am sure to count ten trees as I leave the woodland. I think of my own passport, back home in Harrow, sitting safe and snug in its wooden drawer in the dresser, where my mother keeps all of our important items. I feel safe for one moment.

***

I'm woken from a deep accidental nap by a loud crashing sound downstairs and the noise of a high-pitched girl's voice, screaming. Taking the stairs two by two, I am on the ground floor in a matter of seconds, and can see Ruby being held over the dining table by the scruff of her neck, Keith's red, blotchy face almost spitting into hers.

"Fucking say it!" He is staring straight at her, Jonno looking on. He's not a real fan of violence. Ruby's two friends, I forget their names, are standing, crying. One is twisting her hands.

"I won't!" she squeals, although the position she is being forced into is compromising her ability to speak.

"Let her go!" squeaks one of the girls, the one who had been painting her nails that time.

Keith turns and looks at her. He spits into her face. "Shut the fuck up."

She recoils, using her sleeve to wipe the spit from her eyes. The other girl begins to cry more. I feel a certain disappointment at their reaction.

"And you can button it too!" Keith points at her with his spare hand. Jonno grabs the crying girl and takes her into the next room. She is wailing.

"What has Ruby done to deserve this?" I demand.

It is the first time any of them have seen me.

Jonno is still in the other room with the girl, but Keith looks across the living room to where I am standing at the bottom of the stairs. Ruby is still being held over the table. I can see Keith's arm is shaking from the strain.

"Oh, she's a little snake. A wee little rat. Ratting on us." He lets go of her. She nearly falls headfirst on to the table-top, but catches herself in time. I forgot how young she looks, and even more so now; her eyes red and bulbous.

"I did not rat!" she splutters.

"Tried to though, didn't you, little bitch?" Keith's eyes are almost popping out of their own sockets. "Thought you would try and tell the customer what's happening, didn't you?"

I realise I am biting down on my tongue. Toe-painting girl

is staring at the ground, no emotion on her face.

"But tell Lil here what happened," encourages Keith, pointedly glancing at me and the other girl.

"It doesn't matter," I say. I do not know who I am addressing.

"Ah, but it does," says the bully. He leans to stroke Ruby's long auburn hair. I struggle to remember her real name as it's stated on her passport. Shit. I can't remember.

"She tried to tell Mrs Lee about what a *horrible* time she's having here. How cruel we are. How she misses her home country. She told Mrs Lee that we are running a *sex ring*". He snorts out the last two words with a kind-of spluttery laugh.

Ruby lowers her head. I can see toe-painting girl trying to catch her eye now.

"But what our lovely Ruby didn't realise is that the ancient Mrs Lee is actually one of us. She found it all rather amusing, coming to get a free nail treatment from one of our girls."

He is sneering now, crowing. So pleased with his story. He peers across the room at me, looking for my reaction. I won't give him one. Ruby is hauled into the next room, and I can hear them thumping her. Over and over. I cover my ears with my hands, and the other girl shrugs. I am fighting the urge to go and find the sharpest blade I can. I see Rebecca has come down the stairs too, to see what all the noise is about. She is a fifteen-year-old girl now.

I will not let them get away with this for much longer.

My afternoons are still free for my piano-playing, and I take extra joy in it now that the house is more crowded at various other points of the day, so bloody crowded. Sometimes one of the new women will be having a day off from the nail-bar, more often than not it is Gillian. Her bump is burgeoning, and each time I see her I have to stop myself from asking her how long she's got. She sometimes rests on the sofa whilst I play, one hand circling the rising mound under her ribs, the other poised under her chin. I have found out that she is from Nigeria. She doesn't speak a lot, neither to me nor to the two women she travelled here with, but there is a peaceful serenity to her that seems to calm anyone who may be in the room with her. Her voice, too, is soft and almost husky. Today I am playing *You Can't Always Get What You Want*. It's a tricky number to pull off on the piano. I work away at it for a good few minutes, until I see Gillian gesturing at me with her hands. "A slower song," she suggests.

I don't mind halting the current song for her. Usually it would annoy me. I flick to *Wild Horses* in the music book, even though I know every note and chord by heart. Rebecca loves this song too.

As soon as my fingers begin forming the chords, I can see Gillian knows most of the words and is singing along from the sofa where she sits, hands resting on her stomach, chin lifted for once. At the end of the song I turn and look at her from my piano stool.

"Would you like to be having a girl or a boy?" I ask, too abruptly.

She is swaying even though the music has stopped. Now she is selecting her response carefully.

"A boy," she says, finally.

I smile. "Less difficult?" I offer, even though I don't know what I am talking about.

"No," she says in that quiet voice of hers. "I already have little girl. At home. With my mother."

I don't know why I am surprised at this, but it makes me even sadder.

"Will this one go to live with your mother too?"

I realise how naive I sound, after the words have left my lips.

She shakes her head. "No." Her eyes are no longer on me.

"I won't be keeping the baby." There is a tear prickling on her lower lashes; it threatens to spill out at any moment and wind its way down her perfect smooth cheek.

"The men. They are taking it from me."

I feel a chill course its way through my veins, making tiny hairs on my spine stand upright. The room feels like it's at freezing point.

"No?" is all I can manage.

She shrugs. "What else can I do?"

I stare at the hideous carpet for a while. "We could talk to Jonno and Keith, we can sort something out. I know we can!" My brain is whirring, plotting. The men will not take this child.

"They are selling baby on," Gillian tells me.

I pause to think for a moment. It feels like I have been winded. "How much are they paying you?"

She looks down at her hands. "I can't say." I wonder if it is in the hundreds, or perhaps thousands.

"If you could tell me, perhaps I could help."

She looks up at me, tears glistening on her lower lashes still. "You have money?"

"No, not now. They've promised us money here. In euros. But for now I think there may be someone I could ask." I consider my parents. Or Ali. I have not had another chance again to get hold of the laptop and see if Ali has replied to my message. I also find myself wishing that I had read my mother's message and responded.

She sighs. "It is no use," she says.

I wonder if she is the girl from my dream.

Chapter Thirteen

Richard

December 2006
Islington, London

The relationship with my ex-wife improved over time. We had tried counselling when we were still married, but it hadn't worked. Seemingly, individual counselling was what we each needed. We could call ourselves friends again, at last.

As the children grew older, we found we could lean on each other for support with whatever came our way. She met another man, which did grate at first, but then I learned to get on with it. I had dates here and there, nothing special, until I met Natalie. She was nine years my junior and worked for me (*what a cliche!*). She made me feel young again. I wanted to be carefree, and this is how I felt, for the odd evening or weekend where I wasn't seeing Zoe or George. Zoe liked Natalie straight away; there were no arguments, no suspicion. Nothing.

George wasn't so easily taken with her. "She's with you just for your money," he would say, sixteen years old and believing himself wiser than his years.

"Why, thanks, son!" I would exclaim, and ruffle his hair with as much sarcasm as I could muster. He would push me away and say, "I'm not joking. She's like ten years younger than you. You are so punching above your weight."

He would make sure Natalie was within earshot; working on her notes, ironing in the next room. I think she would like hearing the last comment.

Eventually George succumbed to Nat's charm, and we bumbled along just fine.

George applied to Oxford University, and got in. It was a bittersweet day, that Saturday we left the flat early to pick him up from his mother's. He was excited, but I could tell there was fear under that smooth exterior, enveloped in his maroon-coloured hoodie. He kept picking at his nails, biting them down to the quick. He went very quiet on that journey; Nat sitting in the front beside me, and six foot two George crammed into the back of my old Ford Astra. He'd only packed one suitcase, two boxes of saucepans, a printer, and a duvet. *Did he not think he was going to be staying there for long?*

When we arrived at his accommodation, I could see the relief on his face as he saw other students of the same age appearing as similarly fearful, their parents flanking their sides, shifting boxes and more boxes. He didn't want us to break our backs by carrying his things to his room, so with his usual kindness, he took all of his bits out of our hands, and marched them straight to his room alone. He was concerned about us having to drive home as it was getting dark.

Chapter Fourteen

Yalina

December 2007
Somewhere near Sheffield

My relationship with Rebecca feels strained. I haven't yet told her that they're looking for her out there, that her face is emblazoned on posters, probably several in the area. You'd think Jonno or Keith would have made more of an attempt to hide the evidence, or make arrangements to hide Rebecca herself, but no. They probably only bothered ripping down the one poster. I haven't said that I know she is three years younger than the eighteen she claims to be. With my newfound knowledge, I can see snippets of immaturity, unkindness to others. She has barely said a word to the women who came that night; Gillian, the skinny-legged girl and the mute one. She doesn't ask Gillian how she is, or if she requires a drink, or somewhere to put her feet up. I already gave up my mattress to her by the second night. I should imagine that she doesn't have much longer to go now. I try to swallow down the fear I experience for her in the pit of my stomach. It eats away like a sprawl of tiny maggots, not causing much harm at first, but then really getting into the flesh. I don't know if the men have a plan for when she goes into labour. I naively asked her if she was receiving any antenatal care, and was met with a swift, sad shake of the head. When I nod at Rebecca to perhaps offer her a chair at breakfast in the morning, Rebecca pulls a sullen face, and usually ignores such a request. She has acquired more of a stomp to her walk.

Gillian is not requested to go to the nail bar, or to take part in the night-time activities. I am relieved at least to hear that. Anything else would just be abhorrent, unspeakable. I am hoping she didn't get much of that work in the first place.

It is just the two of us left eating at breakfast one Sunday, when the others are permitted to start work three hours later at the shop in Leeds. They are not allowed to break the trading rules, just like anyone else. The girls are busy throwing their bowls into the already crammed sink, looking for lost shoes, wrapping scarves around their scrawny necks. I guess they could keep everyone somewhere else over the Saturday night, but perhaps there isn't anywhere. The van doesn't come to take them until 8am. The men are always extra nervous on Sundays. The sun is just up, killing off their blanket of disguise, and they know they could be stopped by anyone. This is pure joy to me, this imagined scenario, and I luxuriate in the feeling of the rush of heat; the idea that one Sunday morning, as they race along the country roads in their VW van with blacked-out windows, every single girl in that van could be saved. I could call the police myself, if I had access to a phone. I could email my parents and tell them what has happened to me if I could get hold of that laptop again, and what is happening to these women and girls with whom I share a home. But I don't. I can't.

The idea of calling the house *a home* almost makes me spit out my water with laughter.

I see Jonno is pacing, from the kitchen into the dining room, back and forth, back and forth. I like to see the anxiety on his face, the sweat beginning to disperse on his dark top lip, even though we are in the worst of the December weather and the temperature is yet to hit zero degrees today. "Come on, come *on*," he insists.

He can be pretty soft considering the job he's doing. He could terrorise most of them, drag them by their sleeves into the back of the van, but he doesn't. It is Keith who is more inclined to use his physical brute force, fists almost always curled and ready. Makes me think of Curley in the story about the migrant workers during the Great Depression; brooding, always looking for a fight. Keith is already reversing the van into the driveway alongside the house, which then turns into what would be a garden at the back. He is revving the engine. That makes the girls hurry more than any pacing or growling that Jonno is offering. I grab the moment.

"Jonno, quick question."

He looks at me, exasperated. "What the hell? We're just about to leave."

"It's about Gillian."

"Who?"

There is a stab of embarrassment, and then sadness, in my chest for the pregnant woman who is sitting at our table still, feigning interest in watching the other girls pull on their filthy coats, their falling-apart shoes. *He can't even remember the bloody name he invented for her.*

I nod towards her at the table.

"Oh. Her."

"Yes." I pause, watching the girls leaving through the back door, Ruby leading the way for once, her two friends following closely behind her.

"You need a plan for the baby," I hiss.

He doesn't even look at me but he stops pacing. His eyes are on the van. "There *is* a plan. The baby is moving on."

"I know this. Where is the baby going, exactly?"

He is rolling his eyes, telling me nothing. But he knows where it's going.

I think of the drawers with the paper, the envelopes. Perhaps I can find some information in there, if they are stupid enough to leave paperwork there.

"What about the birth? Where will she give birth?"

He smiles, and I remember that he can still be an utterly cruel bastard. "Why don't you take care of that, sweetie? That could be your contribution to our little set-up here. God knows you do fuck-all. Cos of *that*," and he is pointing to my chest.

It takes me a split second to realise that he means my

81

heart. My mind is beginning to freeze, the edges becoming numb; anaesthetised.

Then he is gone, out of the back door, hastily spinning on his heel to lock it. The key is always taken with them.

I know Gillian has been listening to every word.

"I ask no questions," she says.

"Listen, I didn't know 'til just then that I've been excused from the nail bar work because of my operation. I didn't know."

Gillian turns her kind face towards me; there is such warmth in her chocolate brown eyes. They seem to glow as she speaks. "It's ok. We are friends together here. We have the music together, and we are the lucky ones, no?" I feel like hugging her close, or kissing the top of her head with its fuzzy nobbles, but I refrain, for fear of bumping into her stomach.

"Hey," she says, in a way that sounds very American. "Will you help me with the birth?"

I find myself nodding enthusiastically, although my insides are worms and I can't think of anyone less qualified than me to bring new life into the world.

The piano is still here. It sits proudly, stout, brown and looking as if it's seen better days. The stool, nearly matching, sits in front, its cream cushion looking grubbier as the weeks pass. This morning, early, before he went off in the van, Keith handed me a brown A4-sized envelope.

It simply says *Yalina* on the front of it. "Came in the post," he says, not looking directly at me. Then he is gone. I look at the front of the envelope again. There is no address, no post-mark. It was hand-delivered.

I can feel my heart pumping double speed, hands shaking. There can only be one person who knows where I am living, other than my current housemates. He must have read my message. I try hard to concentrate as I pull open the envelope with clumsy, rash movements, sweat threatening to prickle on my skin. A book of assorted classical pieces. I can't take in the music as a cacophony of invasive thoughts is making me feel both deaf and dumb. My brother. Thinking of me. It makes a spark of life shoot through my body, which is quickly followed by a heavy pang beneath my heart. *Why hasn't he sent for help? Couldn't he have called the police, if he's worked out my address?*

Chapter Fifteen

Yalina

Christmas and New Year 2007
Somewhere near Sheffield

I find I'm being hauled over his shoulder, like a fireman's lift from when I was small and my father would run around the garden with me in this position. I cannot place the garden in my memory, though. It's not the garden I grew up in.

I see my own limbs kicking and punching, and then he is shoving open a door, and we are flying down steps, my head jig-jigging upside down, a wave of nausea engulfing me. The cold air hits my naked arms even though I am hoisted high over his shoulder. I feel the solidness of concrete underneath me as he dumps me on the ground. Lifting my head, I see his huge figure make its way back up the steep stairs and then suddenly the light at the top of the steps diminishes as the door slams shut. I don't hear a key turn, so I try to make it to my feet, but my hip is twisted painfully to one side.

The darkness is stunning me, as is the cold. The temperature down here must be in the single digits. Already I have goosebumps on my arms, and I focus on this rather than try to establish what is happening. All I can see is the garden in my mind. There's a shed at the bottom of it, next to a huge tree, I can't tell what type. There's a girl there, playing with a water feature. Splashing her fingers into the running stream. Raim. She doesn't seem as stocky as I recall, her skin not as dark, but she is very young here.

As I begin to rub the tops of my arms to keep warm, the

door is prised open with a slight squeak and the sudden stab of light temporarily blinds me. Keith has returned, another body hanging over his shoulder. He jogs down the steps as if he is taking part in running an errand; a quick trip to the post-box up the road. Rebecca is dumped opposite me. I noticed she wasn't kicking or punching on her way down.

"Laters, ladies!" He is laughing again. Over his other shoulder are a couple of thin fleece blankets which he throws in the area between us. Then he is gone. I feel for the nearest blanket and hold it to my face.

We've been down here for what feels like a week but is in fact probably only a couple of hours. The walls are watching us, looming heavily, reminding us of our situation.

"I'm hungry," Rebecca says. I can't really see her well in this light, despite my eyes adjusting slightly to the darkness.

"Well, I don't think there's anything down here."

I have tried standing up, despite the pain in my hip, and feeling my way around. The walls are damp and aren't helpful to a blindfolded prisoner. I ask Rebecca to have a look around but she won't. She says she is too scared.

I am looking directly at her figure, diminutive in the darkness.

"They're shitting themselves because you are so underage," I explain. "And they didn't appreciate me questioning them on what they will do about Gillian's baby."

"I don't care that I'm younger," my friend says, ignoring the baby comment. There are slivers of naivety in her voice, "We all do the same job."

I suddenly feel so much older than my years. I suppress the urge to mother her. "It's not about it being fair on all of us. You are classed by the law as a child."

I can't tell if she is looking directly at me or not. She is fumbling around on the floor, trying to find a comfortable position.

"They will go to prison forever if they get caught using you."

Rebecca's response is immediate. "But then where will I

live?"

Her words make me so heavy with sadness; the fear that she won't have a place to exist when all of this is over.

"You will live with me." I sound like I mean it. Perhaps I do.

She doesn't answer, and her snivelling tells me that she is crying. I can't think of anything to say and am relieved to hear the sound of the lock turning at the top of the steps, and the sudden flash of light. He is quick, though, and pulls the door shut behind him. I see him pull his phone out and put on the torch light feature. It brightens up the cellar more than any light at the top of the steps, and for the first time we can see all around us. It looks like Rebecca has been crying for some time, her face flushed red and blotchy. I try to look at the figure moving down the steps but the light from the phone is too painful on my eyes.

Jonno's voice. "Got you some water here," he says, matter of fact. "Don't down it all at once." He puts two plastic bottles in front of the pair of us. From his pockets he pulls out two packets of crisps, winking in Rebecca's direction. "And don't say we're not spoiling you."

He throws the crisps near the water. I want to grab at both but I won't let him have that satisfaction.

"How long are we here?" I still can't look directly at him, because of the light.

He acts like he doesn't hear me. "There's a light switch somewhere in here. So you don't have to sit in the complete dark. Dunno if it still works, though."

Rebecca is reaching out for the water. She is eyeing him. "You're the nicer one. You've always been nicer. Can't you get us out of here?"

He is smiling. It looks almost genuine. "You mean the cellar or out of this game?"

She smiles back weakly. "The cellar."

It hits me again how desperate her predicament is. The need to belong somewhere.

"Not 'til it's the right time."

Rebecca nods.

I will not do the same. "This is ridiculous! Let us out, we have done nothing wrong. I'll…" I can't think of a single threat to use against them.

"You'll what?" laughs our tormentor.

I stare at the wall ahead of me, lit up against the shadow figures of us. It is visibly wet.

"So when will we get out of here?" I try again.

Jonno, stooping, straightens his back. The light from the torch of his phone jigs higher up on the walls. He steps forward a few paces, reaches out to a string hanging from the low ceiling. "This here is your light switch." He pulls on it with conviction. For a couple of seconds, nothing happens, just Rebecca and I looking at each other from our cross-legged positions on the floor. Then there is the sound of a faint flickering; moth wings. A volt of electricity fires itself into a low-hanging single lightbulb, a few feet away from us, nearer the back wall of the cellar.

"And then there was light," I announce. I feebly look at my audience to see if I've received even the most wry of smiles.

"We can keep it on the whole time?" asks Rebecca. I notice she has already tucked into the packet of crisps.

"No, not the whole time." Keith is fiddling with his phone, trying to disable the torch function. Once his laser light is off, we can see the cellar with more clarity, no continuously moving spot light any more. It is a perfect square, perhaps fifteen foot across. There are piles of old broken plastic chairs in one corner, piles of newspapers next to them. A pair of old workmen's boots, layered in old mud, fresh mud on top, are abandoned against a wall. I try to picture the previous owners gardening, fork foisted into the wet ground outside the house.

"When are you coming back?" My friend sounds keen. Not scared.

He is already beginning to make his way up the steps. "Don't keep the light on," he warns. The door opens again with the flash of natural light, and then is closed again. There is the sound of his key in the lock of the door, a twisting of metal, and then his footsteps pound away into nothing.

I do not look at Rebecca, my eyes are still casting around the room. The lightbulb is swinging slightly from Keith's movements. There is nothing soft to sleep on, apart from the flimsy blankets he has brought us, and I want to wrap mine around myself, like a baby.

Chapter Sixteen

Yalina

New Year 2007/8
Somewhere near Sheffield

It must be losing them money, having the both of us kept down here. That's the loss of roughly two to three punters a night, each, nearing a grand. I assure Rebecca of this, even though I don't believe she is as frightened as I am. She is worried about her empty stomach.

I'm ignoring the gnawing pains in mine. You get to a point of hunger, you get past it, and for the record we've not exactly been dining like queens since we were both dragged into this life. The newspapers beneath me aren't dry. I look to the box of papers in the corner. A part of me wants to rifle through them. There's something about the arrogance of the box sitting there, full of dumped *stuff*. I find myself wondering if there is something with our address on there, or anything else of importance. My heart quickens slightly as I consider pulling myself up to wander over there to the corner, but my weak bones just won't allow it.

I think Rebecca is trying to doze. It might be early morning, there is no way of telling. I am wide awake, the cold chewing its way through my bones, and the damp beneath me keeping me moving, trying to position myself in a way that is not uncomfortable.

Rebecca must have turned the light off at some point when I had fallen asleep, and there is only the claustrophobia of darkness now.

I call her name, and she moans a little, still dozing. I call again, and I hear the movement of her body, twisting on the newspaper.

"You ok?" I call.

She gives a little grunt. "I just want to be living with you now. In your home."

I blink, remembering my conversation with her yesterday. A trickle of guilt or something similar is winding its way into my stomach. "Well, we need to find a way out of here first." It's the best I can come up with.

"Can you go pull the light switch?" she asks.

I am aching, pain registering down my spine, but I try to stand. It takes me a while to find my feet. The air is so cold as I straighten myself up, that immediately I wrap my arms around my body.

I walk gingerly, slowly, over to the wall where I think the light switch cord is hanging. The darkness is making me doubt my footing.

"Are you doing it?" Rebecca queries.

I am reminded again that she is a child. Three years from being an official adult. Nine years from my own age.

"Yup." I fumble around in the air nearest the side wall, finding nothing at first. An insect flies and gently hits me in the face, and I realise with relief that it is the cord I am searching for. I pull on it, and again it takes a couple of seconds for anything to happen. The light that flares out from the bulb is still soft, but is enough to light the room.

Rebecca is still lying down. "Do you miss home?"

Her question seems to have come from out of the blue; an obvious sounding query, but one I am not sure how to answer.

"Of course!"

She is watching me make my way back over to my crumpled pile of blanket and newspapers on the floor. I notice the newspapers aren't even damp.

"What will you do when you get home?"

I sit back on my base. Words are tik-tikking through my mind but I can't select the right ones. *Do I miss my family?*

The one I was living with when I was recovering?

I have nothing to lose by being honest. "I'm not sure. I don't know what I will be doing. Or if they will even want me there."

I can feel her face scrunching up without even looking at it. "What do you mean?"

"Just. Families."

"Meaning?"

I don't know how to explain. "Families are...hard work. Not always as happy and as welcoming as you might expect."

Rebecca is wide-eyed. "Why don't they want you there?"

She doesn't get it, of course she doesn't.

I don't even get it. "Just, I don't know. I just don't feel all that close to them."

"Oh." She is staring elsewhere now, her dream snapping and breaking into little shards of glass.

"I mean, you can still be with me, wherever I end up." My words are hollow.

She looks like she wants to shout at me, but she bites her bottom lip to keep any words in.

"How did you end up here?" I shouldn't have put her on the spot.

She sits up, folding and refolding the empty crisp packet in her hands. Not saying anything. She is blinking a lot.

"You don't have to say," I add. I wonder if she is making up a story in her head to tell me.

"It's ok." She looks at me. "I came from a children's home. I think you knew that part. I hated it there. Haven't seen my own parents since I was ten."

I find myself yearning, not for her not loss, but with a jealous jolt that she had an attachment to people she could call parents in the first place. "That must have been hard," I say instead.

It feels like the room is becoming lighter. There are insects batting around the lightbulb, flitting back and forth, their wings hitting the glass.

"Yeh. The people in the children's home don't care about

me. They just do it so they can get paid."

My mind wanders. My *parents*. My *mother. Could it be possible I had come from a care home? That my parents had fostered me? I was fostered. Or adopted. I don't physically resemble any of the others, apart from skin colour. Adopted.*

It seems so obvious to me now. There are parts of the puzzle in my mind, shifting around, trying to find the space that fits. The current piece is almost nuzzling its way into the gap in my thoughts. *Adopted. Adopted.*

Rebecca is talking. "Are you ok? Are you listening? You look weird."

I blink and smile, trying to show her I'm completely invested in her story.

She continues. "So anyway, it got to the point where one of the carers there just...had it in for me. You know what I mean? I mean, I couldn't get anything right. Nothing. And I'd been talking online to this man for a while. He sent a picture." And she pauses, glancing up the steps where the door is.

"What?" I don't know why she has stopped talking.

Rebecca is holding a finger to her lips. She is whispering. "I'm not meant to tell anyone."

I nod for her to continue, and to show that I understand.

"He offered me a job. A permanent job and a life out of the care system. And he told me how beautiful I was. That he wanted to be with me."

I can feel myself raising my eyebrow. "Then what?"

"Then I arranged to meet him on the corner of my street, by the launderette, and we'd go for a date. The date didn't happen, I got into his car and he drove me straight to this empty flat in God-knows-what-town, and then forced himself upon me. The other men came for the same from the next night onwards. I'm talking about Keith, by the way."

After what might be around two days, the door at the top of the steps opens, and stays open. Both of the men stagger down, pick each of us up by our elbows, and drag us back up the steps. My legs are shaky, weak from hunger and from sitting down, but I still make a point of struggling. Rebecca is ahead of me. The men say we don't have to work tonight, and now we are in our room, Rebecca and I, her back on her shared mattress and me on mine. Another girl, the skinny one, seems to have taken it over in my absence but shifts quickly to the floor on seeing me. I lie down, my brain still on over-drive. I wish now that I had pulled my parents' house apart; every door, every drawer, in the hunt to find news of my biological parents. I can't believe I haven't thought of it before. My mother probably has thick browny-red hair like me; my green eyes unusual for Pakistanis. My father, perhaps he has my snub nose. They will have photos of the day I was born adorning their mantlepiece. I just need to find them.

Chapter Seventeen

Yalina

Early January 2008
Somewhere near Sheffield

Some nights are worse than others, just as some clients are easier than others. Tonight is a strange one. The man I am with at 10pm is sad looking. He has not yet had his way with me. I wonder, for a fleeting moment, if he is a plain-clothed officer, here to pretend to want me. I play along, lead him to the stairs. He takes his time to climb each step, and is cautious entering the room with me. I wonder how far we can take it.

He stares beyond my head, and I see he still has sad eyes, and wet traces on his cheeks. I take the liberty of asking what is wrong.

He shakes his head. "I shouldn't be doing this." It is a relief to hear a punter in this game who questions what he does.

He reaches to get something out of his pocket. His hand is shaking a little, he sees me notice this, and puts his hand back down on his lap.

I sit up. There are pins and needles in my arms. "You don't have to go through with it."

He doesn't meet my eye. "But I want to be with you. I just...oh, this is such a cliche. I just want...someone to talk to." He is crying now, staring at me.

It is unnerving; I look away. *Why is he here?*

"You are someone's daughter," he says. "I bet your father is proud."

I don't want to think of my father's reaction. His shame. He would disown me if he knew. That wouldn't be such a bad thing.

There is silence for a few moments. "I have an idea," I say. "I've got another client in twenty minutes, but there is someone you can talk to, if you like." The last thing I want to do is console another human being who is just as cut-up as I am. *Let me enjoy my own misery for a while.*

I stand up and fasten the buttons of my shirt. I motion for him to leave the performance room with me and I make him wait in the hallway downstairs whilst I venture into the room I share with the other women. Only Gillian is there, one leg stretched out in front of her on the floor. It's hard to tell if she's awake. The others are clearly not back yet, the room looks bizarre so stripped of bodies. I think the men are making more money from the women being at the nail bar than they are pimping them out at night.

"Gillian," I hiss.

She slowly turns her head towards me.

"Something out here that might interest you."

She slowly stands, her stomach sticking out in front like a beachball blown up under her top. "What is it?"

I explain briefly to her about the man. She smiles and stretches her back, using the wall for support. I notice her belly is unbearably huge, but cast my eyes to the floor when she catches me looking.

The man is hovering in the hallway, looking unsure, his own eyes darting towards Gillian, and then a slight expression of confusion appearing on his face. I realise I haven't asked him for his money and feel the heat of embarrassment begin to climb its way up my neck. I think he was trying to pay me earlier. I should have just let him.

"You can chat to Gillian, if you like," I say, pointing towards the battered sofa in the tiny living room area. "She doesn't get to see many people. But, um, are you ok to still pay?"

He sits on the old floral sofa. I find myself noticing how threadbare the arms are. I wonder the story behind the sofa, where it was originally purchased, how many owners it's been through.

"Sure," says the man. He pulls a wad of cash out of his shirt pocket, the opposite pocket to the one he had reached to earlier. I find myself apologising as I take the money from him. I go to post it into our money slot in the hallway, locked and only accessible by Jonno or Keith. I wonder how often it is opened. A few times every night, probably. When I return to the lounge, I notice the man's eyes are still red-rimmed. Gillian begins to chat to him in her soft, velvety voice. His hands are still shaking.

Christmas wasn't celebrated here for the others. I am used to no Christmas. The men are in worse moods than ever; they say the work dried up over the festive period. I find myself worrying for them, my veil of a permanent frown slipping to show that I'm concerned. Perhaps I am thinking about how it will affect us girls. Gillian. I couldn't bear to be put in a barn again. Only two nights in that filthy structure within the safe cocoon of summer was enough. A woman can't give birth in a barn. Or perhaps she will have no choice. I wonder where Jonno and Keith will sleep if we have to leave the house, and find myself feeling a stab of pity towards them. Perhaps I *am* suffering from Stockholm Syndrome; fretting about where my captors would live. These past months of being entrapped have brought out a gradual sense of kindness, of empathy within me. Can't be a bad thing. I was a pretty self-serving person before all of this, save the animals I worked with.

***

Jonno is nodding at Keith one Sunday morning before they all head off to Leeds. I feel a slight stab in my stomach, but the other girls seem unaware. They are about to do something, these men.

Keith is grinning my way. "Go round up the other girls," he orders, hand-rolled fag hanging out of the corner of his mouth.

"Huh?"

96

He stops grinning. "Go get all the others!" he yelps. "There's something needs to be said."

I look around the dining table; there isn't room for everyone. Some girls are eating out of their hands on the floor. Gillian is allowed a seat, on account of her condition. Ruby and her two friends are eating dry looking bread cross-legged on the floor. Rebecca sits opposite me, only glancing up at Keith's last comment. The other girls are already about to pull on their coats by the back of the house. I stand and call to them, and they pause, not sure whether to listen to me.

I want to ignore him, walk out the room. That would make him look ridiculous. He jolts his body to make me jump.

"Keith needs a word!" I shout through the door to the utility room.

I see them look at each other, and they abandon their coats in a bundle on top of the old unused washing machine. It makes me realise that nobody has washed any of their clothes in the months we have been here. I wash my underwear in the kitchen sink when the others are usually out.

With all of the girls within one room, I realise what a sorry state we all look. The younger girls, so wan and faded, eyes slightly bulging, a mouth that could tell a thousand stories. Their whole lives revolve around the orders of these two men. Mine doesn't. I am going to be the one who makes it. It's just a matter of *when.*

Jonno is heading for the stairs. Keith stands from his chair.

"Follow us," says Keith. "And no talking or funny looks."

The others follow his instructions and don't risk sneaking a sideways glance at each other. I remain in the living room for a minute or two, savouring having a moment to myself, a moment of rebellion.

The stomping up the stairs by eleven people should be quite a sound, but the girls know to pick up their feet, to walk on tiptoes where possible.

"My room!" instructs Keith.

I find myself running up the stairs, if only to protect the other girls from what fate awaits them.

At once, a thought hits me like a dart between my eyes.

Oh God. *Oh, my God.*

He's going to make an example of me, in his room, in front of all of them. Holy hell. There are beads of sweat rising on my neck, and saliva beginning to appear in my mouth. I can't be sick here. All for that bloody laptop. I knew he would find out.

He pauses as he sees that all of his girls are safely fitted into his bedroom. It looks no different from when I crept into it the first time. Except now it's full of confused people.

Jonno is pulling at a smaller door on the other side of the room, the wardrobe having previously been yanked out of the way. "This," he announces. "Is our safe spot. Ok?"

I don't know if he is expecting an answer.

Keith walks over to the door, keen to be the lead teacher in this scenario. "This is where we go. If the pigs call. You geddit? You hear the doorbell go, ever, and you all need to scarper up here. The wardrobe will be out, ready. You will all go in, and I will be the one to pull it back across."

I hear Ruby is clearing her throat. "Why you think the police come soon? And how much room is in there?"

I'm sure she does it to wind him up.

Keith doesn't answer, but his neck is becoming redder, the veins more pronounced. I think I could pop his head with a pin.

She doesn't stop. "I mean, there are so many of us now. How many can fit in a cupboard?"

Keith lurches forward and grabs Ruby by her arm. "Take a look!" He shoves her towards the little door that Jonno is now holding open; it appears to have a spring-lock.

"It's a *passageway,*" he snarls.

She tentatively takes a step forward, ignoring the pain that must be simmering on her arm, then turns and signals for her nearest friend, toe-painting girl, to join her. They both disappear as they take further steps forward.

"We don't need to go in there right now, surely?" I find myself asking. I'm still shaken, fluids jig-jiggling in the pit of my stomach. Why should I trust these men? They are probably trying to lock us away right now. But before they drive all the other girls to Leeds? That would be a day of lost cash for them.

"We need a practice run, I guess," says Rebecca. *Whose side is she on?*

The girls start walking towards the little door, bowing their heads as they enter.

Soon it is only Gillian and me left, Keith staring us down.

"I don't see why we have to go in," I state.

I feel a shove between my shoulders, and I am falling into the doorway. I expect to hear a door slam and lock behind me, but when I glance back, there is only Gillian treading her own path very carefully. The other girls are squatting on the floor of what is a barely-lit low ceilinged corridor. Rebecca is giggling, as if we are naughty school children on a day-trip.

"No talking, brownie!" Jonno is the one giving commands now. "If you ever need to go into here, if the pigs do come, you cannot be talking!" His enthusiasm means particles of his spit are flying from his mouth. "You can hear voices from this passageway from outside the house. They need to hear nothing!"

I guess he means the police. How kind of him to point that out to us. I make a mental note to be as vocal as possible, should we be trapped in here with the forces coming looking for us. I find I am smiling to myself, and I don't care if they see. I think of shouting now, of screaming out for help. But it's not the right time. It needs to be the correct time.

Keith clears his throat, a warning to us that he is about to lurch into a tirade, a lecture.

"Since some of you seem pretty keen on snaking us out," and he stares at Ruby here, "we need to have somewhere we can hide you away. One of us will be up here with you, so don't go thinking you can just call for help."

There goes my little plan.

Gillian has her hand up like a child in a classroom.

"Yeh?" grunts Keith.

"How can the girls have sex with all those men if they are locked up in here?"

I giggle into my fist. He ignores her question and growls again at the rest of us. They have to be in Leeds in one hour to open up the shop.

Chapter Eighteen

Yalina

Mid-January 2008
Somewhere near Sheffield

New Year's was a non-event. I have hazy memories from before, of dancing in the local streets of my little town, doing the *can-can* and whatever else after the chimes had rung in the new year. I think I can remember my sister dressing up as a maid, or a nurse, and for some reason, pineapple earrings, her wiry body dancing like a maniac. Dad and mum are in the picture too; mum is swaying in line with the other people, hands on the person in front's hips, dad not dancing but trying to catch everything on his camcorder. They are the only ones who have not touched the alcohol in our street. I think it is our street, but I'm not sure I recognise the houses. There are these little fragments of puzzle, fitting together over periods of time, some pieces fitting straight away, other pieces having to be removed again, to maybe try later. I can't place my brother in this street scene. Perhaps he is in the kitchen, clearing up after everyone else.

There is something lying in the dust by the front door. An envelope. Brown in colour. I am searching for fingerprints on the envelope, for any proof of my brother. I wonder if they have threatened him, have seen him lurking nearby, waiting for the right time to post my music through the door. I think of the courage it must have taken, the risk of seeing those men, but still trying to reach me. Their threats are what is preventing him from calling the police. I wonder if they offer death-threats to strangers.

I put the music up hastily on the stand, and call out to Rebecca who, just months ago, would have loved to come and sing with me on the little stool as I played. Her comment the other day, "Gillian is your new best friend now!" only served as a stark reminder of her lack of maturity.

She does appear though, and I try my friendliest smile to reach her. Not speaking, she sits silently on the edge of my stool, being careful not to touch me.

I turn the first page, and I am away. I don't recognise the name of the film, but I have heard the tune before. I can feel Rebecca jigging in time to the music, like she used to.

"Makes me think of my last care home," she offers.

I want to stop playing, to question her, to ask if she's ok, but I daren't. I still don't understand why she wouldn't prefer the security of the care home over this. I abandon the thought deliberately; I'm in the flow of the music, and I can tell she is, too.

After the song, she rests a hand on my knee, looking straight at me.

"Do you know, I'm only fifteen," she says.

"I know," I say, and I hug her. I notice her fingernails are painted red. Perfect shaped blood stains.

I am drinking lager with Ruby and her two friends in their room. It is their *night off,* and mine. I would rather have had the vodka this time, but Ruby says she's out of it. I remember that one of the girls has been named by Jonno and Keith as *Lauren,* but I can't remember the other.

"So I guess you're missing home?" I ask, and then immediately regret my pitiful question.

Ruby glances at the other girls before speaking. One of them nods back at her.

"Nah," says Ruby. "Nothing was great there either." She doesn't elaborate.

Emily is kneeling in a prayer position. I notice she has dark rings around her eyes. "Ruby is the trouble-maker around here," she laughs.

I remember the bruise that Ruby had been given for trying to tie bed sheets together, but I say, "How come?"

Toe-painting girl is walking across the huge room, hairbrush in hand. Her legs are like twigs. "Oh, she likes to have it out with Keith. Or Jonno. She doesn't want to *know her place.*"

Ruby rolls her eyes from her squalid mattress. "And Jonno is from same place as us. He came over ages ago, though. You think he'd be a little kinder to us."

I notice there is another girl, one who arrived with Gillian, in the corner of the room, sleeping.

"I just won't put up with the shit anymore," Ruby states. "They control our lives, they tell us who we have to sleep with, and we can't turn a single man down. They keep the money that we earn. I will get my own back. You will see."

Her friends nod and look down at the floor, almost in unison.

She closes her eyes. "And I miss my friend. They took her away from me."

I don't know what to say.

"Petrova," announces toe-painting girl, joining in again.

I swallow down my mouthful as quickly as I can. "I was with Petrova in the barn when they first threw me in! Blonde?"

Nobody says anything.

"I couldn't get her to leave with me. She just stood there when I broke through the door." The heaviness of the guilt at having left Ruby's friend behind is threatening to ruin my night. I don't know how Ruby would have known her.

I take another swig of the lager. I'm glad it's a Sunday and the men are still out at the nail bar. My head is beginning to throb and swell with sudden floatiness; there are bubbles beginning to grow and then delicately pop within the cogs of my grey matter. I wonder if the other girls can tell I'm not accustomed to drinking.

"So where is this barn?"

I shrug, my helplessness perhaps being conveyed as a

sense of my being non-committal. I couldn't remember how to get there if I tried.

Ruby sighs with purpose. "How the fuck do I find her?"

I say nothing, aware of the other girls looking at me.

"Why does nobody else try to escape?" Ruby is continuing. "What would it take? It cannot be so difficult. We need to find Petrova. I think she is alone."

I cut her short. "You could escape right now if you wanted," I suggest. "The men aren't here. They won't be back for a couple of hours. All the doors are locked, of course, but didn't you say you were going to try a downstairs window?" I am goading her, the alcohol pushing me.

She isn't speaking, just staring straight at me.

"Don't be ridiculous!" I hear one of the other girls say.

Ruby is standing up from her mattress now, looking around. She kicks at a pile of sheets on the floor and grabs at a black sweater, then picks up a half-filled water bottle, and a little book that is underneath her mattress. She glances up at the rest of us who are staring. Secretly, I am hoping she does it. To prove that it can be done. *Go on, go on.*

She is out of the room and down the stairs faster than we can follow her, a cascade of footsteps down the rickety old staircase, sound muted by the red swirls of the carpet.

Chapter Nineteen

Richard

October 2006
Islington, London

He was thriving at university. Made friends, had a busy social life, and was getting first grade results on his course. Well, of course he was. It's George we are talking about here. He was becoming more recognised. The local papers were beginning to mumble, quietly at first, about his talents.

His mum would come up from London too, and sometimes we would travel in the same car, or the same carriage if we opted to use the train. Nat would come too, no awkwardness between her and Suzie, although often they would find little to chat about. Zoe, fourteen to George's nineteen, would usually sit between the two women, whether by design or default I still do not know, her eyes fixed firmly on the pink phone screen held in front of her. She had started to lose her cuteness by fourteen. (Ok, who am I kidding? She had lost it by eleven). George was still the apple of her eye, though. You only had to mention his name and she would jump up like an over-excited spaniel, eyes glazing over, and demanding, "What? What is George doing?" and the inevitable, "When are we going to see him next?"

She would be buzzing with anticipation on the days we went up to Oxford, but then play it as cool as she could manage on the journey up there.

Chapter Twenty

Yalina

Mid-January 2008
Somewhere near Sheffield

She is already in the dining room, trying the top of the sash window. The catch won't budge. I can see her scrawny arms shaking from the strain of trying to open it. She runs to the living room, where the window is slightly smaller and is more risky as it faces the road. She doesn't care. She is trying the clasp on this window too. We are all standing, mesmerised but not helping. The lager is making my head feel heavier, my vision a slight blur. This could be a dream. I could wake up tomorrow and it will be a normal, grey Monday morning where nothing in particular has happened the night before, just the usual men and their usual sticky demands.

I rush to the utility room at the very back of the house, grab a black padded coat. I don't know who owns it. We have to share coats around here. Pacing back into the living room, I thrust the coat at Ruby, who has managed to slice at the window latch with a paper knife she has obtained from God-knows-where. The other girls are hauling the heavy window open from underneath. It is taking three of them just to hold the pane open about a foot, one girl's shoulder shoved under the frame. The window almost stretches from floor to ceiling; you would think this would make it the ultimate escape route, but it seems the more glass, the more of a barrier. Ruby thrusts the coat under her arm, and her little bag over the other arm, and then suddenly she is standing outside, giving us the thumbs-up sign. Her little bag looks pathetic in the great outdoors, a little fish in a big pond.

There is the warmth of elation in my body for her, and for Petrova, should she ever be found. I imagine for a split second the wonderful life of freedom ahead of her. Ahead of both of them. I watch Ruby's tiny figure become smaller and smaller, and gradually disappear from view at the end of the road, an incongruent sense of sadness instilling itself in my bones, and a voice whispers, *You're not strong enough to leave.*

I reply to that internal voice. "*I'm waiting here for my brother.*"

I think I sound quite brave.

***

I have worked out that I have probably had sex with at least eighty men since working here. I say *working*. It's not work. We don't get paid. They say they will pay us, in euros, but that has yet to happen. We use barrier methods of contraception as that's *nice and cheap*, but I would rather be on the pill. I really worry about ending up like Gillian. I haven't even asked her if the baby is from a partner or a punter. My gut tells me it's the latter, so I refrain from asking the question. Sometimes I envy her. She hasn't had to sleep with anyone here, as far as I can tell. She is definitely in the last stages of her pregnancy. The glasses in the kitchen are clean, gleaming. Any food that has been bought is stacked squarely in the cupboards or precisely in either the fruit compartment of the fridge or one of the glass shelves. It feels, almost, like we live in a home, as a family. With a nesting mother-to-be. Although the bedrooms of bodies sleeping on the floors, some on mattresses, some not, would contest to that.

The bathroom is the most smack-you-in-the-face reminder of what we are all having to endure. I guess I could ask for some bleach as one of my favours, but they don't seem to be

106

a thing these days. I haven't requested one in a long time, the other girls haven't either. I will ask soon. I am owed something. But not bleach.

Jonno is shoving his clothes into the washing machine that afternoon.

"No nail bar?" I try, casually.

He doesn't look up, just continues to force a too-large bundle into the machine. I wonder why he gets clean clothes and we don't.

"It's Saturday," he states.

Means nothing to me. They both usually work weekends. They have to, to keep an eye on the girls.

"Ok," I say.

He stands up, hands pressing into the small of his back. He looks so domesticated like this, so harmless. "What do you want?"

I pause for a moment, not sure whether to just come out with it, or to build up to my request. "Do we still get favours?"

It sounds like a blurt, not thought out.

His face is beginning to crack into a smile. Not a pleasant one. "Well, what do you want?"

I point over to the piano. "It needs tuning. I would help pay if I had some cash. If you would pay us like you said you would."

His smile quickly drops and bends into a frown. "Nah. Hassle," is all he says. I assume he is talking about the piano, not our remuneration. He plays around with the dial on the machine. Perhaps he has not washed his clothes since living here. Months and months of yellowing, hard clothes. I imagine them standing up by themselves in his room, like cardboard cut-outs of his body.

"So what do you think?" My words are bold.

His expression does not change. "Nobody comes to the house. You know that."

Rage is soaring through my chest like an arrow piercing through flesh. "Oh, apart from all the men you force us to have sex with?"

He grabs at me, a handful of shirt. "Listen, love. You should be bloody grateful for what you've got here. You've got the sweetest deal. Have you seen where they keep the other girls around here? Have you?"

"How would I? We never see anyone else. We're cooped up here every night. The shower doesn't even work properly. The other women stink. You need to sort this out."

He is laughing, hand still gripping my shirt. I notice he has a bluebird tattoo on his neck, distorted by his tendons poking out, sinewy.

"Sort your own piano out. Would make more sense to burn the damned thing."

A thought pings itself into my brain like a miniature aircraft travelling at the speed of light. A wretched thought, but an idea all the same. I am twisting my fingers. "What if I make it worth your while?"

I can feel his eyes burning into me but I am looking around the cramped utility room. I notice red tiles on the wall that I had not noticed before, one in every six tiles adorning the shape of a rose, thorns lingering under the petals.

"What?"

"You know what I mean."

He is laughing, the noise of the washing machine barely covering the sound. "You must want that bloody piano to work! Come on then. Whilst we've got time."

I feel like laughing out loud. I know he is the softie of the two. The other one has already forced himself on me. Not to mention the other girls he's done the same to. Jonno is a *polite* sex-ring leader. He waits for me to suggest it.

"Your part of the deal first," I state. Maybe I should put my hands on my hips.

I can tell he is thinking it through. I study his tanned skin, darker around his face than his arms. I wonder if he is Hispanic.

"Not gonna work for me."

I raise an eyebrow; I am calling the shots here. "I need to see that you mean it. You could just do me and then not provide my favour."

He is studying me now. I wonder if he is thinking how brown my skin is, too.

"And no offence, but you obviously have forced us all into this scenario with a bunch of lies. I mean, how can I trust you?"

He pulls himself up taller, so he is towering over my five foot two frame. "Listen, brownie. Do you want me to just take it for myself anyway? Like my pal does?"

"You wouldn't." I am risking a lot here, goading him.

He is walking out of the utility room, into the kitchen. I don't know if the conversation has finished. I follow him through.

"So?" I venture.

"So. I'm thinking about it. But the answer is probably no."

I feel like screaming, but I don't. I keep my composure; I say, "Sure thing."

He looks back at me before he begins to ascend the staircase. "And if you keep banging on about it, you can work days too, like the others. Dodgy heart or no dodgy heart."

The words are swimming in front of my eyes now. *My heart is fine. I'm not the one with the dodgy heart.*

Chapter Twenty-One

Yalina

Mid-February 2008
Somewhere near Sheffield

I don't know if I will go through with it. There is sleeping with random men at night because you simply have no choice, and then there is sleeping with your power-hungry captor for a favour. A person who has made each waking moment of your life something that is just a claustrophobic, drunken blur, out of your control. Someone who is threatening to take away the one element which helps you to survive. I am weighing up the options. The scales in my mind are silver, they're weighted with guilt and disgust on one side, pleasure and beauty on the other. I cannot tell which side is the heaviest. When I told Gillian, she hissed and shook her head in that way of hers. I didn't think she'd approve. But I have been through worse, much worse since I have been held here. Men I would never even look at on the street, much less give them my body, have demanded unpleasant things from me. Men who seem to have crawled from the darkest corners of the earth in order to get a quick moment of physical release. It makes me think less of them. Of men in general. I know my brother would not be one of these men.

Most nights I think of Ali. Not when I am *working*, but afterwards. I lie on my mattress, often the last back to the shared, obnoxious smelling room that used to just house Rebecca and me.

I wonder what he thinks I am doing. I sometimes think

about if he had replied to my message online with instructions, or explanation. I want to know how he found where I was living. I want to tell him how thankful I am for the sheet music he has sent to me, twice now. Something inside me curls up into a tight ball when I envision him encountering either Keith or Jonno at the door. But especially Keith. If only I had the courage to ask Keith if anyone had called for me. Or maybe Ali just dropped the music through the door without even trying. My mind is whirring; *He has told the police, and they are lying in wait. It's just a matter of time.*

I find the house is quieter now with Ruby gone; I am missing her voice, and her bolshy way. The other girls from her room are silent, I forget they are up there in the evenings after their days in Leeds, and before the men come. I find empty bottles by the bin that nobody empties, and I can smell unwashed bodies from a draught that follows them from up the stairs. Without Gillian, I would be alone. With people, but alone. Gillian is in her very last days before the birth, I am estimating. At night, when she thinks we are all asleep, I hear her crying. I think it is crying. It's a snuffling kind of sound. She moans somebody's name. During the day, she grips her stomach as minor ripples cast their path across her bump; a foot, a hand extending itself. It's all I can do to stop myself from imagining where this baby will end up. The naive, or hopeful part of my brain is imagining him or her being sold to a wealthy European, or American couple, unable to have a child of their own. A white-columned mansion in Missouri or Iowa, orange trees planted with care punctuating a long, meandering path to the front door. I know Gillian tries not to think of where her baby will end up. I wonder if it would feel like losing a part of your body.

Jonno winks at me whenever he can. He knows it is repulsive. It is his own little control-freak thing. Sometimes he will mouth the word *brownie* at me, or give a tug at my headscarf. I wish I had never opened my mouth about the favour. I haven't even had the time to play at the piano for the past few days, and the music is feeling further and further away from me; a trivial delicacy that I just can't afford. They've got me washing clothes now, during the day. It wasn't me who complained, it was Gillian. The smell of the putrid clothes from all of us girls is making her feel her morning sickness again. Or evening sickness; that's what she used to experience mostly. She apologised profusely when I was the one nominated to wash nine women's clothes. After all, I don't work at the nail bar. I have *had it easy*, they are quick to remind me. The other girls were asking after my heart, my operation. The men must have mentioned it, a reason for why I'm not dragged to the nail bar every day. I told the girls the truth, that I had suffered from a congenital defect since birth. Something that had to wait until I was mid-twenties until it could be operated on.

The thought of my stitches make me feel sick. There is no mirror in this stench-hole of a bathroom of ours. I am grateful. I don't need to see where I was sewn back together, where the deep black bruising took seven months to begin to dull. Where the memories of my childhood used to linger.

I am woken by a low groaning sound in the early hours. I have only just got rid of my last customer, one who didn't seem to want to go home. He reminded me of the man I am meant to call *father*. At first I think it is Rebecca, sleeping under the window, but when I sit up I see Gillian grasping her stomach. She is rocking on the carpet, backwards and forwards. Immediately there is simmering anger in my veins at the man who put her in this position and at the two men who are ignoring it.

"What's happening?"

She just glances at me then continues her rocking, complete with low groans. I fumble with the light switch, and the other two girls open their eyes in confusion.

"Go back to sleep!" I say, and I move across the room to guide Gillian to the door. It takes longer than anticipated. Once I have her in the hallway, she manages to stand straight, hands against the wall. There are beads of sweat populating on her forehead. I see she is wearing joggers, and make a mental note that they will have to come off at some point. There is no time now for me to consider how important my role is. It's been playing at the back of my mind since she arrived here, like a sand timer, sucking away the minutes.

One of the other girls comes out of the room on tiptoes, she motions with her finger to the upstairs of the house. "I shall go get one of the men," she suggests. Her legs are like sticks of liquorice poking out of her over-sized t-shirt.

The response that sparks out of me is unexpected, raw. "Don't you dare!"

She looks bewildered, and I manage to reach over to place one hand on her shoulder. I hope it looks reassuring, rather than a patronising notion. "Let's do this alone. We don't need the men."

I try to imagine this is a scene from perhaps a homely village back in Pakistan. *Just the women. This is women's work.*

I feel Gillian look at me, fear snowballing in her features. She still hasn't spoken. My gut instinct is to call an ambulance, some other agency to take the pressure, the expectation away from me. There is no phone. And that would be the end of us, should I give away our location.

Gillian is beginning to rub her stomach aggressively. It strikes me as amusing, the resemblance of a comedy bear in a kids' tv show, trying to demonstrate hunger.

"Do you need a seat?" is all I can come up with, and notice skinny-girl is still staring at the two of us.

I point for her to go back to the bedroom; she dutifully obeys.

I notice Gillian is nodding to my question, and I make sure she has enough of her weight leant against the wall for me to leave her and find a chair. I grab at a dining room chair from the table. These pieces of furniture make the house we are living in seem normal, sophisticated, even. They are neither. Most of the chairs are wobbly, with a cracked leg or a seat which is hanging off by one screw. There are three different types of chair out of the four which host themselves around the table. The table doesn't match anything either. It is made out of some cheap plywood, on closer inspection, dents nubbed out of the surface, never cleaned. Still, the moment we were transported into this house, I felt safe. *Safer*. God knows where the others had come from. I think back to the boy in the van again, the one who had pissed himself. I will never know his whereabouts, or from where he came. Or what the men would want from him. Well, I can imagine but I push that thought away as Gillian lowers herself on to the least-broken dining chair I can find.

Her features are beginning to ease, a smile is almost stretching itself on to her lips again.

"It's getting better," she says.

I look at her body. She is starting to relax, her arms flopping to her sides.

"Is it meant to?"

She is smiling properly now. "False alarm, I think."

I can't think of anything to say. I'm not a doctor.

My face must be crumpled with concern, as she laughs and puts her soft hand to my cheek. "It's ok, it happened last time," she says.

I help her up from the chair and walk it back to its place at the table. It wouldn't do for me to leave a piece of furniture out of place downstairs. Suddenly I feel like throwing the damned chair at the wall.

Jonno still hasn't got back to me about the favour. The hours I have been sitting listlessly at the piano seem a waste of time; the notes are dull and muted, like a duckling calling to its mother in the wrong voice. I cannot play a single piece without it sounding like a child is doing it. I open the top of the piano and look inside. I don't know what I'm looking for. There are hammers and strings. All look fine to me, sitting there, waiting to be instructed what melody to chime. Shutting the lid, I sit back down on the stool and try to think of something else to occupy my mind. The washing only takes up an hour or two of my day. Gillian is napping, recovering from her false contractions. A thought flashes before my eyes, like rapid gunfire. The laptop. I could check again. I realise I am grinning inanely even though my heart is beginning to race now. I don't know if either of the men are in the house; it is Saturday. There seems to be no order any more in whether both men travel to the nail bar; occasionally one will stay back at the house. It seems to be happening on more of a regular basis now, perhaps they are being considerate in case Gillian goes into labour suddenly.

Or, most likely, they are lying in wait, a vulture quick to the scene of the new-born hare, talons ready, wings spread to take flight.

The staircase always seems to take longer to climb when I know I am not meant to be doing it. It is a mountain, a lack of oxygen the higher I climb, although I know really that my shortness of breath as I approach the top floor is fear. I put my ear against the door of Keith's room, the room where we must drag ourselves to obediently, should the authorities come knocking. Nothing. There is a tick-tick of perhaps his bedside alarm clock but nothing else. Confidence overcoming fear, I push gingerly at the door, remembering how it sticks to the carpet. My muscles lock. He is sitting at the dresser. My brain tells my feet to shift backwards but they are reluctant. I cannot help but stare. He is on the laptop. I can see the blue hue of the website page, his right hand lurking over the mouse pad. I'm pretty sure that even Luna, who is curled up and licking her paws on his bed can hear my heart going off like an undetected bomb in a village. She is staring directly at me but doesn't make a sound. I decided to break eye contact with the cat; she miaows, questioning my lack of interest. Keith glances sideways at her briefly. I shift one foot behind me, careful not to fall backwards down the narrow stairwell, and, turning back to the scene, notice all of the drawers of his dresser are hanging open, and the contents thrown upon his already sullied floor. He's been looking for something.

Chapter Twenty-Two

Yalina

Early March 2008
Somewhere near Sheffield

They haven't mentioned Ruby. Well, only once. It gives the rest of us hope. Perhaps too much. Each one of us is plotting, planning. We don't talk about it, but I know each one of us considers just how easy it was for Ruby to get away. You'd think they'd have secured each of the windows, battened down the front and back doors, but for a while I have been questioning their levels of intelligence. I escaped easily enough to go and bury the girls' passports. It wouldn't take much planning. Or *any*. They have us down as too terrified to make the move, too psychologically controlled by them.

The only thing stopping me at the moment is Gillian's impending situation. I don't know about the other girls' reasons, and then a bolt hits me like a pain between the eyes; *they can't return to their home countries.* I should return their passports to them. I just didn't want the men to unscramble our bedrooms and find them. I am scribbling a note down on the back of a piece of old newspaper; *I will be gone from here by mid-summer.* Back to my parents, and my own passport, lying safely inside our sideboard like a newborn baby in its nest of blankets.

Gillian is in the early stages of labour. It's no false alarm this time, she says.

Jonno is hovering in the kitchen, messing about with

newspapers, so I tell him. He doesn't look even slightly concerned. Just looks at me and says, "I've thought about your deal thingy. It's a yes. Just gimme a minute."

My mouth is opening, closing again. My eyes are on my friend, labouring on her hands and knees. Her clothes are stuck to her back with sweat. She has been wearing that same top every day for as long as she's been here, pulling more and more taut at the sides with each passing day. Her joggers have been tucked under her bump for the duration of her stay here. Now it's time for her to pay her way. And for me to pay mine.

I realise Jonno is waiting for an answer.

I say nothing, but he is beginning to look more aggressive in his face, frown lines becoming more pronounced, the sneer in his mouth more prominent.

It makes my stomach heave for a moment, the thought of what am going to have to put myself through. "What, now?"

"Yes, now."

I remember the details of the deal I had tried to make with him. "Erm, the deal was that you organise and pay for the piano tuning before I do anything for you." The relief is mopping at my spine, where sweat is beginning to form. I have bought myself some time. I have bought Gillian the assistance she needs at this hour.

He grins. "Done it, brownie."

Gillian is beginning to moan as she moves backwards and forwards on her knees. An animal caught in a snare, the sounds are spine-chillingly unignorable.

I cast a look back to Jonno. He is getting his phone out of his back pocket. I fantasise about grabbing it, running, yanking that front window up and open. But Gillian is almost howling, her eyes on the threadbare carpet, as if she is the only person left in the room. I wonder how women go through this alone.

Jonno is showing me the screen of his phone. There is a text there. I try to focus my eyes on the writing, there is a receipt of some kind, sent by Brent Yorkshire Pianos. An appointment for the tuning of a piano. This Tuesday.

Gillian has stopped her noises, is sitting back on her heels and sighing. She smiles across at me.

"It stopped?" I try.

She gives a little laugh. "They are contractions. They come and go every four minutes now. I've been counting."

I look back at my captor, putting his phone away again.

"Happy now?" he asks.

I'm not sure if he means that Gillian has stopped being in pain for the time being, or that I can see there is a piano appointment booked.

"I will believe it when I see it." There was too much confidence in that voice, and he doesn't like it. He grabs at my throat this time; my weight is hoisted upon the wall.

"Woah!" calls Gillian, perhaps only just aware of Jonno being in the same room. I don't need her to panic.

He lets go of me, but his face is so close I can see every pore of his skin and smell his earthy breath, mixed with stale smoke.

"Let's go," he says, and he turns to walk across the room.

"After the tuning," I try.

He turns and looks at me. "Are you for real?"

"Yes. My friend is in labour, and how do I know you won't just cancel the appointment after I've played my part?"

He looks to the floor and back up at me. "Women take fucking ages to push a baby out. Look at her."

I glance at Gillian, who is now lying flat on her back, breathing deeply, eyes fixed to the ceiling. She looks as though she's just experienced the most luxurious massage of her life.

I follow him up the stairs.

He is pulling my top over my arms as I hear my friend beginning to groan again from the ground floor. She sounds louder this time. I look at Jonno for his response; I try the most effective pleading eyes I can muster, but he resists eye contact. His mind is on the prize, and only the prize. Shame begins to fill me up inside like an immense heat, as I admit I have chosen my own desires for a piano over this out-of-control situation for my friend. I push him away, I say *I have changed my mind,* but he is naked now. My lower half is still clothed, the deal is not on; I am protected by the jeans I wear. I can't hear Gillian now; the pain must have eased, and I shout in Jonno's face, "I don't want to do this anymore!"

He is pinning me down, the weight of his body on my lower half too much to fight, but I scramble and try to scratch my nails into his face. He tosses his head and my aim misses. He grips me even harder, so that I cannot move at all. I focus on something else, either on the ceiling or a faraway thought. My jeans are off. I dream of the places in the world I would love to discover, when I get away from here. Japan. The USA. I could hire a huge American car and do Route 66. I stop these thoughts as rage courses through my veins; rage at myself for not fighting more. I try to raise my right leg to swipe a foot at him, but again, I miss. I am screaming, and he is doing nothing to silence me. Hopefully another girl will appear at the door, and this will be over.

But there is a burning pain and then he is having his way with me. I turn my face the other way to avoid his gaze, but my arms are still struggling. I notice there are lace curtains adorning the window of this performance room, perhaps supplied by another generation, cream and woven into a beautiful pattern. Like a wedding dress from the nineteen fifties. A spider has made her web along the side of the curtain, delicate loops and weaves against the fabric. It is difficult to tell when the lace ends and the web begins. Rage is flickering at the edges of my thoughts again, and I use my suddenly-free arm to sock him in the mouth. Now there are drops of his blood on my top, and I feel a swell of pride at the wounded man in front of me. Success. He doesn't get opportunity to hit me back. Once he has finished I am halfway down the stairs, pulling jeans over my ankles. I hear him shout something about a *bloody Paki.*

When I get downstairs Gillian is in the same spot, back on her hands and knees, swaying.

"What should I get for you?" My voice is wavering. I don't know if it's the guilt or the uncertainty of the situation.

I grab self-consciously at my headscarf, check it's still there. I could just remove it. There is nobody here that would care.

"Anything." She is growling, a low, bassy sound. "Anything for the pain."

Jonno has followed me down the stairs; perhaps heading for the bathroom. His hand is covering his mouth.

"What can we give her for the pain?"

At first he looks as though he's not going to answer. Then he gives a shrug. It's doubtful whether Gillian will notice his wound.

"Stay there," I say to Gillian, although she is not going anywhere. None of us are.

I bolt up the heavily-carpeted stairs to the middle floor, and let myself into what was Ruby's room. The other women aren't in there. I hastily advance to the bottom of the mattress where she used to sleep, but there is no sheet there covering any lager or vodka this time. *Christ.* I try the wardrobe at the side of the huge room, but it lies empty, save for a few empty carrier bags and coat hangers. From downstairs I hear my friend groaning. I wonder what Jonno is doing.

After raking through sheets and abandoned clothes, I come across a nearly empty bottle of cheap vodka, perhaps the same bottle as Ruby offered me the first time. Grabbing it by the neck, I fly down the stairs. My friend is lying in a puddle on the carpet by the sofa.

"My waters broke…" she begins, but the pain is too much for her to endure.

I twist the lid of the bottle in my fingers and motion for her to drink what's inside.

"Straight?" she questions.

I nod, not knowing what I can possibly find in this house to dilute the drink.

She opens her mouth and I pour the vodka on to her tongue. She is thirsty, and swallows what I pour immediately. I see her face scrunch up with the bitterness of the vodka, and then she relaxes a touch.

"You need to get your trousers off."

I note the irony that my own have only just been pulled

back on.

"Can you help?" she gasps.

I grab her joggers at the waistline and yank them down. They are drenched.

"Where did Jonno go?"

She cannot concentrate on my question. Her chin is down on her chest; the groans are like those of an animal; primitive.

"I need to push," she is moaning. I position myself between her knees and make myself look at where I need to be. Already there is a crowning head, full of black hair, and my friend is lowing, a cow in distress.

"Push, Gillian!" I encourage.

But the top of the head disappears, and Gillian drops her body to the floor with exhaustion. "Can you see it?"

"I *did*."

I grab a tea towel from the kitchen and dampen it from the tap, mop it upon her forehead.

"It'll be another few minutes 'til the next one," she says.

I sink down to my knees. "Are you ok?"

She is smiling, bright white teeth arced in a perfect mouth. "Yes."

I feel burning between my own legs, and bunch them closer together as I sit.

"Are you ok?" she queries.

At first I don't say anything, not knowing if she is aware of my ascent up the staircase with Jonno.

"Yep. Don't worry about me."

Jonno appears from the back door, shutting it behind him and locking with his key. He can do it in a split second now. He is not touching his split lip any longer.

"Have any of you been in Keith's room?"

I glance at Gillian, still reclaiming her breath.

"No. Why?"

"It doesn't bloody matter *why*!" He is grunting. "Just he mentioned that he's lost some stuff from his room. And we all know that you two are the only ones here most of the time."

121

***

The heat is beginning to pulsate in my neck, my jaw, and work its way up.

Gillian picks this time to begin to moan again, flips herself forwards on to her preferred position of being on all-fours.

I can see Keith look at her. "Is she gonna be ok?" he fires at me.

My reactions are as quick as gunfire. "I don't know. *IS* she?" Then I rest my hand on the small of my friend's back, rubbing.

She is moaning, lowing again.

"Gillian, you need to be on your back," I suggest, not knowing what else to do.

"Nooooo," she groans. "I need to sit up."

She is squatting now, her long top covering her thighs and her modesty.

Jonno is just staring.

"Are you going to just stand there and gawp?" I am almost screaming. "Call a bloody ambulance, will you?" I am not scared of him. Not at this moment.

He is shaking his head no, pulling his phone again out of his back pocket.

"Are you calling them?"

He doesn't respond. Gillian is groaning like an animal still, wounded, hurt. She is in her own world; her nostrils flared, saliva flicking from her mouth. Her chin is pushed down into her chest and she is groaning, a long, never-ending mewl from the depths of something I have yet to experience.

And then there is movement, and I rush to grab the child that has so quickly exited her body that my friend and I have no time to even glance at each other. There is blood, water, all kinds of waste pooling around my friend's knees, but she is not looking. She takes the red bundle of flesh from my hands and brings it to her face. She is kissing it. For a moment, it doesn't cry, doesn't move.

Jonno is staring at me, I can feel the heat of his gaze. Neither of us would know what to do with a dead baby.

I picture the woodland all at once, the grave where the passports are buried. The baby would have to go in there. They would be neighbours.

I am waiting for the child to change colour. I have seen blue babies on tv, the ones who didn't quite make it. This baby is a delicious browny-black.

She tips the baby up to get a view between its tiny, puny legs.

"It's a girl," she says, and the baby gives a shriek that makes us all start. The relief at the sound is palpable.

I glance at Jonno, who is still standing where he was. His mouth is hanging slightly open. "Now do something!" I shout, and then he is scrolling on his phone.

It occurs to me that I should take the child, wash her, and then run. But Gillian would not be able to keep up. Perhaps I should do it alone. Run to the nearest hospital, wherever that may be.

"Can I use the phone? It's an emergency!"

"No way," calls Jonno, who is now wandering through the kitchen in an attempt to get out of the back door. Probably to ring Keith.

"Scissors!" says Gillian. She is holding the grisly cord up to me in her spare hand.

I make my way into the kitchen just as Jonno is locking the back door shut again.

There is a pair of steel, unused scissors lying in the sink. They've been in there for weeks, with piles of plates and bowls that will never be washed. We have taken to eating straight from the packet now, or from our hands.

I don't want to be the one to cut the cord, but there is nobody else. The blades cut into the sinewy substance and I have to apply more pressure than I had anticipated. She motions for me to cut it nearer to the baby's body too.

"And the placenta!" says Gillian.

I look at the blancmange lying sodden on the towel on the carpet. It could be a pig's liver. "What do I do with it?"

She shrugs, immediately looking so sad, her huge brown eyes no longer filled with the ecstasy of five minutes ago.

A rattle of the back door shows Jonno is back, his cheeks ruddy. "Keith is on his way. He'll be forty minutes."

I can feel my shoulders sink. For Gillian's sake, I was hoping he was calling a hospital at least. I refuse to look at her.

"Jonno, we need to get rid of this," and I am pointing at the pile of placenta.

He pulls a face. "What?"

"Or we can cook it and eat it."

I'm not sure if Gillian is delirious. She is staring into the baby's eyes, swaying slightly. There is a white paste smeared all over the child, obscuring part of her face. She looks like she's been prepared to be roasted in an oven.

He is staring at me, waiting for guidance.

"Anyone would think you'd never done this before." I don't care if I piss him off. He's had what he wanted.

"So what the hell do we do with it?" his voice sounds almost desperate. "We can't keep it in here. It stinks."

"And the baby's fine, by the way." My voice is sullen, dropped.

He goes back into the kitchen and grabs a plastic carrier bag, then brings it over to us. He hasn't looked at the baby. "Put it in here," he orders.

I can see the swelling of his top lip. It makes me smile inanely. I know he can see me smiling but he doesn't question it. I am winning.

I ignore his order, wait to see him lift the gloop with the tea towel and drop it into the carrier bag himself.

"Now bury it in the woods," I say. I like the authoritative tone of my voice. The weight of the bag takes Jonno by surprise, and it nearly hits the floor.

All at once I have little patience. "Can you just go bury it now!"

He glances at me then is making his way towards the back door, fumbling for the key. I see his arm is shaking. He tells me he won't bury it in the woodland. I try to argue with him, tell him he must, right in the centre of where the trees stand. His butchered mouth drops into an 'O' shape and he is

124

shaking his head no. He says he cannot do that; he can't. I think for a moment that he is going to faint, but he rests his hand against the wall to steady himself, blinks several times. I don't think I have seen him like this.

I look at Gillian, about to suggest we make a run for it, but she is going nowhere. There is blood leaking out of her, and a gaze held in her eyes that tells me there are only two people present in the room, and I am not one of them.

Chapter Twenty-Three

Yalina

Late March 2008
Somewhere near Sheffield

The baby has gone. They let her stay for four days, and then she was gone. Gillian didn't get to say goodbye. She spent her next few days curled up in a ball on her mattress in the room, crying. I hate them, those men. They wouldn't say where the baby been taken to. I try to console Gillian, put my arm around her, but she doesn't register my presence. In the built-in cupboard of our room, I find baby blankets, one blue, one white, which look like they've never been used. She must have stashed them with her when she was brought here.

The days are longer, and the light streams through the floor-to-ceiling windows for a yawning stretch in the mornings, as well as the evenings. I am playing piano, back to a Beatles number I became familiar with in the weeks before the melancholy of the house seemed to follow me everywhere. The keys hit the hammers with clean precision, the notes sharp. At least he kept up his side of the deal. I don't know how much the tuning would have cost him. None of us were allowed to be downstairs when the man came, but I hovered on the first floor landing, ears pricked, taking in the muted deafness of the notes and experiencing them becoming music again. I realise I am playing *Yesterday* and the lyrics succeed in making a lump form in my throat; I quickly flick through to the next page of the music book. Already I am reminiscing about the days here last year when there wasn't such an obvious void in the house, such pain. Well, there *was* pain, but of a different sort. I am beginning to think about when I will make my escape. I have had evenings chattering about it to Gillian, and sometimes to Rebecca, but each roll their eyes, as if to say, *it will never work. You are crazy.*

I remind them, not for the first time, that Ruby escaped without so much of a mention from the men, but they say she was more *streetwise* than me. This stings; although I am not sure why. I am picturing the walk to the edge of Sheffield and down the hilled road past Meersbrook Park, and into the city. Around six miles. I'll have to travel by night, not like the last time. And I'll need some cash. I can worry about the details later. I pick up the sheet music of Brahms that Ali sent to me, and I forget everything as my hands take control of the keys, and the music has its way with me. There may be crying in the room beyond this one; I wouldn't know right now.

Gillian will have to go out to work soon. They say I will, too. When the time comes I know I will fight it out with them. It is March and my operation was a year ago. I am healed. I should be feeling compassion for my friend, child wrenched from her womb, but I am worrying instead about myself. I will not have the chance to play the music; the other girls only being allowed one day off from the nail bar each week.

Keith lets himself in through the battered back door, turns, and quickly relocks it again with a key he forces back into his pocket. We have not made eye contact for some weeks. As he leaves the kitchen and staggers through the dining room, his eye meets mine and I look down.

"Got your pride and joy sorted, then?"

I nod, eyes on the music sheet.

"Looking forward to joining us at the bar?" His tone is mocking, cruel. I notice the papers I am reading from are crisp, pure white. New.

"Sure."

He is standing closer to me now. I can smell stale cigarettes.

"It'll be a shock to your system, that's for sure!" He is laughing again, enjoying it.

I nod, not turning. I don't know what he wants.

"Do you ever fucking speak, brownie?"

"Yep," I say, and turn now to look at him.

"We should've never bloody bothered with you. More trouble than you're worth. You've barely made us any cash. But that's gonna change." He pushes my head scarf back to expose my hair. It makes him feel a sense of power, that much is obvious.

"I never asked to be here. I was meeting my brother at the station. You remember?" I am fighting back the anger that is twisting inside me.

"Oh yes. The brother. Well, we got to you first, didn't we dear?"

My brain is hurting, turning cogs to find a different line of conversation. "You can't make Gillian go to work so quickly."

He is raising one eyebrow, creating vast lines on his forehead. There are acne scars on his cheeks, perhaps from adolescence. "Excuse me?"

"She's just had the baby. She's in bits."

"And that's my concern...why?"

It is useless. Of course he wouldn't care.

"And I guess you'll be trying to get out of work next?"

I swallow down the sigh that I was going to outwardly exhale. "I wouldn't dare." I am rolling my eyes.

He is grinning again. "Unless you want more clients at night?"

I shake my head, *no*. There have been slightly fewer men at night, and I don't wish for more. I wonder if he and Jonno are worried about the cash drying up.

"We could strike a deal if you want?"

I look away from him, the dread of what he is about to suggest engulfing me like a cloud of toxins.

"I mean, Jonno got a nice little deal out of you, didn't he?"

I know his face is holding a sneer, I can feel its heat next to me. They have discussed it; the piano deal.

I say nothing.

"I mean, if that's what it takes to keep you stuck here all day with that...that thing." He is nodding at the piano.

"Just once?" I venture. It might be worth it for one time. I will just lock up my mind again. Like I always do. I try to picture which performance room he will take me to. I quite admired the lace curtains in the one Jonno used.

Now he is laughing properly. "You've gotta be kidding me!"

My shoulders sink, weighted with disappointment; sandbags balancing on them.

"A regular thing. It's gotta be worth it for me. And you're such a pretty little thing." His hand is stroking my cheek, and instinctively I slap it away. His paw connects with my face again, with force. The sting makes me hold my cheek like a victim, but I won't look at him. The coolness of my fingers is soothing the smarting heat. I think of lashing out at him. Perhaps a decent kick in the balls.

"Don't push me away again."

I don't react, still dreaming of hurting him between the legs.

"So what's it going to be?"

Someone has walked into the room and is standing in the space between us.

"I'll do it," she says, so quiet that it's barely audible. Rebecca.

***

Keith turns on his heel. At first I swear he looks repulsed, but a smile breaks out on his pallid face; he flicks his eyes to me and then back to Rebecca. "Ok, darling. That'll do nicely."

Adrenaline is fizzing somewhere in me, coursing its way through the map of veins in my arms and legs. "No! No, Rebecca. You're not going to do it. Stay with the nail bar. It's better for you."

She is glaring at me. "I'm sick of that place. The heat, the smell, the bending over for hours. You try it."

She doesn't get it; she thinks I am trying to get out of working.

"Keith, no," I try. "She's fifteen, for God's sake!"

His eyes are cold, a rabbit caught in headlights. "She's eighteen."

"No, Keith. Fifteen. You and I both know it."

He is immediately in her face, yanking her arm towards him. She recoils with a small yelp and I find myself running to her side.

"She didn't tell me that!" I am screaming now. "She didn't! I read it on that notice you left out the back with the newspapers. I know she's recorded as missing. The authorities are looking for her, you bastard."

He pulls himself up straight. There is a long pause. "You." He is staring straight at me now, "You - always snooping around. I don't know what to do with you."

I hold my tongue, to stop myself coming out with something sarcastic. Instead I say, "So what are you going to do about it?"

Rebecca is on the case. "What do you mean? It's not like they're going to hand me in, are you?" She is directing this at Keith.

He is staring out of the window at something; the trees swishing in the wind in the far distance. I can hear the whistling through the leaves. He doesn't reply.

"Keith?"

He turns to look at her. "Maybe it would be for the best. You know, if you just...left. Just returned back to where you came from. Get you off my conscience."

"I didn't realise you had a conscience." I couldn't help but butt in. I am ignored.

Rebecca turns to me, eyes jutting out of their sockets. "Yalina, tell him. He can't send me back!" She tugs on Keith's sleeve. "Jonno won't let it happen. And I was going to live with Lil when you're done with us. She said I could."

She is blinking back tears, looking at me now with her pleading-dog eyes. She could be twelve. "Well if you want

130

me gone, you'll have to get rid of Yalina too. We come as a pair."

I am cringing inside. *What is she on about? He'll never buy that.* But for a moment, in the pause that follows, my brain triggers a feeling of desperate excitement; a firework. A chance.

"No way. Not going to happen," says Keith. He is peering over me on my stool, glancing at my music. Rebecca is hovering closer. "Keep playing that damned music," is all he says.

Chapter Twenty-Four

Yalina

Mid-April 2008
Somewhere near Sheffield

I'm getting progressively more skilled at playing this stuff; I know it. Sometimes the girls from my room or the floor above come out of their rooms before work in the evening to listen. The men don't care, most of the time. I've been nailing Tchaikovsky's 6th Symphony, as well as The Nutcracker. It still works without the violins and oboe. The girls perch on the edge of the battered sofa, or sit cross-legged on the floor of the dining room. Not one of them laughs at my manic hands or head jigging in time to the music. It seems to transport them, to somewhere further away than here at the edge of the city, or the Peak District; away from wherever we are. I wonder if the Polish and Romanian girls are thinking of home. Whether Gillian is thinking about Nigeria, where her little girl is waiting for her. I wonder what Gillian's real name is. My hands cover the keys in timings I have never been able to keep to before. When I reach a part with a diminuendo, you can hear only the faintest of breathing in the room. The girls are waiting for the next part. Me, I'm still waiting for my brother. I wonder if he is ever near the house when I am playing, his ear pressed to the wall.

***

"Chisimdi," says Gillian. "That is my real name." She is speaking properly for the first time since the baby was taken. "And I named her Adaeze."

Her eyes are small, puffy. Her voice croaks. She tells me she hasn't had a proper wash of her body since the birth. Too weak to stand. Not wanting to wash away the only reminders of her child's arrival.

"They're going to make me work soon," she says.

I know this already, but I don't say anything.

"They think I can just continue with life, just like that."

The rage is coming in waves; I don't know how she can stand to feel like this every day, and how the men couldn't care less.

"I just want to fade away." Her voice drops away, words carefully landing on the floor like unwanted feathers. She looks at me. "Can you help me to?"

Words churn in circular motions around my head but I can't select any to articulate.

"No, Gillian!" I give what must look like a false smile and correct myself. "Chisimdi."

"It's ok. I know you can't. I'm just thinking out loud. My apologies."

I hoist my arm around her neck. It feels too casual, too flippant and quickly I remove it. "It's ok. Anyone would be feeling the same. I'll get us out of here."

She is smiling, the gentle smile I recognise from her pregnancy, when the idea of the baby being taken was far into the future. She must know I am just saying words, meaningless words, but there is gratitude emanating from her.

"You are a star," she says. It sounds funny, coming from her, but I don't laugh. It wouldn't be the right time.

"Listen," she whispers. "I cared not at the time, but I think you girls may not be here too long. I don't really care what happens to me." The last sentence takes away any joy from the first.

She is staring at me. The hairs on the back of my neck are tingling. "What do you mean?"

We are sitting at the only two good chairs at the table. I've not played the piano today, and my hands are itching to get back to it.

"When I was alone in the bedroom last week, I think it was Thursday, but I don't know, I've lost track of the days, I heard something outside the window. I couldn't even stand to have a look." She stops speaking, gazing out towards the kitchen at the back.

I wish she would hurry up and spit out whatever she is going to say, then I hate myself for being so impatient with her.

She is fingering a knot of wood with her middle finger; back, forth, back and forth. "There were two men peering through the window."

Chapter Twenty-Five

Richard

March 2007
Islington, London

The call came at 5:22 in the morning. I'd been dozing, attempting to think about getting up for the past twenty-two minutes. I was alone that night, Nat was working away in Bournemouth. I grabbed the phone, no real thoughts entering my mind, and batting the cat away from my face.

The caller asked if I was Richard Stokes. I affirmed my name. They told me that they were the police, calling from Oxford. It's at that very moment that the adrenaline release happens; something in your brain commands the rest of your body to prepare itself for fight or flight.

"What? What's happened?" I was not giving them a chance to speak; I did not want them to say anything despite my hurried question asking.

"It's about George. I'm so sorry but he's been in a road traffic accident. Would you be able to make it to Oxford this morning?"

He was still alive. I don't remember throwing on my clothes, or the jacket that I only ever wear for special occasions. I just remember reversing the car out of the drive so fast and with so little care that I nearly knocked down the early morning runner who was jogging past the end of my drive. I held my hand up in apology and bolted down Leonardslee Road at a speed I don't think was even reasonably legal.

The journey felt like it took hours, but I was there at the Royal Oxfordshire hospital in less than ninety minutes. George looked like he had been in the most awful fight, but in reality he had been knocked down by a car as he made his way back from the nearest off-licence. A witness to the accident said there was broken glass all over the road, and an alarming red stain that wasn't just wine.

He was hooked up to a certain number of tubes, and a ventilator mask was half-covering his face. The nurses told me he was in a coma and that as a result, he was unconscious and unable to speak. They said there was the possibility of him being brain-dead if he did wake up.

My ex-wife and Zoe turned up in the next hour, faces blotchy from crying, and neither able to put a coherent sentence together. I remember feeling angry at them for giving in to grief so quickly, for admitting that it was all over. It wasn't over for George, he was only a first year at university, and plenty left to prove.

"Am I meant to be saying goodbye?" asked my daughter. Her words made me choke a little in my own throat, then I felt as though I was gagging uncontrollably.

"No!" I exclaimed, too quickly.

Suzi was looking at me, eyes furious. "We need to be honest with Zoe," she said, watching our daughter hovering near the doorway to George's room. "We're staying in the nearest Travelodge tonight," she added, and stopped to squeeze my hand. This took me aback, it had been several years since the touch of my ex-wife. I wondered what Nat would make of the situation. Nat, still on her way from the coast.

She arrived at the hospital just after Suzy and Zoe left, breathing hard as if she had run the whole way.

"I'm so sorry. Couldn't get out of bloody Bournemouth. Roadworks. Doesn't matter."

She stopped talking as soon as she saw George, and a fast-flowing trail of tears began to make its way down both of her cheeks. I noticed it messed up the layer of skin-coloured makeup she had applied.

"I ... you didn't say it was so serious," she added. I didn't realise I was the bad guy here.

"I didn't know what to say," was my response, a bit pathetically. Again, I felt the rumblings of a burning rage in the pit of my stomach; another woman to deal with who had already written George off.

"He's going to be ok," I say.

There was a nurse in the room, she spun on her heel, not waiting to join our conversation. "The prognosis is serious," she butted in. "These next twenty-four hours are going to be vital."

Why do they always say that? Surely if a person is not going to make it, then they will not make it immediately?

Nat was looking at me like I was an alien, just landed beside her. Clearly, she was livid. "Why didn't you say how serious this is?"

She pretty much just repeated what she'd already said.

With my rage about to spill over, I simply shrugged and avoided eye contact with her. I focused on George, his breathing, the in-out simplicity of it all. All we have to do to keep going is breathe. It's not that difficult. Or perhaps it is.

The dumpy-looking doctor of the ward said that the police were coming that evening to update me on what happened. I was dreading their appearance.

When they did arrive, they removed their helmets and bowed their heads, as if coming to tell me my son was already dead. I didn't stand, but remained on my plastic chair and offered my hand. They politely shook it, and fumbled around next to the bed, seemingly embarrassed.

The younger cop began to speak first. Perhaps this was his first *bad news announcement* but seeing as we were already gathered around my injured son's side, there couldn't be much else he could tell me.

"Hello there. I'm Detective Constable Phillips. So sorry to meet you at such a time," he said, or something to that effect. "We wanted to let you know about the accident George here was involved in."

I nodded, looking at him briefly, then my eyes returning to

137

my son.

"It seems, unfortunately, that your son was the victim of a hit and run. A witness saw what happened but couldn't remember the registration number of the car. She said there were two people in the vehicle. That's all we know at the moment."

I remember the older police person taking over then, a woman. "The accident happened at about 1am. We worked as quickly as we could to contact you."

Was I meant to feel grateful?

I don't think I said anything.

I remember Nat trying to make the police feel better about their job. "Thanks, officer."

A silence swirled its way around the curtain hanging loosely in my son's hospital room, words trickling down to the floor and away out of the door.

Chapter Twenty-Six

Yalina

Mid-April 2008
Somewhere near Sheffield

She doesn't say anything else, and I have to stop myself from pushing her on it.

"There was a car parked on the road. The two men must have come from it."

I don't know what she is saying. "What does this mean?" I ask. My heart is thudding. *Ali.* He's come back to the house to get me. Last Thursday. It must be Tuesday now. *Why has he taken so long?*

"I know what you're thinking," says Chisimdi. "It's probably nothing. But I don't know. I have a feeling about this. I've only thought about it this morning. I couldn't think of anything else since Adaeze. You understand."

"I do." I hold out my hand and rest it on top of hers on the table. "So who do you think the men were? Don't you think they could have just been some clients? What did they look like?"

She is gazing at me with that smile of hers, friendly but sad around the edges. "They did not look like clients. Not at all."

I don't know how she can say this. None of the men we see are the same as each other. All ages, all sizes, all races.

She senses my doubt. "I mean it. They weren't clients."

I want to ask if one of the men looked like Ali, but I don't want to sound ridiculous, and I can't think how to describe his photo anyway.

"What? What are you thinking?" Chisimdi as a name suits her perfectly. She never seemed like a Gillian to me.

"Nothing. Just, that...I have told you about my brother Ali?"

"Yes. You said you reconnected with him online after your operation. You were going to meet up with him." Her eyes flash. "You think it was him! One of those men who came."

There is a hot flash of embarrassment up my neck, it is creeping into my cheeks. I can't think what to say.

"What does he look like?"

I am contorting my mouth, not sure how I can describe what I don't really know. "Mid to late twenties. Dark hair, dark skin like mine. Browny green eyes, I think." I am cringing, realising how awful it must sound, that I don't know exactly how old my brother is, nor the colour of his eyes.

Chisimdi is looking upwards, as if checking her brain for memories. "Well, I can't say strictly what colour either of the men's eyes were. But I think they were both white men, dark hair. I could be wrong. Maybe in their thirties."

My heart doesn't sink, but it's not singing either. There is no way of telling if it was my brother.

"You don't know how old your brother is?" She is finally grasping it.

I stand up from the table, pushing my chair away.

"I don't know if I have told you this before, but I've been in touch with him. He's going to find me."

She pulls me into a seated position again in my chair. "It's ok. It's going to be ok."

She doesn't believe that he exists. Or perhaps she doesn't think that he will bother to find me. My problems are nothing compared to hers, I shouldn't be even talking right now. I say this.

She is crying now, hugging me close from her standing position. It is an awkward stance. I feel annoyance at her tears; I do not want sympathy. It's not required.

"It might have been your brother. But how would he know where we live? And why wouldn't he have called the police instead of coming here himself?"

Hearing her voice my concerns out loud make them seem more real. It just confirms how stupid my longing has been.

She can see disappointment in my face, I'm sure, for she suddenly says, "It will be him, I know it. We will get out of here together."

I hug her by way of a reply, but doubt is forming inside of my body, drip-dripping its way through my heart and into my stomach.

Two men. *Two men.*

Chapter Twenty-Seven

Yalina

23rd May 2008
Somewhere near Sheffield

I'm becoming so sick of the work. It eats away at you. Night after night, man after man. We have seen a surge of Indian men lately, a few Pakistanis. They request me specially sometimes. I hate them for it. Wakefield and Leeds accents. They are rough with us. I hate these men even more than the white ones. They could be family, ordering their daughters, wives and sisters about as soon as they get home again. Not letting them out of their sight, because they know what men will do. But it's ok to do that to us.

They want their money's worth. I have mentioned this to Jonno, but he just smirks, ignores me. It's never worth mentioning anything like this to Keith. I've heard them talking in the van about the money that this new cohort of men is bringing in. It makes them easier to deal with. Sometimes I think, and plot, of cutting the brakes in the van. I imagine them on the country road of the Snakepass, no girls in the back, Keith going to brake and finding there is no resistance; that his foot falls to the floor as the van hurdles off the side of the cliff. There would be no funeral. His body would be too mashed to identify.

In the afternoons I stick to playing the piano, shifting from left to right on the tiny stool as the pain from the previous night smarts between my legs. My mind wanders to the men

Chisimdi told me about; their car. *There were two men. Peering through the window.* The thought sends a little surge of joy through my limbs, but I won't permit my brain to consider it any more. It still could have been some potential punters. Or just some people lost on their travels. *And why would Ali have had another man with him?* There is annoyance in my bones too, at Chisimdi. I try to shake this feeling away. *Why didn't she take more notice?*

Just above my eyeline, on the top of the piano, something waits for me. Its rectangle shape makes me stop breathing for a moment. I reach for it as a shot of adrenaline courses down to the ends of my fingers. It's the same type of brown envelope as before. Before I even open it, I am rushing to the bedroom I share with the others. Chisimdi is there, combing her knots of hair into bobbles. She starts work tomorrow.

"This envelope." I can barely get the words out. "When did it come?"

She turns her head slightly to look at me, comb digging into her afro roots. "Envelope?"

"This!" I say, too aggressively, shaking the thing in my hand. "Did you hear those men post anything through the door that day?"

She is doing that thing where she looks up into her head, searching for a clue. "Sorry, I don't know. I was in and out of sleep." She sees my crestfallen face. "Sorry, Yal."

I realise that I am the only girl here with her original name. And that my *mother* had called me Lil for short.

"So...nothing. You didn't hear the letterbox?" I know I am pushing her too much.

She takes the comb from her hair and sits up straighter on the mattress. "Sorry," she says again.

I repent. "It's ok."

"What is it?"

I pause. "It's music. From Ali." I wish my shaky voice didn't make me sound so weak.

A flash of teeth as she grins at me. "That's fantastic!" Then in a slightly less positive tone, "How do you know it's from him?"

I want to lash out at her; my friend. My friend who has been through so much. My friend who has lost her two children, perhaps indefinitely.

"Because it is. Because I asked him to send it to me."

She opens her mouth to protest, and then closes her lips again. She is smiling at me, a smile of compassion.

"I told you I messaged him online, to ask him to either come save us or at the very least to send me some classical music sheets."

This time she doesn't query why he wouldn't have contacted the police. But I can see the clouds of doubt drifting in front of her dark eyes.

I leave the bedroom and make my way back to the piano, lowering myself onto the stool. My fingers tear at the end of the envelope, and I pull out with caution a slim booklet of Tchaikovsky's symphonies. Luna appears from the bottom of the staircase, and steps lightly onto the edge of my stool, sprawling her body out on my lap. No permission needed. I stroke her soft back and she purrs, tailing jutting out in pleasure. I think she needs the music too. She turns her head to look at me. Often, she spends her days in either one of the men's rooms. I often overhear them talking to her, mumbling. I wonder what she sees in those rooms, what she hears, what she knows.

**

It's painful watching Chisimdi getting ready for work. She has been given some black clothes to wear; a long oversized shirt and pleated trousers that are way too wide at the waist, despite her still-protruding stomach from the pregnancy. She tells me she has only just stopped leaking milk from her breasts. You don't consider these things as a non-mother. I know the men wouldn't have given this sort of thing any consideration. She seems shaky as she slips on her only pair of shoes near the back door. Even they are too big for her. Rebecca is being kind. She is waiting for Chisimdi, whilst the other girls are already loading themselves into the van out the back. It's 5.40am and I would never usually be up at this hour, but I felt my friend's dread in the pit of my own stomach all through the night. I am calling her Gillian again. I wouldn't want her to receive punishment for my loose tongue. I don't think the other women are aware of her real name; I think she may prefer it that way. I realise, as I watch my friend being almost manhandled into the back of the van, that I do not know any of the women's real names. It makes this whole scenario seem more made-up. Like it's fiction, and that their real names are waiting for them in another life when all of this is over. This whole life is a made-up story. I don't know what it means for me.

Gillian can see me through the back of the doors of the van, her deep brown cow eyes avoiding mine. I glance at Rebecca and she looks away too.

After two straight hours of perfecting two of the Tchaikovsky symphonies, my hands ache, and I need to rest. I am sore from a particularly nasty punter last night. I don't know if we all should be checked by some kind of medical provision at some point, but I know this will never be permitted. With nobody else in the house, I realise I can do just about anything now I don't feel responsible for being by Gillian's side any more. I do feel a sense of betrayal at leaving Rebecca, the child who has come to depend on me, but perhaps the others, or Gillian can support her now. My heart is quickly pumping as my brain is going faster than it ever has before. *What do I need to take?* I am thinking so quickly that it only takes me a minute to grab the shoes I wear each day and one of coats lying in a pile by the back door. I check the lock on the door: securely bolted. I pad through the empty house to the never-used front door. Locked. Returning to the kitchen at the back of the house I put one knee up on the sink to hoist myself to the window I escaped from last time - not bolted again. *These men are mad.* I climb through the small window and land with a crunch on the ground. There is a searing heat through my ankles but I am able to stand after a couple of moments. The sun is high in the sky, and I am feeling positive. I cannot believe that I haven't tried to just leave like this before. As I step towards the road that goes past the front of our house, I am careful looking left and right; not because there will be any traffic from the right, because it is a dead-end, but in case there are people. Spies. I can't imagine being able to walk away so freely but here I am, in the middle of the day, no constraints, no hands pinning me down. Crossing the narrow road, I'm sure there are a hundred eyes on me, but am not sure if they are animal or human. There is safety in the field I am entering; tall wavy grasses to hide my form. I will not risk the walk along the roads again. I think of slinking down further in the grass, to squat as I walk, or go commando on my belly. If anyone was going to see me leave, though, they would have seen me by now. I am thinking of Ruby, confident and self-assured Ruby as I slowly begin to mend my way across the next couple of fields. There is wind rushing past my ears as my feet crunch down on the earth underfoot. I feel alive. I scream *I am out!* inside my head. One day soon I will scream it out loud.

The air is warmer than I had anticipated and I peel off the coat I am wearing, sling it over my shoulder. I don't really know which direction to travel. I find myself thinking I should have escaped just as the van had left for Leeds early this morning.

I have been trampling through fields and areas of woodland for a couple of hours now. Even though there is excitement buzzing in my ears, sitting behind that there is a sense of creeping sadness for the piano which I may never play again, and for the girls who I promised I would take with me. In the distance, a concrete viaduct looms tall over the fields which submit to it underneath its sprawling arms. I imagine the happy families visiting for a walk on a Sunday, the children craning their necks to look up at the monstrosity.

I let my legs give way and collapse in a heap in a yellow tall-grassed field. Glancing behind me, there is no sign of the house, or the road. I could be anywhere. Three hours ago this would have filled me with ecstasy, but my initial wanderlust is beginning to wane, and the heat of the day is making my mouth dry, however much I try to ignore it. I realise I didn't even bring the few coins I had left in the pocket of my only other pair of trousers, let alone bring a drink. I dump the coat, my shoes kicked off within seconds. If I owned a pair of socks they would be kicked off too. I laugh out loud at the idea of wearing socks these days. *What a luxury…* then curse myself for being so spontaneous, so underprepared and think of the hundreds of pairs of eyes watching me, mocking my stupidity. Lying back, I close my eyes and try to ignore the raven nearby, screeching at me to reconsider my great escape.

I wake from a mangled dream of sweat and visions of people who are not my parents, and sisters who aren't my sister. *Where would I even go back to?* I think of my father and can barely picture his face, his stature. All I know is his controlling manner, his obsession with respect, with reputation.

Would I return to the same job? The thought of cleaning out animals' cages and taking dogs for daily walks makes me crave my current piano-filled afternoons at the house, despite the life I lead there. These months have changed me, made me more *adult*; I want to look out for others now. I find I am standing, stretching out my arms, and beginning to retrace my steps through the grass. I am not thinking; my feet are leading me back, a silent dog yelping at my ankles.

The house is as silent as when I left it, and the window above the sink in the kitchen remains propped open for me to manoeuver my body through. The van is not back, and won't be for a few hours. I feel the lightness of sheer relief as my first leg hangs through the window, finds the surface surrounding the sink, and supports my weight so I can swing my other leg down. When I land on the floor, I make more of a noise than I had expected, and I find I am holding my breath, waiting for someone to call to me.

I don't bother going into the bedroom. I don't have anything to dump in there. As I am about to flick through one of the music books at the piano, I see the form of Keith sitting at the table. My heart stops for a moment. He looks up slowly. "Nice trip out?"

I don't say a word, my eyes desperately trying to read his face. I can feel my heckles beginning to rise. Fight or flight. *Fight!* screams my mind.

"Well?"

I cannot tell how angry he is. *Why couldn't it be Jonno who stayed behind today?* I thought they had both set off in the van, but now I think of it, I couldn't really say. My hands are beginning to shake a little, though not with fear. It is rage again. My brain is clunking slowly into action. *Harm him. Hurt him.* I am quickly scouring the surfaces of the kitchen for a potential weapon.

"What are you doing here?" I am the one in charge.

He is smiling a distorted smile at me. His skin is so pale it is like cheap paper. I can see the heat underneath his paper skin; swirls of red capillaries that nearly match the carpet in this place.

"You were expecting me not to be here?"

I am standing in the doorway between the dining room and the kitchen. I don't know if I should try to bolt out of the kitchen window again or to face him. The adrenaline is causing my thinking to manifest into whispers of words, *fight, hurt, harm him.*

"You're a good girl, brownie," he is saying. "When I saw that window left propped open, I knew you had done a runner." He is massaging the stubble on his chin. "So I waited a few hours."

I can hear my breathing. I try to slow it down, quieten it. I want to ask why the window is never locked. I want to tell him I'm the only girl here who is not afraid. For some reason, I find myself yanking off my headscarf. The cool air is welcoming to my head.

"But here she is. She returns! She knows life outside will be worse."

I want to tell him that I know there's a whole world out there where people care for others, where life is good, and where there is a future. Where women get to be with their own children. I want to tell him that he has no control over some of the women in this house. That I have discovered their passports and buried them for safety.

"Why are you frowning at me like that? Are you not happy for the work that we give you here?"

I find myself choking on a little sarcastic laugh. "It can only really be called *work* if you were to *pay* us for it."

He jumps to his feet and makes my limbs jolt with the suddenness of it. He is in my face. I can feel the wall against my back.

"You *will* get paid. Just not yet." A pause. "Are you going to apologise for that comment?" His voice is raspy now, his eyes pulled into slits. *Weasel.*

"No."

Still, he is not touching me, not hurting me. Just so close I can smell his breath, the leather of his jacket. "You think you're gonna grass on us?"

I could call his bluff. "I'm not sure."

"You're not sure?"

"Someone knows I am being kept here."

He stands up straighter, his face no longer in mine. I can tell he is panicking under the thin layers of paper, not sure whether to believe the girl standing in front of him or not. He covers his fear with that smile again. "Oh, really."

I notice it is a statement and not a question. They like to speak like that in this house.

"Yes. Really," I say. I am beginning to feel the scales tip ever so slightly more in my favour. It feels nice to hold a little bit of control.

"And who would that be?" he demands, in the coolest voice that he can probably muster. It's not fooling anyone.

I won't show my hand. I can't let him know. That would defeat the whole purpose of Ali coming to find me. I say nothing, but I won't break eye contact with him.

He's not going to let this go. His face cranes down towards

me again. "You will tell me what you are talking about, or you will get what's coming to you."

You will get what's coming to you. The echoes of the man I should call *father*.

I am aware I am not blinking.

"You know what I'm talking about. The same thing as last time. But worse."

He means the attempted sex. The attempted forced sex. In Ruby's room.

"I can run away. I practically just did."

He is laughing now, but there are beads of sweat forming on his brow.

"Or the police will come soon, anyway." I don't know why I have said this. I wanted to scare the man, get him out of my face.

My arm is yanked and I am being dragged to the door of the basement, easily opened with his other hand. I am struggling, spinning myself around to try to spit at him. My body is pushed down the steps in front of his body, my feet moving so fast they barely touch the steps beneath them. It feels like I'm falling. I land at the bottom and the smell of the damp, wet walls hits me again. He lifts his giant hand from my arm. "You stay here until you decide to tell me what you're talking about. I'll give you another chance now." He looks at me, waiting.

But I won't say. I am looking around for some of that newspaper to sit on again.

He gives me one last glare and stomps his way back up the steps. The door slams, the key is turned, and the light from the doorway is gone.

I am on my own this time.

Chapter Twenty-Eight

Yalina

24th May – Ramadan. 2008
Somewhere near Sheffield

Jonno hasn't been down here. It's been Keith both times. I am in some kind of alternative universe, not just under the house I have been living in for a year, but in a universe independent of other forms of human life. The temperature isn't as painful as it was last time, but the confinement is. What those ignorant men don't realise is that they picked a perfect time to stick me down here; Ramadan. I need to be fasting; being starved down here suits me just fine. The lack of food in my system usually causes my brain to work more slowly anyway. I can just pause my brain and my thoughts and concentrate on something I can see on the wall. I think of those lace curtains. It would have to be in a performance room, though, not here. That would be hitting rock bottom. I hear myself give a little laugh out loud as I find myself wishing for something to happen in a performance room rather than for this whole cycle to stop.

The door opens, and there is the light at the top of the steps. I can see Keith standing, staring down at me. He pauses before he begins his descent, a bottle of water gripped in one of his hands. I know he wants to find disappointment on my face at the lack of provisions he has brought with him.

He squats opposite me, teeth glinting. I wonder if he is going to punish me for having the light on. *Bring it on.*

"Come on. Aren't you sick of being down here?"

I'm not going to react. I purse my lips.

He is reaching out his hand to touch my cheek, and I turn away a little.

"You don't want me to do what happened last time." He pauses, corrects himself. "What nearly happened."

I think of telling him that I've just agreed with myself that I don't care one bit. It's the location I'm picky about.

He isn't going to shift. I keep my face turned away, and out of nowhere I feel a slap of hot venom, propelled from my captor's mouth. It hits me at the corner of my right eye.

"You are fucking vermin, you know that?" He is rocking back and forth on his heels, still squatting right next to me.

The drip-drip of anger is stirring somewhere at the base of my spine. My father's face appears in my mind, watching me, blaming me. *You must have led those men on.*

"I don't care what you do to me!" I have nothing left to lose. "Do what you want, I know I'll be getting out of here."

Now he is facing me, he has shifted over. I notice the door is swinging open on its hinges at the top of the stairs. *Run for it,* my head is saying. But my feet are glued to the spot, his bulk blocking my exit route.

"Who?" he asks, for the only the second time since I've been down here.

"You don't know him." *Oh God, here we go.* I want to tell him. I'm compelled to. There are guns lined up in my head, a hundred of them, waiting instructions to fire.

"Tell. Me," he orders.

I cannot look at his face since he spat at me. My body is sitting up straighter. I will use my one card. He can't go looking for Ali anyway; even I don't know his whereabouts.

"My brother," I say. I can hear it repeating in the damp air. It's out now. I've said it.

Because I am turned away from Keith's face, I cannot see an expression. He merely repeats the words I've said back to me.

I'm unsure what else to say now, but he is standing, finally, no longer squatting in front of me. "Your brother." He says it again. It's a mocking tone. "The one you were meant to meet."

"Forget I said anything," I quip. My words are futile now.

"Yes, I remember you talking about your brother."

"Well." I am swallowing lots. "He's coming to get me out of here."

He's not saying anything now, but there is a sort of cracking sound. He's laughing. "This is the one who was going to meet you?"

"Yes."

"The brother of yours who has been sending you the music books?"

My heart is in my ears, pounding. There is a cat chasing a mouse round and round in my head. "You knew that?"

He isn't laughing now, more smirking. I hate his teeth, gleaming with their stained ochre hue. *There's a gold tooth in there.*

"Sure."

I picture him opening the envelopes and then resealing them. Nothing is sacred in this house, this game. I want to spit back at him.

"So you know that he's around," I comment, trying to tip the scales again to my side. I hate the clipped sound of my speech.

"Yeh. He's around, alright."

I know something is not going in my favour. Keith is not folding; his arms are folded but he's not defensive. He is leaning towards me again, smiling that smile. "Did you enjoy the music fairy coming? I was hoping you would."

Chapter Twenty-Nine

Richard

March 2007
Oxfordshire

So, turns out they were right; the doctors, Nat, and Suzi. George passed away that very night.

I was with him, but I'm ashamed to say I was napping when he took his last breath. I am trying to not blame myself for this, the way Suzi is blaming herself for leaving the hospital that night with Zoe. They had to go and find somewhere to rest.

I didn't know how to tell them the next morning when they arrived at the door of this room; that he was already gone, the bed cleared and new sheets fitted. Suzi's face had looked to me so hopefully, a look of *oh, has he been moved to another room?* I remember just shaking my head very sadly at her, averting my eyes away from my daughter who I could not bear looking at. The sounds that followed next are just too unbearable to replay in my already grief-stricken mind. Let me just tell you, you don't want to hear the sounds of a fourteen-year-old girl when she's informed that her nineteen-year-old idol didn't make it. I think I may have placed my hand on each of their shoulders, before leaving the room to deal with my own shock. Looking back now, perhaps I should have cradled them both in my arms, as Nat had done.

Nat had stayed at the same hotel as Suzy and Zoe that night but somehow had arrived in the early hours to support me. I suppose I had pictured my ex-wife and daughter enjoying an almost leisurely breakfast at the hotel, taking their time over choosing whether a continental breakfast was the right choice for the day or a slap-up full English. I had envisioned Suzy straightening her hair in front of the modest hotel bedroom mirror, smiling at her reflection and passing the straighteners to our daughter, so they could both enjoy their twin ironed locks. My counsellor says this is my way of dealing with the grief; to point blame at others who are close. But I'm not blaming them. I'm just wondering why they took so damned long to make it to the hospital that morning whilst our son had already been dead six hours. It doesn't matter. None of it does.

**

We weren't even given the chance to arrange his funeral straight away. There was too much other stuff to think about. The sheer responsibility of it all was making my head ache, getting in the way of me even beginning to think about grieving. I expect it was the same for Suzi. We had to work together on this one. Come up with the right answer. Do what would be right. They were pushing us, pushing us. Time was limited.

Chapter Thirty

Yalina

Late June 2008
Somewhere near Sheffield

The other girls are working tonight, Chisimdi included. I must get used to calling her Gillian again.

The pieces all fit together now; Ali not appearing at the train station, one of the men taking me instead. Even the appearance of my *brother* online at a time when I felt the most vulnerable is so glaringly obvious now. I am hating myself more than anything. Who would fall for such a trick? Maybe I knew, deep down, that the prospect of having a brother coming to save me from my existence was all bullshit. A fantasy. It makes me want to need my real family more; the family I left last year. Their faces don't jump into my mind as a source of relief to me. They are just faces. Three faces of strangers, made slightly more familiar from the time I spent with them in those weeks of my recovery.

It's hard to eat, hard to swallow down the uninspiring dry bits of bread. We make a right pair, Gillian and me. My hope is waning. Well, I suppose for Gillian there is the far away hope of returning home one day and being with her daughter. I want this to happen for her, I really do. But I just wish I had a real family to dream about myself. Perhaps I should have had a child, probably not *the done thing* in my family's social circle; pregnancy before the wedding, but the gift of someone I would have had a real genetic attachment to. Someone to

156

long for. Someone to need me. Or a partner, a boyfriend at least. I never asked *Faiza and Mo* if there had been a love interest. I sincerely doubt I would have been allowed near a man, anyway.

The days are long and hot, the nights longer. The men don't stop arriving. Gillian doesn't speak about the nights. She doesn't get as much work as some of the other girls here, but I still hate to think of her being used for this purpose. Rebecca seems to attract more of the punters; she rarely has an hour off before 1am, let alone a night off.

I should be working on my escape plan, but there is no energy left in my bones now. Nothing. I seem to enjoy working myself into a cycle of rage, thinking of how stupid I was getting caught up with the idea of a brother online, a brother who was going to meet me at a city station up north. I think of Keith, slipping those music books into those innocent looking brown envelopes, sealing them closed, laughing at me as he posted them on the dusty unused doormat, or on top of the piano. I wonder if Jonno was in on it too. Probably. It took me a few hours to realise, with an increasing dark cloud of dread building over me, that Keith would have known I had entered his room to get to his laptop. It makes the hairs on my arms stand when the next penny drops; that he would have read my desperate message to *Ali*, asking him to find me, to rescue me. I guess maybe that was the real reason for the unceremonious dumping of me in the basement. A chill passes through the veins in my body as I consider what they may have in store for me next.

There is a job to attend to. At a factory. Seems it was too risky at the nail bar; Keith commented on some apparent *snakes* who were seemingly intent on *spreading gossip*. He doesn't say if he knows who. Perhaps we will find out in due time.

It means the end of the shop, a pop-up variety, open to whoever wanted to pay the rents and then promptly leave again. From what I hear, the other girls are relieved. They were sick of it; the long hours. The fumes. They sound almost cheery at the thought of something new. I cannot share their enthusiasm. There is a heavy tombstone of dread inside me, the thought of forced mundane work, taking me away from my music, my sole reason to exist.

"I wonder if there will be men there too," coos Rebecca. My stomach curdles. You would think she would have had enough of menfolk. Especially her, with so many clients at night. And her age.

"You *want* men there?" Gillian is as appalled as me.

Rebecca is looking upwards, the three of us about to go to sleep in our room. The time is 1:10am. "Do any of you ever think about meeting someone?"

I am staring at my feet. The thought doesn't really cross my mind. "No."

Gillian doesn't respond. The other girls in the room are already asleep, skinny girl's legs sticking out from under her one beiged-with-filth sheet. I haven't made enough effort to recall the other girls' fake names. *Is Lucy one of them?*

"Well, sometimes *I* do," says Rebecca. "Don't you each want to get married and live happily ever after? Have kids?"

I risk a sideways glance at Gillian. She catches my eye. "I have been married," she says. "It was not good."

I find myself wondering if that husband was the father of both of her children. I have never found the courage to ask.

"He was the father of my eldest daughter," she explains, reading my mind.

Rebecca is just staring at her. "Well, you wouldn't have married if it wasn't for love?"

Sometimes she really shows her age. I feel a stab of sadness at her naivety, not for the first time.

Gillian is clicking her tongue, something I have not heard her do before. She seems angry; there is a violent flash in her eyes, her usually dark doe eyes. "We do not always marry for love in Nigeria. My parents sought out the marriage for me. They wanted me to marry into a wealthier family than I was from. Well, let me tell you, I would rather be poor any day."

Rebecca hugs her knees, pulling away. She could be

158

twelve right now.

Gillian continues. "My daughter has not met her father. She never will."

I have not seen this bottled up heat begin to force its way from my friend's body before.

"And now I come here for a better life for her, so I can send the money home, but there is no money. And they make me pregnant and take my baby away."

She is scowling at Rebecca. "So please don't tell me you will be happy if there are men where we are going to work next. I for one will not be happy."

We start today, Tuesday. The girls are chattier than usual as we get dressed; same filthy clothes, same sole-peeling-off-the-bottom shoes. It is hot already, the sun just poking through the clouds, and I can smell days-old sweat from some of the others as we climb aboard the van. I've never been in this particular van before. I was brought here by different people. I forget the no-talking rule and receive a sharp slap from Keith across the back of my legs as I try to find a space to sit down. I knew I shouldn't have worn the only pair of shorts we girls share. I try to slap back at him but he catches my arm and twists it to near breaking point. I hiss. There is less room in the back of the van than I had envisioned, or maybe there is just no room now that I have joined the masses. The men have assured us we will receive proper pay - ninety euros a week, each. I'm not sure if this is a lie, told to jig us along with enthusiasm for the new job. The others aren't nervous, they smile wanly at each other from the hand-made wooden bench in the back. Some of the others are sitting cross-legged on the floor. There's not a lot of light, save for some that reaches through from the front. A flash-back of the van journey that delivered me flitters before my eyes. Those girls, their haunted eyes, their filth. I look at the girls I live with and realise they are no better, I have simply become accustomed to it. In my mind, I try to fight this. I don't ever want to succumb to thinking this way of life is the norm.

I believe they have given me a place on one of the benches to be kind. I see Jonno look over at Keith and wink.

After perhaps half an hour on the road, the van halts and we are all thrown forward. It must still be long before most people are awake. Jonno walks around to the back of the van and opens the door. The girls stop looking at each other. Another man appears by Jonno's side, an unknown. Each of us stand up and hop out silently, no gravel underfoot, just the dried grass from weeks of being flattened by the overbearing sun. It is the first time I have been properly outside since I visited the woodland near our house. The light burns at my eyes, but a neon surge of happiness streaks through me as I notice the sharpness of the blue sky above us, and birdsong. I wonder what type of bird is lighting up the land with its song. Perhaps a thrush. I used to know so many types of bird, could list perhaps seventy from the British Isles. I could differentiate the songs between the common robin and a blackbird. I would pause and listen as far away, a Greater Spotted Woodpecker gently attacked the trunk of cedar in a distant forest. Alarmed, I am pulled by the wrist by the stranger, whose name, I garner, is Greg. I don't believe for a minute it is his real name. He is clearly Polish. It's the same accent as Ruby's was. Ruby. Her name spins, almost dances, around in my mind like a mirror on a string, and there's another surge of joy as I think of her rejoicing under this sun, this radiant blue sky every day.

We are filed into the factory, which is really a form of an abandoned warehouse; dark, high vaulted, no windows. We don't speak. We are handed blue hair nets by some other girls who are there. Nobody is in a uniform, so we don't know who the other staff are. I guess we are the staff. I have not worked since the days before my operation. I like the idea of it, but a voice inside me says it is just the temporary sheen from the sun that has bleached my spirit. We are told to remove any jewellery; not difficult since anything of value was taken from us long ago. Rebecca has managed to stand behind me in the line as we prepare, washing our hands with cheap-looking wipes. There are boxes and boxes of potatoes ahead of us. I've heard in the next room it is fruit. We do not get a choice where we are to work. Glancing up, I see Jonno, pacing up and down the aisles of boxes. Keith is standing by the double doors we entered through, bolting them shut. There is an old analogue clock on the wall, stating it is 5.55am. It makes me think of a clock that may have been hung in a classroom somewhere. I don't remember my school days. I try, but there is nothing there in my head. I am grasping at nothing again, sand spilling through my fingers.

A woman, small in stature, is hovering by Rebecca and me as we sit cross legged on the dirty floor. There are no chairs here, and I see Rebecca turning up her nose. She must already be missing the nail bar.

The woman, gruff-voiced, tells us to pick up the potatoes and begin looking for flaws. Good potatoes go in the large box to the left. Misshapen, rotten ones to the right. I wonder who is picking these vegetables out of the ground. Perhaps that will be our job next.

The woman has not told us to put on plastic gloves like the other girls here are wearing, and Rebecca and I both receive a sudden slap to the back of the head for this. We don't know the man who has administered this, but we see it is the one named Greg. He pauses before thumping the woman who is supervising us too. She won't forget again.

After nearly five hours of sorting good potatoes from bad, my wrists ache and my bladder is complaining. I turn to the woman who is still standing over the girls on this aisle of boxes. There are nine of us from the house. On the other side are around another fifteen women, people I have never seen before. They look the same as us; tired, too thin, resigned to their current situation. I wouldn't say any of them look British. They are careful not to catch my eye. I want to know how long they have been working here, and where they come from. *Where do they sleep*? I realise with a degree of embarrassment that perhaps some of them are living here; I see blankets and the odd pair of shoes stacked up all in one corner. There are no mattresses. It makes me think how lucky we have been, some of us. One of the men's words rattle through my head, *you don't know how lucky you are.* I remember thinking at the time that he was out of his mind, or was just plain mocking us.

"Please, I need the toilet," I say to the woman. She must be around my mother's age. *Faiza.*

She is shaking her head, very slightly; so slightly that I might have missed it, had I not been so desperate for a response.

"Please," I whisper. It is the first time I have said *please* to one of our captors. The men will not hear me say it.

She points with one finger to the clock above the doors. "One o'clock," she says, barely audibly. I see Jonno look over at her.

I continue for another two hours, my eyes sometimes grazing over Rebecca's head to catch a glance at Gillian. Her head is always bowed, her hands busy.

***

It is so tempting to talk to the others as the front doors are unbolted and we are herded outside. I cannot see any buildings that could house a toilet anywhere. It's just this solitary warehouse.

"Where are the loos?" asks Rebecca. She is stopping herself from ramming her hand between her legs like a six-year-old, hopping from foot to foot.

The men and the one woman from the building walk towards their car, parked a few yards away. The sun is glinting from one of the men's gold watches, temporarily blinding me. They don't seem to worry that we will drift away somewhere. They are used to their workers being institutionalised.

I watch the other women from the warehouse disappear around the side of the building. The girls from our house are simply standing there, stunned under the sun, taking in the air, the sky. I follow the women I do not know around the side. They are pulling trousers down, squatting. Some of them have thought to wear a skirt. They do not look away.

We are handed crackers to eat, an orange, water in plastic cups. I see the two men and the woman eating McDonalds, leaning against a van. Jonno and Keith are with them, chatting, laughing. I can smell the burgers from where we are standing, and my mouth becomes a pool. The crackers make our mouths more dry than they were before. The oranges are old, I guess they may be from the *bad* pile from another part of the factory, but they are still refreshing. It has been over a year since I have tasted anything like citrus fruit, and I let the juices run down my chin, smiling. Rebecca is watching me, sucking her own orange like a small child, savouring every drop as if it were candy floss.

The journey back to the house isn't until 8pm, and I can tell Keith is nervous about travelling. It's still daylight. He is sharp with us, practically throwing me and the women in the back of the van and shoving the doors closed in a matter of minutes. I am seated on the floor for the journey. It would have been the ultimate luxury to be sitting on that bench that Gillian and toenail-painting girl managed to grab for themselves. Before too long, we are back, and I am surprised to feel the intensity of relief warm me up as we file our way in through the back door. I kick off my shoes and let the other girls overtake me. They head straight for their rooms, upstairs or my shared room on the ground floor. It must be around 8:30pm now. I find I am settling myself on my piano stool, my fingers grazing the keys, eyes jerking up to see which music I left on the stand last. The punters won't be coming until 9:30pm. I have one hour to dream myself away from this mess.

Chapter Thirty-One

Yalina

Early July 2008
Somewhere near Sheffield

Each day at the factory feels longer and longer, and the novelty of the new has worn off for the others. I know they wish they were at the nail bar. I sometimes go into my own world, whilst I am sorting the potatoes; *good* and *bad*. It's as if the others aren't there at all. I suspect the men are making obscene amounts of money now they have all nine of us working there, and doing the dirty work at night. They don't care how exhausted we are, that we can barely keep our eyes open. Most of us are only getting around four or five hours of sleep at night, if we're lucky. I used to sleep for hours, after the night shifts in the performance rooms. Now I struggle to think straight, and it affects how I work, how I function. We no longer care about having to take a piss outside, against a wall, or in the middle of the field. It's become the norm.

Rebecca has been particularly clingy with me on workdays; she hovers to get a space next to me on the work floor. I find her hard to take. Today, though, she is keeping her distance from me. The others have noticed and raise their eyebrows in jest, or in interest. She is hovering closer to the wall of the factory, where the men are. She is trying to get their approval. That's what it is.

Our bedroom stinks in the heat. For obvious reasons we are not allowed to open a window; it has been bolted shut from day one. Six bodies in the room, and each allowed a shower once every two or three weeks, depending on the men's moods or if the shower is choosing to function. My own armpits are best left unmentioned; it strikes me as desperate that there are men who are willing to pay a lot of money for forty minutes of our time. I don't even know how much money; sometimes 60, other times 70 euros. What I do know is that Keith and Jonno have kept to their word, and have paid us each ninety euros this week. Gillian's face was a picture of pure elation, for a moment. I could see her thinking of her little girl, whose name I don't know, and her mother, receiving the money in the post. Or perhaps travelling to their nearest Western Union dept in the next largest town to theirs. God knows why they have started to pay up. Perhaps to keep us sweet. Maybe they were worrying about the men at the window that day. I didn't know Gillian had told them. Perhaps I should go and unearth the passports of the girls, in case someone has made a tip-off to the police, and we will be set free soon. I imagine the shift of the expression on their faces, the ecstasy of knowing they are free, safe now. That they can return to their home countries, the places they had abandoned in the hope of a better life here. I picture Chisimdi with her new baby daughter, her hands gripped around the child, never letting go. The blankets from the cupboard wrapped around the baby. I should feel elation too, but I don't. Just a weighted cloak resting upon my shoulders.

***

Gillian is not doing well. When we rise in the mornings, she does her best to keep her head down, and is the first to bolt from our room to try to find a morsel to eat from the kitchen. She avoids our stares. Sometimes there is nothing to eat, just old fruit brought back from the factory, some bread, some whatever-leftovers from the takeaway or pizza the men had the night before. They never order food in for us. We are getting more gaunt by the day, our collarbones more pronounced, our knee bones protruding more. There is less

165

food than there was this time last year, and most of us have come to rely on finding whatever we can within the factory during our one break. Mary, the quietest member of my shared bedroom, gives a yelp of excitement during one such break, as we see she has risked travelling further away from the warehouse to relieve herself. *"Strawberries!"*

She hasn't shrieked it loudly enough to alert the men, who are again leaning against their van during that thirty minutes of freedom, half a field away. They continue to munch on the fish and chips from their greasy paper bags; the one woman from the factory occupying the front seat of the van, not joining in with whatever conversation the men are having. I wonder how she ended up here. She is sipping on a red can of Coke.

We all scramble over with delirium at the word Mary has thrown up into the air; our eyes, our hands searching through the bushes where she is standing. We find the red fruits, hidden behind prickly leaves, an abundance of red. We don't even check to see if anyone is glancing up at us or checking their watches. Like school girls, we yelp and giggle, as we each pick the fruits delicately from their stalks and slip them into our mouths. The taste is electrifying, and for a moment, nobody speaks. The taste of the strawberries is all-consuming. The silence sizzles. They say that taste and smell brings up the strongest type of memory, and each of us are now settling on the grass next to the strawberry bushes, piecing together the floating parts of our lives before; a summer picnic, a slice of Wimbledon on tv before heading to the garden in flip flops. It would have been a moment of undeniable ecstasy, those five minutes of discovery and secret consumption, if I had not seen Gillian standing alone by the factory wall, head jolted up to the sky, mouthing words; unheard, desperate words.

On the ride home in the van, some of the girls are still upbeat about their fruit findings. I know the joy was not in touching the illicit fruit, but from keeping it a secret from our captors. Gillian does not join in. Her perfect shaped face is

166

balanced in her hands, and she stares at the rubber layered bottom of the van as we snake our way through the hilltops of the Peak District. I can tell she feels my gaze, but she does not turn towards me. I have not had opportunity to speak to her for some days now. She has black pinch marks around the tops of her arms, which she does not try to conceal. I know she is thinking of her baby. I should have made an effort to have remembered the date of Adaeze's birth. I can't ask her now. Instead, I look back to the other women, smiling, joining in with their attempt to pretend we all lead normal lives and that today was a *good day*.

The next morning, Gillian does not rise with the rest of us. She is a darkened shape on her mattress, twisted to face the wall. I am pulling on my t-shirt, ignoring the putrid smell of it as it passes over my head. Rebecca is darting around, looking for something, not noticing anybody else. The other girls rise, dress and leave the room in silence. I can hear them clunking around in the tiny kitchen at the back, opening cupboards, then closing them again. The eternal and fruitless hunt for some food. I hear the tap come on, the noise almost deafening for a moment. I look down at my friend, calling her name. She does not stir.

"Gillian!"

Nothing.

"Chisimdi," I try.

She doesn't move; her eyes are closed. There is the threat of something heavy hovering over me, something that makes me want to bolt from the room. When I rose two minutes ago there was still the lighter feeling of the camaraderie of us girls from yesterday, the fuzziness of feeling together. It takes less than a second for that to dissipate.

I can just about see that she is breathing, and the relief hits me like a twenty tonne truck.

"Chisimdi," I try again.

She opens her eyes. They are fixed to the ceiling.

"Are you getting up for work?"

She remains silent. Only her chest is slightly moving, up

and down. Up and down.

"Are you ok?" Ridiculous question.

I squat down next to her. "I know you're in a bad place. I know that. But maybe coming to work is the best distraction. And…you know...the money."

She sits bolt upright. "The money!" she spits. Her face is turned to mine now, her large eyes bulging. "The money! Ha!"

I shrug back into myself. There is a bit of her spit on my arm.

"Don't go talking to me about the money. There was money that week. And that was it. That's all we are going to get!"

I don't reply. Her eyes are fixed on me.

"Do you know what I am talking about?" Her tone is accusatory.

I shrug uselessly. My mind shifts to the conversation I once overheard in the doorway; one of the girls and Jonno. *Debts.*

"They are *making us pay our way.* They call them *debts.* For our travel costs over here. For that horrendous fucking ...journey." She spits out the 'k' sound as she swears. I've never really considered her journey here before.

"I'm sorry," I say. There is nothing else I can say. I'm not the one being charged debts.

"So, the money...it's good for nothing. One week of ninety euro. That's it. The rest is going straight to *them.*" She practically growls the last word. "I'll never be able to send anything home, and worse than that, I'll never make it home. They've stolen my passport."

I am aware of the other girls getting ready to leave the house, the back door being unbolted, the voices becoming more quiet as they venture through the kitchen. Keith's voice questioning, "Where are the other two?"

I gesture towards the back of the house at my friend as we both hear his voice.

Her eyes are still out on stalks. No tears now. "Are you kidding me?"

I shake my head no. Of course I'm not kidding. We have to go.

"I'm not going," she says, echoing the opposite of my thoughts. She lies back down on her mattress. "I'm going to leave this place."

I am aware of time marching on. "Leave?"

She blinks. "Yes. I'm going to run away today whilst you're all out."

"But...they'll find you. And make you pay. They found me when I escaped from that barn."

"Ruby got away, didn't she?"

I am about to nod in agreement, but then I realise that we don't know for sure that she got away. They could have captured her and sent her to a different ring. Somewhere worse.

I straighten up, ready to join the others. I don't need more punishment. I take one last glance at my friend and turn towards the door. "Bye, then." I say, and then I step towards her to give her a hug.

She reaches out from her mattress to hug me back. This may be the last time I see her. I don't ask if she is going to try to find the baby. Instead, I give what must be a pitiful smile and race through the house; I am the last out of the back door. Keith is scowling at me, and he slams the door behind us, twisting the key aggressively. He doesn't ask where Gillian is. I climb into the back of the van and find myself a tiny space on the floor amongst some of the other girls. Rebecca is staring at me, willing me to say why I am so late. I don't speak. The absence of Gillian is enough.

It's difficult to concentrate today and it's not because of the tiredness so much. I am happy for her. I don't know where she will go or how. She might stick out more on her escape route, being the only Nigerian woman wearing almost-rags in the Peak District, and barely a pair of shoes on her feet. The men could follow and catch her easily.

The factory woman has poked me in the ribs twice today already, and it is nowhere near our break time yet. The other girls periodically glance my way, noting my slowness, my ineptitude for the job. After another hour of struggling to tell

169

potatoes apart from one another, the man I didn't know from before marches over to where I am sitting cross-legged on the floor. He grabs me by the elbow, wrenches me up into a standing position. I am aware of at least eighteen pairs of eyes on me. He shouts something at me in a language I don't understand, and I am pulled through a set of double doors into the next part of the warehouse. It's the stench that hits me first, then the rows and rows of eyes on me again. These women are Asian; Chinese perhaps. They are wearing the same blue hair nets yet they have matching blue masks over their noses and mouths. The silence is so raw that I wonder if the man has knocked my hearing out. The women quickly look back down again to the task they are doing. There are mattresses piled up high against the walls, and again, no windows. I find myself wondering if they have to do the work that we do at night, too. *In here?* The man drags me to the end of a line of women and gestures for me to sit on the ground again. He points at what the others are doing; skinning chickens and removing their gizzards. They do it with such a speed that it is taking a moment for my eyes to register what they are doing with their hands. The smell of the room is making my stomach stir, and my limbs feel weak. I quickly jump to my feet and find myself vomiting not two feet from where the man is standing. He yells again in his language, and I am hit around the back of the head.

One of the women pulls down her mask and says pointedly to me, "He is telling you to clear up your own mess." She pulls her mask back into place, eyes back again on the poultry she is detangling.

I stand for a moment, staring at what is in front of me. These women, this is their life. They work here, sleep here. Bits of paper towels are being thrust into my hands by another woman who is also standing to the sides of the workers; she must be this side of the factory's poking-lady. I am on my hands and knees absorbing the puddle of vomit whilst my fellow workers look on, yanking at the chicken bodies. Something worms itself into my head, a memory, of when I was little; responsible for raising the chicken in the garden at home. I would feed them seed each morning, look for eggs under the bushes, pulling at the leaves. Sometimes the chicken would hide their eggs in the most bizarre of places. I picture the garden at home with Faiza and Mo. A small enclosed patio, no plants.

Chapter Thirty-Two

Yalina

Early July 2008
Somewhere near Sheffield

I find I am humming a Beatles song on the journey home, thoughts of Gillian on her journey to freedom improving my mood. The chicken work was disgusting; the sinews of the creatures stuck in my mind; their goosebump skin slithering over my blue-rubbered hands. Tomorrow I can go back to the potatoes, they said. I am relieved but still cannot stop myself from thinking of the Chinese women with the facemasks. *How long have they been there? Are they here illegally?*

The girls in the van are chattering slightly; the men have the radio on in the front, it is unlikely they can hear anything. One of the girls I don't know very well asks me how it was *in the other part of the factory.* I pull a face ·and she almost laughs. I want to ask her name but feel it is too late now. She asks how long I have been playing the piano, and where I learnt to play. I like her very Slovak-sounding accent. Holding up one finger, I mouth *one year; only since I have been in the house.* She makes her eyes bulge open dramatically, and mouths the words *wow, no way?* I tell her that I taught myself. I wonder if this is true.

I imagine Gillian to be in another county by now, far away from the Peak District and its light and dark coloured hills set flush against each other, so it is a shock when I enter the room I share with the others and find her lying on her side, mouth open like a fish. She is barely conscious. I pull her up to a sitting position with the help of the others, and hope that the wall will hold her straight. There is a white paste streaming from her mouth, mixed with saliva. "Chisimdi." I am calling her name. I try again. The others are looking at me, waiting for me to work miracles, perhaps wondering why they have not heard that name before. I motion for skinny-girl to go to get her some water. Still, Gillian is not opening her eyes properly, and I fight the urge to shake her.

"What is wrong?" asks Rebecca, feeble at my side. Her foot kicks a small bottle on the floor, and she grabs at it. The label is written in another language but most likely would have housed tablets. "Oh."

My brain is shutting down, I don't know what to do. I try to think of what they would do in a hospital to help her, try to remember the countless episodes of Casualty I used to sit through on my own. There is only a blank tv screen.

I look at my friend; pale, eyes not moving. She's not alive.

Chapter Thirty-Three

Richard

Late March 2007
Location not stated

We were all in charge of organising the funeral; me, Nat and Suzy. I didn't want sole responsibility, nor did I really want the women to try to take over what I felt would be the very last scene of importance to George. I didn't want anything to go amiss; the extent of his talent, his genius, and his kindness. The two women in my life didn't feel it was appropriate *to go on* about his inimitable achievements, and instead thought the emphasis should have been spent on how he always put others first. They chose the music (not songs I had ever known my son to listen to) and Zoe chose one that she had used to dance to with her brother when they were both little. That part of the ceremony would have tested the most hardened soul. No matter how hard I screwed up my face, the tears were still pushing, bustling their way out of my eyes. It is the most bitterly painful thing to lose a child, and not just any child. A child like George.

***

I was there, in the next room, waiting for it all to happen. I had thought I couldn't focus on anything else, but I needed to in order to keep my own sanity. The family was there, obviously. They had a load of belongings with them. They were just in the next hospital room from mine, a door kept locked when they were pacing back and forth in the corridor, but left open the rest of the time. Security didn't seem to be top of their agenda that day. This hospital barely seemed any different from the last one; green painted walls, linoleum floors mopped with disinfectant at regular hours by cleaners who would smile at me one minute then seem frustrated that I was in their way the next. It took hours; they were right. Suzi seemed less patient than me, chewing at her nails, twisting her hair in her fingers. Zoe didn't come with us. It didn't seem right.

It was easy enough to do what I had to do. Guilt didn't come into it, not at that point. A five minute task, completed when the others were too fraught to even notice. I wasn't going to give up my son that easily.

Chapter Thirty-Four

Yalina

Early July 2008
Somewhere near Sheffield

"We need to make her vomit!" Rebecca is further ahead than I am. "Try salt water!"

I run through the house to tell the girl to make it a salt water. She looks quizzical so I snatch the glass from her hand and fill it up myself, searching the cupboards above my head with my free hand. They are practically bare, apart from a few miniature seasoning jars, probably left behind from the previous occupants, and some rice. Finally, salt. I pour more into the glass than is really necessary, and head back to our downstairs bedroom. Gillian is coming round, her eyes rotating in an almost comedic fashion.

"Here, make her drink this," I say to Rebecca, who is closest.

She takes the glass from my hand and holds it to Gillian's lips. She makes no attempt to drink the water herself, so I find myself holding her body slightly away from the wall so that I can just about tip her head back a little. Rebecca carefully pours the liquid into her mouth, and I move her chin up, the action making her head loll back. She is coughing, spluttering. For the first time we hear her voice; moaning and making choking sounds. After a few moments of it, I realise what she is saying. I try to ignore it.

"You must swallow some," I tell her, trying to sound like I'm giving sage advice.

She is beginning to shake her head violently, and I step back. She is furious; a horse with searing eyes, teeth bared, frothing at the mouth. "Why are you trying to save me?" It is a screech. The other girls step back from her too, I can see one of them is crying. I still cannot remember her name. *Lucy.*

"Chisimdi, we will get you through this, we will." I am kneeling next to her now, and I motion for the others to leave the room. Rebecca hovers with the glass, eyeing me; uncertain, a child looking at her mother for guidance.

I am stroking the side of Gillian's face, but she is not looking at me.

"You should have left me to die!" Her body is doubling over, she is rocking back and forth. The birth all over again.

"No!" There is no point in my screaming back at her, but I am doing it all the same.

"You need to be sick," I add, my voice becoming more gentle, and to my surprise she takes the glass from Rebecca's hand. Rebecca stands and leaves the two of us alone.

Immediately Gillian swallows as much water as she can, and grabs at her stomach. This time, no baby. She is sick almost at once, on top of the plastic bag that I had grabbed from under one of the mattresses. I clear up the mess, folding the bag around itself and run to the kitchen to find another.

The other women are standing together in the hallway, the crying girl mopping at her eyes with her sleeve.

"Why would she want to do a thing like that?" Rebecca can never cease to amaze me.

I blink. "Well, I don't know, Rebecca? Why do you think? Perhaps because she has just lost her second child? Perhaps because she is used at night by disgusting men and then is driven to some factory in the middle of nowhere to sort potatoes for no money?" My own voice is making me tremble. I feel my cheeks beginning to fuzz up with redness around the edges. From the bedroom behind me I can hear Gillian vomit again; she is an animal, wounded. I pace to the kitchen for the bag and walk right past the other women. Rebecca follows me into the bedroom. I could swipe at her.

"Sorry," Gillian snivels. "It might all be ok for you lot soon. Remember the men."

I don't say anything, just nod, and make attempts to clear up the vomit.

Rebecca looks at me, then straight back at Gillian again. "The men?"

Gillian is sitting against the wall, head tilted back. She says nothing.

I clear my throat, attempting to break the silence. "Gillian saw a couple of men outside the other day. It's probably nothing."

Rebecca is not moving, not looking at me but staring straight into Gillian's eyes. "Men? Why didn't you say?"

I don't think she has breathed for a few seconds. Her body is rigid, her arms frozen. Finally, she blinks, and we hear her feet pounding up the stairs.

***

"Listen, we will find where Adaeze has gone. We will. *I* will. It can't be that hard."

I have no idea where I am grasping these words from. It must be sheer desperation.

Gillian rolls her eyes at me, a gesture that would appear rude from anybody else, but just smacks of resignation from this particular person.

"I can get someone to help me. I don't know...Rebecca perhaps?"

Her eyes create a comedic roll deliberately this time, and we both laugh. "Perhaps not," she says, still smiling.

"I don't think she'd make the most astute of detectives," I confide.

"And the fact that she is Jonno's little lamb."

I stop to consider for a second. "You think?"

"I know."

"I guess she's always bleating by his side. Never wants to get on the wrong side of him."

"She wants a father figure, is my guess."

I sit back against the wall too and absorb what Gillian is saying. There is something about Rebecca neither of us understand.

"Anyway, please rest tonight. I will see if I can make sure you have no clients." My heart sinks a little as I consider what I'm going to say next. "I can take yours for you."

She reaches out her hand and strokes it down my cheek. "You are a true friend," she sighs.

I smile, a weak smile, wavering at the edges.

"I will be at the factory with you all tomorrow."

I don't want her there, but I do. I need to make sure she is breathing.

**

Tonight, I cannot stop my brain from whirring. It is a machine, won't stop. I have to take this upon myself. There must be paperwork somewhere, a note, anything. I don't know how easy it is to get rid of a newborn baby but surely there must be a trace. I need to go to the men's rooms again but time is no longer mine during the days. I have no free time. I could tell them straight about Gillian, about her suicide attempt, and that I need to stay back to look after her. *I could lie and say she has promised that she will keep trying until she is successful.* The last thing they would want is an illegal worker's body on their hands.

The plan worked. At 5am, when the others were silently dressing for their day at the factory, I waited until I heard the heavy footsteps of Jonno leaving the bathroom. I accosted him on the landing, towel tied around his waist. I have never seen him topless before. There were darkened tattoos spawned over his torso, previously red and green artwork turned to a muted grey and turquoise colour. If he was embarrassed at me seeing him, he failed to show it. In as few words as possible, I explained about Gillian. I could see the shroud of confusion pull across his face, until I described her as *the one who had the baby.* I told him about what she had

179

tried to do, and that surely the sensible thing was for one of us to stay with her today so she doesn't try again. Today is a Friday. I convinced him that she would be better, ready for work by Monday. He nodded, agreeing. I saw him make his way into his room. He stooped to nudge a red bangle bracelet from the floor, kicked it under the bed.

Chapter Thirty-Five

Yalina

Early July 2008
Somewhere near Sheffield

I wait until they've been gone an hour, long after hearing the van reverse its way over the tiny stones and onto the road. Waiting an hour ensures they will all have been at the factory for an hour, hard at work. I know I will somehow be punished for missing a day's work; Gillian too. When I get to the top floor of the house, I push on the door to Keith's room, but nothing budges. There is a shiny new brass lock which has been fixed to the door by an amateur's hand. A glance to the other side shows me that the room Jonno sleeps in has had the same treatment. Groaning inwardly, I lightly jog down the stairs so not to alert Gillian to my lack of success. I go straight to the piano, neglected in recent weeks, and lower myself gently on to the stool. I don't need the music books. I let my hands touch the keys and then the music begins, almost by itself. It must feel like that one forbidden drink to an alcoholic, or that one last hit of heroin to a junkie. I cannot describe it. The blood inside me is sparkling, dizzy.

I don't know how long she's been sitting here watching me. Gillian, cross-legged on the carpet. Her finger traces the swirls in the pile.

"You can still call me by my real name if you like," she says from behind me.

I have only just stopped playing, and turn, where I see her

for the first time.

"I have hope," she says. "I woke this morning, and you were there with me, and the sun was shining through the window. I know she is alive, wanted. I know she is not dead."

I don't ask her how.

Her eyes are waiting. I have not yet mentioned how my search for information went. I need to keep on looking.

"Any joy?" she asks me, directly. Her phrasing of things is becoming more British.

I smile, trying to imply that perhaps there is good news.

She beams back, hope in her eyes, and my stomach drops a little. I will find something, I have to. I am aware that time may be the most important factor here; that perhaps each day that passes takes Adaeze that bit further away. There is no way of telling if she is even still in the same country.

"Wild Horses," says Chisimdi, and she is at my side, pushing for space on the stool. I don't need the sheet-music. Jagger and co are pretty much ingrained in my muscle memory.

She is napping on her mattress now. Yesterday must have taken a hit to her system. I know I won't bother trying the men's rooms again, there is nothing I can do to get into those locks. I sit at the table and try to think. My feet lead me to the door of the cellar. The key is in the lock but the door pushes open anyway. The musty smell makes me almost gag, conjuring the memories of my days spent down there. It feels odd to be walking down the steps voluntarily, not by force or over someone's shoulder. I leave the door wide open at the top, knowing there are no men in the house but am still wracked with the fear that it will be slammed closed and locked. I don't know what I am looking for. Papers, perhaps. I have to make my way down the steps in half-darkness until I can find the cord hanging near the side wall. I pull on it and remember to wait the few moments until the spark of light appears. I blink to acclimatise to the new surroundings. There are the plastic chairs and the cardboard boxes in the left-hand corner of the room, but I'm not sure anyone would leave important paperwork down here. Shuffling through the layers and layers of single sheets of newspapers, I don't find anything about the baby. I have a disgusting heavy feeling twisting at the bottom of my spine proclaiming *there is no paperwork for the baby.* At the bottom of the box, my fingernails hit something. I pull at it. It's a little book, just like the ones I buried in the woodlands. I find I am blinking tears of relief away. She has long black braids in her photograph but I would recognise those eyes, that mouth anywhere.

When I get back upstairs, after closing the cellar door and leaving the keys jangling in the lock as they were, I discover she is still asleep. I find myself wondering if they are going to make me work tomorrow. Probably, and I don't mind. I will do anything for her.

They all arrive back a couple of hours later. Rebecca is first into our room. She wrinkles up her face to declare how much it stinks in the heat, no windows to open.

"I bet this smells worse than the chicken factory," she states, looking directly at me. I'm sure she finds it a source of amusement that I was dragged into working in the other part of the factory that day. She doesn't consider, though, that chicken factory is the daily life of those Chinese women who work there, who live there.

"Sure," I respond. Some days I grow tired of her childish talk.

"And how are you?" she asks Gillian, sounding particularly robotic.

Gillian gives her polite smile. "Getting there."

Rebecca looks straight at me. "Has she been sick again?" The authority of a nurse. I am trying not to smirk, so I smile down into my fist.

"No. And Gillian can speak for herself."

"I'm only trying to help," she muses. She sits down with a *floomp* on the edge of one of the mattresses. "So, I may as well tell you."

I tip my head back, eyeing her. *What now?*

She senses my negativity. "It's nothing bad. I thought you would be pleased, in fact…"

Gillian is sitting up, folding her arms. It looks odd, both her legs and her arms folded.

"They've said I don't have to work the nights anymore."

Gillian and I glance at each other. I don't know what to think. I think I am relieved.

"Why now?"

Rebecca pulls a face, almost a pout. "I thought you would be happy."

I move forward to hug her, but she doesn't look receptive to this.

"They said it's all too much for me," she continues. "The night-time work, the factory during the day."

"I told them that ages ago."

"Well, now they've listened. I'll be free at night." And she stands up to do a little skip in the air. I *am* happy for her, and I'm relieved that the men have finally taken into account how hard it all was for her. There is a little drip-drip of bad feeling I'm trying to ignore at the back of my mind that tells me they are still in it for themselves, and not the fifteen-year-old.

Chapter Thirty-Six

Yalina

Early July 2008
Somewhere near Sheffield

The heat is almost unbearable. The rooms never get cleaned, but I sometimes try to clear the piles of shoes from the floor, and attempt to dust with a top that is just about to have its bi-monthly wash. The others don't seem too bothered about cleanliness any more. Rebecca never was, Mary and skinny-legged girl keep their heads down and don't do anything. Gillian, now her baby has been and gone, has stepped down from her nesting duties. I think about Adaeze a lot. I don't tell Gillian this. I wonder about the world she has entered, and how it's most likely she will grow up and never know her real mother, or what situation she was born into. I take this last thought as a positive. I consider whether Gillian will tell her other daughter back in Nigeria that she has a baby sister, or if this will be kept under wraps for eternity.

Whenever I feel so heavy that I feel I can't work, or function any more, I take to my piano. Sometimes the others will still gather around on the carpet into the evening, before the men come. It will only take Keith to appear at the bottom of the stairs, phone or shaver in hand, to make me stop. I usually just let myself slither off the stool and away into the utility room, where I pretend to fold washing. They are getting less and less tolerant of my playing. I don't blame them. They are here to control us, not get music out of us. I usually have one hour after a day at the factory to do whatever I want, before the night-time work.

Gillian asked me if I had found out anything yet. I think I managed to fob her off with a "Let's wait and see." I didn't want to get her hopes up, but I couldn't bear to see those huge brown eyes blink in despair at my lack of information, the perfect arc of a smile wiped off her face. She must be thinking about it all day, every day.

***

The next morning we are awoken by one of the girls in our room flapping, hopping around the room. "They're here, they're here!" she is squealing.

It takes me several seconds to come round.

"The pigs, the pigs!"

It strikes me as amusing, hearing her Eastern bloc accent using very English slang.

Gillian and I are paused, half sitting up on our mattress, elbows propping us up. My heart is lurching, my stomach suddenly thrust from one side to the other.

The girl is standing at the window, peeking from the very edge of it, her hand shaking. I glance at Rebecca, wondering if she will leap for the light switch. Her eyes are wide, scared, a bush baby caught in a forest fire.

"I see the police car!" squeaks the girl again.

"We must all get upstairs, like they showed us!" It is Rebecca speaking. She can be such a kiss-ass.

The rest of us have frozen, but she is picking her way across the room, motioning with her hand for us to do the same. Gillian is standing already, smoothing out her filthy sheet on top of her mattress.

"There's no time for that!" whispers our youngest girl. She is already at the doorway.

"Should we hide the beds?" skinny-legged girl is asking. It's a fair question. *Not if we want them to know we are here.*

I am the last to leave the room behind the other women. It is getting light. I think that, if I can wait, just a few more seconds, perhaps it will all be over. There is a quiet hammering sound from the very top floor; Rebecca is waking up the men. Within what feels like seconds, Keith is running down to me, motioning at me with his hands to scurry up the stairs. His face is a picture. I try to preserve the moment; my captor's features composed of clouds of fear, and nothing else. It's good to see him so vulnerable. For as long as I physically can, I remain still at the bottom of the stairs, my feet refusing to listen to his instructions. He grabs at my elbow from a couple of steps above me, and I am yanked up. Still, I fight him, struggling, elbows everywhere. When I eventually get pulled to the first floor, there are no other girls around, only Jonno. The pair of them manage to lift me up to the top floor and into one of the bedrooms, where we were shown the secret passageway some weeks ago. The wardrobe has already been yanked across to allow access to the door. I am the last one to be shoved in. As Keith forces his way in after me, the door is closed and I can hear Jonno clumsily shift the wardrobe back in front. He must have to go and hide elsewhere. I only just manage to squat down to my feet when I hear the front door. It is them. They are hammering. I can see the hairs on my arms standing to a point, the goosebumps underneath. This is it. *Come get us.*

Chapter Thirty-Seven

Yalina

Mid-July 2008
Somewhere near Sheffield

They only tried knocking at the door a few times. *Oh God, how I wish they had battered it down.* We are still stuck up here, though. It has been a couple of hours now, but we are not allowed to move until the men are absolutely sure that we are in the clear. Rebecca has been chatting in a whisper for practically the entire time. She hasn't received a slap from Keith, but there is still time. My feet are fuzzy from having been squat down on them for so long, with no room to even sit cross-legged, and I find I am moving my weight from one foot to the other without realising. Rebecca is talking about her birthday, and how she wants to celebrate it. She is looking at Keith from the corner of her eye when she asks if perhaps there would be some way to get hold of baking ingredients. I know she doesn't want to ask outright for a favour. She is hoping he is taking the information in. He is staring at his phone screen, pretending not to hear her. Keith is not as malleable as Jonno, and we all know this. Rebecca knows this. Nobody seems too interested in hearing about Rebecca's yearning for birthday cake. She insists that she didn't even mention her birthday last year, and I think she is right. All at once, there is a spike of electricity through my system as I try to recall if I mentioned my own birthday to anyone last year. It occurs to me right then that I am completely unaware of when my birthday is. I feel like I'm about to pass out, but a body squatting next to me is holding me up.

"You doing ok?" It is toe-painting girl. She doesn't tend to speak much. She is looking at me closely, eyes shaped with concern.

"Yes, fine," I snap, without meaning to.

"It'll be ok," she whispers to me. "We have it easier than most girls caught up in these rings."

"Yeah, I know, I know," I tut. My sarcasm is almost deafening. "We don't know we're born."

We are up there another hour before Keith gives us the signal to leave. I can hear Jonno moving the huge wardrobe away from the door that is holding us hostage. Soon, the door is prised open. I am the nearest girl and stand to make my way out of the passageway. Just as I am about to step through the small doorway, I hear women's voices behind me. They are yelling; screaming the word "Help!" at the top of their lungs. It kick-starts the adrenaline in my system and I turn to see who is calling out. I remember when we tried out this emergency procedure the time before; how it had made me want to scream for help, just to see if anyone could hear, like the men said they could.

I have never heard the word screamed so many times.

The passageway is too dark and too narrow for me to see who is at the furthest end of the line-up of us women, I can feel my eyes straining as the light filters through.

Just minutes ago Rebecca had been singing.

Mary, Mary, Quite Contrary,
How does your garden grow?
With silver bells,
And cockleshells,
And pretty maids all in a row, row, row,
And pretty maids all in a row.

We are the maids; lined up, sometimes beautified, waiting to be chosen. It's strange what your brain suddenly throws at you when you realise things are about to change forever. She's stopped singing now.

In slow motion that feels like swimming through treacle, I am pulled out of the doorway to make room for Keith forcing his way back in. He needs to get to the screaming culprits. The other girls in the line are almost crushed against the wall as he battles his way past them. Finally he has their arms, skinny, already bruised, clutched in his huge bear paw and is tugging them back through the passageway, in front of all the other girls who are too squashed to move. It is the girl who I think is called Lucy. The other woman is Gillian.

***

Rebecca seems a happier child these past few days. I say child, as that is what she is. Nobody likes to go to work for a potato factory in the searing heat of summer, rammed like cattle into the back of a van with blacked-out windows, but she is free from the burden of the men now. The nightmare of the 9:30pm men. She is missing Gillian from being in our room, like I am. Both the Lucy girl and Gillian have been gone for three days now. We don't know where. I suspect that they are still in the house, in the basement, but the men are leaving us with not a moment of freedom to ourselves, lest we go searching for our friends. I'm sure Keith and Jonno are not stupid enough to realise that, again, they are losing money from each day the women are down there. If that's where they are. We continue as normal, the rest of us. We dress in silence, clamber into the van, still hoping for a seat on the narrow bench, pleading in our own heads that the day will pass more quickly than the one before. Despite this, the days are feeling longer, and the sun is relentless. It doesn't seem to take a break. The heat in the factory is indescribable, made worse by the smell of the chicken from the other half of the warehouse. I have not seen the Chinese women again. There are no sounds from their end. Perhaps they have been released. The men have secured the middle doorway that was once half-open with locks on chains.

I am startled by a black helicopter up there today; noisy, circling, circling. I like its silver doors, flashing light from the sun. I can't hear the whispering chatter of the other women under its clamour, and for this I am strangely grateful. Flat on my back, I move my arms up and down, pretending to signal to the police helicopter, the grass underneath me flattened out like a snow angel. The helicopter doesn't come closer but continues its circular progression in the sky. Its noise seems to be turning more urgent now. I sit up and I am waving, more and more frantically. The helicopter jilts a little and moves down in the air slightly. It has seen me. The noise is so loud it is causing me to cover my ears. The other girls notice now, and they are running under the aircraft, waving and shouting. It comes further and further down, circling. We jump. We yell. The women are covering their ears like me and shouting at the same time. I am back in the passageway of the house; the two women screaming "Help" at the top of their voices.

I glance over at the van where the men are. Keith is giving us cut-throat gestures and the blackest of looks. I let my arms drop to my sides. The other girls stop suddenly too. The helicopter lifts its tail and accelerates high into the air now, no longer circling. There was a jittering in my stomach two minutes ago that has now come to a halt. I bite my lip as the aircraft lifts beyond the trees and tails away, out of our reach. Not today.

Chapter Thirty-Eight

Yalina

Late July 2008
Somewhere near Sheffield

The men are restless, Keith especially. They haven't been able to relax since the helicopter incident, or when the police came knocking at the door two weeks ago. I feel like telling them that they should breathe a sigh of relief; they obviously got away with it. The police have not been back. If they were so concerned at the time, they would have broken down the door. But they didn't. Keith gathers us in the living room one Thursday after work. All I want to do is try to wash myself a bit under the cold tap in our disgusting bathroom. There are dirt stains on my arms which have been there for at least a couple of weeks. My pits stink. There is still no sign of Gillian and the other girl. It makes me feel sick when I think of what might have happened. To distract my train of thought, I point out to myself that I have already forgotten the other girl's name again. *Damn.* My memory for names used to be brilliant. I remember at high school I could name every single student in the year, first and last name. When I try to do that now, there are just letters flipping around in my mind, like Scrabble pieces thrown in the air.

It has been a while now since we saw them last. The childlike part of me is wondering if Gillian has been reunited with her baby. There is no way that this can be true, and it makes my heart so heavy that I find I'm screwing up my face, trying to concentrate on what Keith is about to say. He is clearing his throat and I am now glancing across at Rebecca to see if she found it comical too. She is not looking at Keith or me; her eyes are fixed on Jonno, and he is nodding back at her. The other girls are hugging their knees, waiting for Keith to speak.

"Right," he says, trying to glance at each one of us. "I won't beat about the bush. Basically, we can't stay living here. The pigs are on to us. I'm pretty sure they'll be back again, and next time they'll use force to open the door. Luckily the front window of the downstairs had the curtains closed, like I told you to do, so they couldn't see nothing."

I take a glance around at the girls on the floor. Some of them are frowning. Toe-painting girl is shaking her head.

"We're moving tomorrow. No choice."

A silence for a few moments.

"What about the mattresses?"

Keith is not blinking but is scratching at his stubble. A couple of the girls are looking tearful, but they say nothing. I wonder when he will get Gillian and the other girl out from the basement.

"Where are we moving to?" It is my voice. I hadn't meant to speak.

He turns his head to look at me. "Wherever we can find. Some of you will need to be separated; you know, go to a different place."

Toe-painting girl is crying now. I wish Gillian were here.

"We're leaving at 5am tomorrow. Make sure you're up or I'll get you up myself. Anyone tries escaping and I'll kick the shit out of you. The usual." He is laughing, looking across at Jonno, who laughs too, partner in crime.

I am trying to find the courage to ask my burning question. I don't care if he throws me in the basement again. At least I'd be with Gillian. I make myself count to three. "Where are the other two?"

Keith shoots me a death stare, only lasting a split second, but a stare all the same. He motions for all of the girls to get up off the floor. "Now go get yourselves cleaned up for work tonight. The men have commented on how much some of you stink. They're not paying for that." He looks pointedly at me again.

I stand and walk out of the room before anyone else does. He's pretty much given me permission to have a wash. I linger in the tiny bathroom, an over-used towel wrapped around my body. As I turn the shower head on, I remember that it barely works any longer, and instead have to make use of the tap that pumps out yellow water. There is no soap or shower gel of any sort, yet we are expected to look and *smell* attractive to the men. Sometimes I will smear some red lipstick on my lips, my cheeks. It makes me feel a bit sick so I've stopped doing that lately. The other girls are welcome to the high-heels too. The towel is barely absorbing any of the water on my body so I stay in the bathroom, patting myself with my hands until I feel more dry. I step out of the crumbling doorway next to the utility room and make my way through the small kitchen. The house is ringing with silence. Everyone must be upstairs, although the clock on the wall states it is not near 9:30pm yet. The girls most likely are in their rooms. I am faced with the door of the basement as I make my way out of the kitchen and towards the dining area. I can feel the chill of the cold water droplets making their way down my chest and legs as I walk on the balls of my feet towards the door. The key is still hanging from the outside. I crane my neck around the corner behind me just to check the men aren't waiting to catch me, and then I try the door handle. It turns silently. The idiots must have forgotten to lock the door the last time they went down to give supplies to the women. I am grinning wildly, one hand grabbing on to my towel. When the door is open I see that the bulb is not on down there. The light from behind me spreads itself through the air of the basement like a laser, giving a dusty glow of mottled gold down into the room. I can see the piles of newspapers down there, abandoned in the corner, and the box I had rifled through. There is a morose feeling to the room. Dank air; a haunted space made darker by the eerie lack of humans.

Chapter Thirty-Nine

Yalina

Late July 2008
Somewhere near Sheffield

Once again we are crammed into the back of the van. There are a couple of our mattresses in here with us too, tipping this way and that with each corner on the road. It is not yet light, although the black sky is lightening gradually through the front of the van, highlighting dark circles under the eyes of the other girls, bruises on limbs. They haven't told us where we are going, or who is getting separated from whom. The tiredness behind my eyes is preventing me from even caring where we are being taken. If anything, I am just grateful we are not heading to work today. One day off, that's what we've been told. The heat is already creating a ripple effect in the road that I can just about see if I squint through the windscreen, a fair distance away at the front. Rebecca is nodding off in the back of the van; lucky enough to secure herself with a seat on the tiny bench, her head bumps now and then against the side of the van as it stumbles across bumps and potholes in the road.

We are only driving for around twenty minutes. I can hear the men quietly arguing with each other about the best place to stop. I am not too tired to question their motive of travelling in daylight, although it's at a time when most of the world is still asleep. Perhaps they didn't want to miss out on the money from last night's punters. We still haven't received another penny since that token ninety euros they gave us weeks ago. That must have been just to keep us sweet. I remember Gillian's face lighting up, the joy of the thought of being able to send this money home to her mother and daughter; the slightest crack of light in the darkened cave. Now she's not even here. I have to hold on to the threat of great wracking sobs that are threatening to take over my chest. The van is reversed and then lunges forward again before suddenly stopping. The men are talking to each other in lowered voices. I can tell a couple of the women are trying to catch some of the words; their heads tilted to one side like robins perched on a fence, listening. I can't tell what is being said. Keith gets out of the driver's seat and walks around to the back of the van. The door is flung open silently, and he stands surveying his brood of women for a moment. I think he is trying to work out who is who. He takes a step forward and pulls toe-painting girl by the arm. She stands but turns to stare at the rest of us, tears brimming. He pulls her down to the ground from the van and stares at the rest of us. The others look to the floor of where we are sitting. It's as if they are dumbfounded by the beauty of the rubber grooving beneath our feet. Sometimes I wish they would stand their ground. Like I am meant to. Keith steps up into our space again; he is looking straight at the other girl who shared the room with Ruby and toe-painting girl. She stands voluntarily and lets him take her by the elbow. There are now two girls standing outside the van, looking at each other, with relief or shock I cannot tell. I stand up from my seated position and toy with the idea of jumping out too, but the door is slammed shut and we are in almost-darkness again, our eyes taking time to get used to the sudden lack of light. The remaining women scoot along the bench to take up the new space. I sit down again, wondering if we will ever see those girls again. Keith opens the driver's door and gets back in, engine still running. I almost laugh at him fastening his seatbelt. I turn, straining to see where we are, where those girls have been left, but all I can see is a long street of red-bricked terraces. We are on the edge of the city, or else making our way

196

towards somewhere more central. I try to catch Rebecca's eye now she is awake, but she is not looking at me. Her chin is perched on her hands, eyes on the men in the front, waiting loyally for their next instruction.

Another twenty minutes or so go by and then the van glides to a stop. Both of the men jump out this time. They take a while to open the back doors. I am almost desperate to see where we've ended up, my tiredness no longer inhibiting my thoughts, but the men's bulky bodies take up the view at the back of the van. Keith signals with his hand for us to get out, and is *shushing* us before we get a chance to take a breath. Finally we are standing on tarmac, not knowing what is next for us. I am following the women in front, they are walking around to the side of a row of terraces, and climbing a black iron staircase attached to the side. I notice how dark the bare heels are of the girl in front of me in her flip flops. At the top, we are ushered into what looks like a kind of flat; a living room area with a kitchenette at the back. There are burn stains in the carpet under our feet, and a smell that catches you at the back of your throat. Most of us are looking at the men, awaiting further instruction. Keith is busy looking around him, rubbing the back of his head, noting who is visible on the street outside before closing the door behind us. Anxious. Already I am missing the house, its huge windows with the light looming through. The piano.

"There are two bedrooms to the side," says Jonno, pointing left and right. Choose where you go. We'll bring in the mattresses in a bit."

One mattress per room. I still haven't tried to stop my tears. Rebecca is attempting to put her arm around me but I shrug it away. I don't want sympathy. I'll be out of here any day soon.

This place is disgusting. All I can think about is the house, the music, the beautiful fields and woodland opposite. Some of the other girls are fighting back tears too.

"Where do we do the night-time work?" asks someone.

My heart sinks even further into my soul. I had not even

thought about that. This time I'm point blank refusing. Especially as this may be my last night here.

Jonno is pointing down to the floor beneath us. "Down there," he says. They've got it all sorted out. "There are a few rooms down there that you'll use."

The other girls are beginning to wander around the limited space. Skinny-legged girl lets herself drop onto one of the brown dated armchairs, not looking anywhere.

"So go make yourselves familiar with the place," says Keith. I wonder if he is meaning to sound like someone's dad.

I go first, taking the room on the left from the living area. A bare room with a window so small it looks like it's been designed for a child. The carpet is stained with cigarette marks and God knows what. There is an abandoned phone wire coming from the wall. Not a morsel of furniture. I can't be bothered to try the other bedroom, so I just hover back in the living area again. The other girls continue investigating, whilst one of the men goes to grab the mattresses from the van outside. I note Jonno is on watch at the door, his eyes surveying the street for any potential passers-by. It must be around 5:45am by now, and still quiet. There is a loud whoop and laughing from the other bedroom, and I find myself pushing my way through the doorway of the room where the other girls are collected, suddenly keen to find the source of excitement

She is sitting cross legged in the middle of the room, black knobbles of hair, her perfect teeth exposed by her grin and her dark eyes crunched with laughter. Next to her is the other girl. I hear skinny-legged girl called her *Lucy*. Gillian sees me and almost screams with joy; I go to her and we embrace. I'm ignoring the bruising on her face, her neck, and realise I had not really stopped crying since we entered the flat and I'm not going to stop now. She is even thinner than she was before; gaunt arms exposed in a vest top I have not seen her wear. The other girl, Lucy, is smaller looking than I remember.

There are so many questions to ask, but the men appear in the room, one of them throwing a mattress upon the floor and giving us looks that make us immediately stop in our tracks.

We have to prevent ourselves from giggling as he leaves the room to grab the other mattress. It is light relief after all these weeks. I am reluctant to let go of my friend, and she is grasping me with both of her hands around my waist and her head tilted upon my shoulder. All I can gather is that she was put in the basement for one night with Lucy, and then moved here, with a few little beatings in between. They have slept in the two armchairs in the living room at night. The work has continued for them once the sun has gone down, it's just a different location. Lucy says she recognises some of the punters from the house.

Keith walks into our room, cracking his knuckles. *British bulldog.* I wonder where the men will live in this new little setup. As if reading my thoughts, Keith, standing over the huddle that is me and Gillian, announces that he and Jonno will be living downstairs. He adds that the door at the top of our metal staircase will be locked at all times. Then he leans forward and pulls us up, takes us out of the bedroom. The other girls are pulling on their shoes and flip flops.

"No point wasting time here," is all he says.

We are setting off to the factory, as usual, despite promising us the day off.

Chapter Forty

Yalina

Late July 2008
Somewhere near Sheffield

It feels like there are sparks of ecstasy shooting through my mind, having her back. That day at the factory passed more quickly than the days there without her. It was reassuring to glance up and just see her kind face looking towards me as we went about our work. The new accommodation is taking a little time to get used to, and the rush to leave the previous house means I don't have any of my music books with me. This sits heavily with me, and I lie awake at night, after being with the clients, thinking of the piano I have left behind. I imagine a family moving into what was our house, their grimy hands touching the piano's keys; not treating it with the respect it is due. Playing *Chopsticks* on it. Children pumping the pedals up and down with their too-small, aggressive feet. It creates a yearning, stabbing jealousy inside of me. I have to go back. I don't know how, but I will. I cannot continue to live this life without my music.

There is no table to sit and eat at in our new residence, so we sit on the floor with our bread. There is no butter, and the fridge doesn't seem to work. The girls are talking to each other, sometimes trying to include me in their conversation, but I am not listening. I am trying to take in what Keith is muttering to Jonno. He is talking about going back to the house later, to pick up some of his things. He's going to go this evening and come back before light. I can't decipher when. Rebecca is giggling next to me, talking about some trashy TV programme she used to watch when she was in care. She glances at me, tries to make me join in. I must be scowling, as she calls me a name and turns her shoulder to me, making her conversation exclusively between her and skinny-legged girl. I don't care. Keith is talking about what he needs to collect from the house in muted tones to Jonno. *Once it's dark.* My heart is speeding up. I'm going with him.

I've got Rebecca to tell Jonno that I'm hideously sick, that I can't stop vomiting. He'll listen to her, he always does. She comes tip-toeing back into our new room to tell me he bought it; that I don't have to work tonight. I don't know how she does it. He listens to every word she says. I watch as the other girls get ready; newly washed clothes for once, but the same clothes, the same shoes. One of the girls has brought make-up with them; their only possession apart from the tunic-dress they wear each day. I think this may be one of the most sad things I've encountered up here. I watch them colour themselves in; grey eyes, pink cheeks, red lips. I am on the periphery tonight. Already I have checked to see where the van is parked. Further than it used to be from the house; we do not have a driveway here nor the luxury of a dead-end road in the country. The girls go downstairs at 9:30pm on the dot. That hasn't changed. I listen to them thudding down the stairs; you would think they are wearing heels from the cacophony they are creating, but they're not. I wonder if that's what Keith is hoping to go and collect tonight from the house. Dressing up clothes for his girls. I lie back on the mattress and realise it's the first time I have been alone for weeks. There are cobwebs hanging from the Artex ceiling, and what looks like a bee's nest yellowing in the corner of the room. I try to think of mum, of dad. There is a woman, tall, blonde hair. She's not Faiza. Dad is in a suit. Dad doesn't wear suits.

I'm having to hover by the open front door at the top of our metal stairway to check that Keith is not leaving the house just yet from his downstairs room. I am beginning to shiver, despite it being July. The stars have been out already for a couple of hours. I always thought you didn't get stars in cities; too much smog, but there are plenty here. Perhaps we are not in the city at all. Leaning over the banister, I am searching for any evidence of a street sign, but there are none in view. It's time. Rebecca has already run out there to open up the van with keys she managed to steal from the windowsill. I walk with a certain speed down the circular staircase and almost jog across the little path and the road to the layby where the van is parked. Luckily, the front of the van is facing towards the house, so even if the men were watching, they wouldn't catch me climbing in the back through the open doors. The little bench is too cold, so I curl up on the floor where I've sat so many times before. The area feels vast without the other girls to fill it and I wrap my arms around myself for warmth. I have been waiting around forty-five minutes before I hear footsteps close to me and the beep of a car remote key. It locks the car and I hear Keith swear to himself as he has to beep the key again to reopen it. Holding my breath, and pinning my thumb nails into the palms of my hands, I let myself breathe once I realise he's not coming into the back of the van to check anything. The engine starts up, and we are moving. He's not secured his seat belt this time.

The drive seems to take forever, and I don't risk trying to get a peek at the way we are travelling. I find I am curling myself into a ball, as small as I can, here in the musty back of the van I am so accustomed to. He must know the old house is still empty. Once we are parked on the drive, he picks up his phone and I can hear from the tone that he is making a call. As he waits for the other person to pick up, I can hear my heart beating in my throat. *How can he not hear that?*

"Alright?" he says, into the phone.

I cannot catch what the other person is saying, but they are talking for a while. My face is flushing crimson, burning up my neck as I realise that Jonno may be on the other end of the call, reporting me missing from my room.

Keith doesn't flinch with the information, just strokes the stubble on his chin. He does this when he's thinking hard. "Listen," he says. "I think I'm going to stay here for the night. Too tired to drive back straight away."

I am sitting back on my heels, they are beginning to hurt. *Will I have to sleep in the van?*

"What else did she say?"

There is more talking from the other person on the line.

Keith laughs. "Original!"

He says his goodbyes and hangs up. Opening his door, I can hear his feet crunching away on the stones that lead to the kitchen door at the back. My hands in prayer position, I am pleading with God that he doesn't open the back doors of the van yet. He doesn't. I hear his key in the lock of the kitchen door, hear it swing open and close. I am doubting why I am here now. I'm not going to be able to play the bloody piano. Just take the books. It almost doesn't seem worth it now. I sit back against the wall of the van and wait for the lights upstairs in the house to go on.

Perhaps I won't, or shouldn't, travel back with him. Especially if it's morning and light, although I have no idea how I would ever find that house again. And then it hits me.

I am free again. I can run, go to the police and report the whole ring. The music books don't seem quite so important right now. I can't stay here in this van. I push one of the doors open and creep out, the door clicking back shut behind me. The cold of the air nips at my bare arms and makes me shiver, and my jaw is chattering. I'm not even going into the house. I'm going straight to the city centre, even if it is a six or seven mile walk in the middle of the night. Hopefully I can get the attention of someone if I stick to the road, but that was how I got caught last time. A light at the top of the house turns off, and I quickly run to the safety of darkness under a tree next to the wide driveway. I can see a figure walking through the downstairs of the house, pacing back and forth, on the phone again. Keith exits through the kitchen door and unlocks the van from where he is standing. He is only holding a stash of papers, some clothes. He looks towards the road, eyes scanning for something, finding nothing. I am barely breathing as he jumps back into the van, reversing it right past in front of me and the tree I am squatting under. I can smell the fuel burning. He is driving slowly, and when out on the road, stops. I cannot think what to do. Far away, I can see the blinking lights of the city, beyond the peaks that glow purple and yellow in the sun. They don't glow now. A car appears around the corner at speed, pulls on to the drive. Jonno gets out, and someone else; a girl I don't recognise. She is wearing a pink hoodie and brand new-looking pink trainers. The girl turns to glance at the house, laughing with Jonno, and Keith gets out of his van on the road to walk to the two of them. I hear a peal of female laughter and for a moment it feels like the girl looks straight at me, under my tree. Her face is instantly recognisable, her baby-faced features. Let off from the night-work because she is so young.

Once the van is gone, and the car containing Jonno and Rebecca, I am completely alone. Standing is uncomfortable, after crouching under the tree for so long. I don't know why they were all here. And for so short a time. I cannot return to be with them all. I am shaking so hard that I can barely get my limbs to move. It must be like teaching your body to walk again after an accident which half paralyses you. I am staggering. *Am I drunk?* I find my way into the road and cross, into the fields opposite. My brain is trying to make sense of what it just saw, cogs turning the wrong way and coming up with nothing. She is my friend. She is the girl I have been protecting this past year or so. *They have just broken her down and got her on their side.* I can't afford to think about it right now. I need to get to safety. There are no clocks around but my guess is it's around midnight. I feel a pang as my mind wants to think about Ali for comfort. Ali who doesn't exist; Ali who was just a trap to get me caught up into all of this. I don't know who I can trust any more. I can't even find the nearest phone box and call home. I don't know where home is. I have a Brahms waltz circling round and round in my mind. It's meant to be a comfort but it's haunting me.

Chapter Forty-One

Richard

April 2008
Islington, London

I went there once. It didn't really work out. I wasn't emotionally ready for it. The whole journey took up more time than the minutes I spent there. I suppose it was worth it, in a sense. Just to be close. In my wallet I kept the ticket from the very last show. *Show.* I would always get berated for calling them that. I think I must have sounded old. *Why do you even have to come?* That's what George would say, embarrassed. I guess he was only eighteen. He didn't seem to mind his mother being there though, front row seats, with Zoe. I would sit further back, hidden behind the rest of the white middle class theatre-goers. Except this wasn't theatre at all. It was real.

Maybe I will go there again. Be more mentally prepared. Be ready to do something about it this time. Say exactly why I was there. I've got to stop being so cowardly. *What's the worst that could happen?*

Chapter Forty-Two

Yalina

Late July 2008
Somewhere near Sheffield

I slept here in the field last night. I must have done. My bones ache, my muscles are locked. God-knows how many insects have found their way into my mouth over the past few hours. My mind keeps ticking over but constantly landing on Gillian. *Chisimdi*. Perhaps the only person I can trust in this entire world. *Who knows if she is a trap, too?* She could be on the men's side, masquerading during the day as one of their workers, but really is one of them by night; new trainers and hoodie. My stomach is in knots. I want to return to the new place now, to see if she is real. If she isn't, then I am alone in this world. My parents aren't my parents, my sister not my sister. Rebecca was a piece of bait, used to make me stay, to look after her, look out for her. And it worked. I need to get back to that house. My mind is ticking, ticking.

My only ticket back to the new place is the hope they'll return to the original house again tonight. Thoughts of reporting them right now are crumbling away into nothing. I'll have to go to wait by the house this evening. I need to make sure Chisimdi is my real lifeline. I swore Adaeze would be returned to her, that I would find out what had happened. I have yet to fulfil that promise. I think of the other women, wish I had made more of an effort with them, too. A neuron smashes into another neuron in my brain, and at once I remember the passports I buried for safety in the woodland. Not far from here. If the girls are to be free soon, they'll need their passports. I jump up to my feet. I kept meaning to retrieve them. Tonight I'll be waiting for my captors to take me back to my personal hell. Probably receive a beating or time locked away. It'll be worth it to see Chisimdi, to give the girls their freedom back. Perhaps I can make it worth my while, worth the other girls' while.

The woodland is only three or four fields away. The grass is damp beneath my feet as I stomp. I don't remember any rain last night. Grasping at my top, I find it is saturated; with rain or sweat, I do not know. It is making me shiver, knowing how wet my clothes are. The fields of heather in the distance lift my heart a little; the greys and lilacs set out like squares of a patchwork quilt. The woodland feels further away than I remember, but I am not coming from the direction of the house this time. As I approach the trees, I make myself walk around so that the road with the house is behind me. I remember to pace ten trees in. There are twigs crackling under my feet. I look back and see I have left footprints in the ground which is soft from the recent rain; a Hansel and Gretel trail back should I forget the way I came. There is still a slight mound from where I kicked back the earth over the hole, no grass on top. Again, I have come unprepared. I find a stick and begin to dig, only a couple of inches at first. Nothing. I use the toe of my shoe to try to knock some of the earth out of the way. The ground is not hard, it gives way easily, but there are no passports. I stop digging and look around me. Definitely ten trees in from the front of the woodland, as if I had walked from the house. I survey the rest of the ground around me, it lies undisturbed, untouched; weeds and leaves covering the earth. The mound where I am digging is bigger than I remember. I continue to dig, further and further until I am sweating, my brow wet and becoming sore from my wiping it countless times. I decide to stop. There is nothing here. Someone must have been watching me that time, and the passports have now been taken. Defeated, I hear my own voice groan. The exhaustion from lack of food and proper sleep takes over, and I sit for a moment on the damp ground, a sense of unease hanging over me as I consider waiting for the van to return to the house tonight.

Maybe I buried the passports further down. I stand, weariness twisting in my hips, and begin to dig again, using the toe of my shoe, and the stick. I look around for a wider stick, or a branch, I need something more weighty with a bigger end. My eyes fix on to a loose looking branch nearby which has been trying to poke my eye out for the past five minutes, and take great pleasure in pulling and yanking it away from its body. Eventually it snaps, and I fall backwards. I kneel in the dank soil and thrust its sharp end first into the ground; digging, poking, scratching away. I am like a mad woman. Sweat is leaking under my breasts and the back of my neck. I keep digging, and then I stop. I don't know why I was so desperate to keep going. Perhaps we all would have been better off not knowing.

***

Her polka dot top is near-ruined, the white spots on the red barely recognisable through the mud stains. The red trousers are muted, a burgundy now. I cannot see her face. I have left it covered with earth. She is still wearing those little ballet pumps, now browned from the ground. I am back in the chicken factory; those bodies, plucked, sinewy, lifeless. The vomiting starts and exhausts me further. I should cover her back up, but I can't.

I don't remember walking the fifty yards or so back to the old house. I'm just sitting under that tree again now, next to the drive. There are chunks of sick still in my hair, and the shakes have yet to leave. The most desperate thing is that we all used her as our role model; *the one who got away.* The brave one who wasn't scared to go.

How I am meant to sit in that van with those murdering scum is beyond me. I am praying it isn't Keith. I know it would have been him who did that to Ruby.

It is Jonno who turns up, and someone else. The van took five hours to arrive. It appeared through the end of day's new darkness; the smell of the fumes hitting me in the gut. I don't move from my cross-legged position under the little tree. I'm hoping that maybe they see me.

Chapter Forty-Three

Yalina

Late July 2008
Somewhere near Sheffield

They take a while to turn off the engine and get out. Neither of them see me. From the rear view of the pink hoodie and new trainers, I know she is one of them. She always has been. It's difficult to know what I feel more disgusted about, but the retching is about to come back, and I don't need them to see me like this. I watch the lights go on in the house, see the bodies moving up the stairs to the top floor. *Are they looking for the passports?*

They walk out of the back door a few minutes later, clothes slung over their arms, bedding too. My brain comes to the memory of the grave I had created, now empty. *They already have the passports.*

Cynicism has cornered my thoughts; everything is a trap. Out to get me. Ali was a trap; the first, most fundamental one. Rebecca, the second.

She is the first to catch my eye. I am still sobbing, squatting here, saliva wiped all over my chin, my face. My nose is dripping. She gives a little laugh, looks over to Jonno; the look of collusion that I had not chosen to recognise those times before. He is temporarily dumbstruck, eyes boring into me, and then away. He opens the van doors at the back after walking past me. The clothes are shoved into the van, and the doors are slammed shut. He treads over to me. I have no energy to stand. I just need the lift back.

"What the fuck." He is just staring again.

Rebecca looks at me, then at him. She gives another little giggle. "Seriously, what the hell are you doing here, waiting for us? Thought you were gone forever."

I want to tell them both that I know of Ruby's fate. But I can't say anything. I pull myself up into a half standing position, one arm held out towards the brick wall behind the tree. Jonno walks around from the back of the van and lurches at me with his right arm, his fist making contact with my left cheekbone. The force of the punch sends me down onto the ground again, my head nearly touching the wall. My tongue is checking to see if my teeth are all still there. *Yep. All there.*

Rebecca is standing right over me, laughing. She looks at Jonno again for approval. He gives a little guffaw of a laugh to appease her. He's not going anywhere yet.

She holds up one of her feet behind her, like a horse getting shod. "Yeh. New trainers. You like?"

I can't speak anyway. My hand is busy rubbing blood from my cheek. One of his cheap rings has grazed the surface of my skin, but there's no more damage than that.

"Jonno got them for me. And this." She is pulling her hoodie out to the front.

I find myself nodding. *She doesn't know I already saw her last night.*

She is leaning forward, pulling me to my feet, like a friend. I manage to hoist myself up, arm around her shoulder. Like when I played piano and she would sit beside me, hogging most of the stool. I take baby steps towards the front of the van, her lithe body holding me up. *She must know about Ruby.*

"You're shaking," is all she says, as she looks in Jonno's direction.

He is walking around to the driver's door. I am expected to climb back into the van. Instead, I brush off Rebecca's hold and begin walking towards the road. I can create quite a speed, and I am not looking back, not tossing any glances over my shoulder. One of them will follow me, once they've realised I'm not climbing into that bastard van again. I begin to run, conjuring up energy into my legs, my feet. I am not running away. Just running.

Chapter Forty-Four

Yalina

Late July 2008
Sheffield

He is on my tail, and I find myself zig-zagging away into the first area of woodland I come to; bracken and tall grasses getting shoved recklessly out of my way. I can leap over any stump or branch, my body weightless. My first look behind tells me he is metres behind, slowed by the size of his own body, sweat gathering on his brow and chest. He is panting, hard of breath. His eyes are a blur as he is yelling out my name over and over. I wonder if he is going to give up the chase as he pauses, hand firmly planted on a beech tree, leaning over to catch his breath. It makes me slow down temporarily, but I shouldn't linger. We can't be too far now. Perhaps only half a mile or so more to go. The darkness doesn't seem as difficult to plough through now, my eyes have become accustomed to it.

He is mumbling as he staggers past the trees, words about Rebecca that I no longer care for. Words about *having always done the best* for us.

Once again he has stopped, is flailing around on the ground picking up little rectangles of card that have carelessly scattered to the ground, pieces of puzzles.

The passports.

I toy with the idea of sprinting towards him so I can salvage them, but think better of it, and keep up my pace. I can just about see the top of the viaduct looming towards me in the near-distance. There are lights in the ground, attractively embedded in some Derbyshire-styled stones at each end of the structure. When I eventually get to the middle part of the length of the structure I stop, and allow myself to bend over, catching my breath like Jonno had done only moments earlier. I can see his figure catching up with me, becoming larger, more detailed. I am not afraid. I have no need to run any more.

He has a look of surprise on his face as he gets near me, slows to a stop a few feet away. Neither of us say anything for several moments. I have caught my breath, but Jonno is still breathing hard, the passports clutched in his right hand. They make a broad spectrum of colours, something quite beautiful to match the suddenly-beautiful surroundings we find ourselves in, lit up like a setting for a Halloween party outside.

"Stunning, isn't it?" I say, staring out over the view. I can see the lights from little cottages atop the hills, the vales tailing away into the distance, under the stars.

He is staring at me, still struggling for breath. "Why did you stop?"

I am smiling now. There are long shadows drawn over his face from the lights. *Clown eyes.*

"I said, why did you stop running?" He is losing patience with me.

"Give me those," I say, nodding at the little books in his hand.

He glances at them as if he had forgotten they were held tightly in his own grip.

"Yes, those."

He is shaking his head at me, frowning. "You're off your rocker."

I stop looking at him, turn my head to stare into the distance. The twinkling lights of the city are spread out like a patchwork blanket to our left. I twist suddenly and kick his right hand, successfully knocking the collection of passports out of his hand. He is immediately on the ground, scrabbling around to pick them up, precariously close to the edge of the viaduct. Within a split second I stamp on the back of his neck and he is flat on the ground completely, but I can't see his face.

"Don't do this," he says. His voice is muffled into the ground.

But I am not listening. More than twelve months of rage has taken its toll in my head. I loosen the grip of my foot and let him stand slowly, pretending to prepare to lurch for the passports in his hands again. He is staring down at his grip, making sure there is no way this little girl can steal them from him. He's not expecting what happens.

It's dark down there. There is no movement. It would be a long walk in the dark to go and check if he was still breathing. I doubt he is. The fall alone will have been enough.

Chapter Forty-Five

Yalina

Late July 2008
Somewhere near Sheffield

"What the hell was all that running off about?" Rebecca is curled up in the front seat of the van. I wasn't sure if she would still be here on my return. "And where is Jonno?"

I come up with the excuse I have been planning for most of my walk back to the house. She seems to buy it, for now.

I turn the key and start the engine, and we edge out of the driveway. I feel like a queen in a carriage, for a split second. The van feels so high up when you have a view out of the front.

She turns to look at me. "How did you end up over here anyway?"

"I came back here last night. I wanted my music books. And to play the piano." It sounds feeble. It is, but it's also the truth.

There is a wrench of pain inside me; laughter at the thing that has kept me going this entire time. Folding my arms prevents me lashing out.

"Last night? So you slept here, in the garden?"

I am shaking my head no. "A field. By the woods.". Any sign of her believing me would relax me right now. We both stare straight ahead as we leave our dead-end road.

Rebecca is warbling away next to me. It's as if she's forgotten for a moment that she's completely betrayed me, and that Jonno is now missing. "So you came to the house to get your music books, and then you slept in a field. You know it rained last night?"

I don't respond, just continue driving.

She sits back, looks out of the window. "You know I could have slept in a proper bed every night," she offers to me, by way of showing what a good, solid friend she was.

I don't have the energy to respond. I can only see the sullied red trousers, the almost invisible polka dots on Ruby's top. Her arms. The mottled colour of them.

The unevenness of the road and the speed of the van is making me nauseous again. I hold my hand over my mouth.

"Are you going to hurl?" squeals Rebecca. I answer her question by vomiting on to my lap, some of it spilling over on to her legs.

Rebecca is disgusted. "I'm not cleaning that up. Skank!"

I don't let the van slow, just race through the streets. I can see the stars again, like last night, just like at the viaduct only minutes before. I wonder if they were out the night they got rid of Ruby, watching like witnesses in the silence.

"So, I stayed on that filthy rotten mattress every night, and I didn't even have to," she is continuing. "Listened to your bloody mental piano playing. Just so you would want to *care* for me."

I am covering the pile of sick with my hands and I clear my throat. "Just so I would stay, and not run away to report you all." It is the first thing I've said for a while.

Rebecca says nothing, just stares out of the windscreen.

It occurs to me that Rebecca and Jonno were together. A couple. He would still have been taking advantage of her, at her age. *Disgusting.*

"So how old are you?" I am doubting everything now. But I'm almost past caring.

"Eighteen."

My mind is reeling, spools and spools of tape ribbon dragging from one side of my mind to the other. "But the poster. I saw a battered poster in the utility room. It said you were fifteen. They are looking for…" and I stop. She is smirking, eyes lit up.

"Right." I say. The nausea is back. I wonder for a split second if I could be pregnant. Chisimdi talked about the non-stop sickness. No. I've been fastidious with the contraception.

"So, you or Jonno created that poster and shoved it in that room knowing I would see it. To fool me."

She doesn't say anything, but the smirk is still plastered to her face.

"Then I would feel sorry for you being so underage." I don't need to look at her for affirmation.

I am slowing the van down, pulling over. We come to a stop. I can see the rows of red brick terraces ahead of us, and a swarm of butterflies take flight in my stomach, lifting the nausea slightly.

"So you two… you and Jonno…are a couple," I suggest.

Rebecca bursts out laughing. "Gross!"

She straightens her face. "No," says Rebecca, undoing her seatbelt. "He's my Uncle. Uncle Jonny."

I can feel my shoulders slump back into the seat. There is an unexpected stab of something in my gut. Jealousy. A family member to share with, depend on, laugh with.

"Where did you say he was again?"

I don't say anything, just shrug, and she doesn't seem bothered. *Stupid, ignorant Rebecca.* I'm amazed she trusted me to drive her back to the house again. I could be driving her anywhere. To a police station. But not to admit to my crime. I can't do that.

I jump out of Rebecca's side of the van. The house looks the same. I wonder if Chisimdi is working downstairs or asleep.

Chapter Forty-Six

Yalina

Late July 2008
Somewhere near Sheffield

I unlock the door of the upstairs with the key attached to the
van keys and we step inside, Rebecca first. She walks about
the house in a different way now; strutting like a peacock.
She kicks off the pink trainers and makes no attempts to tidy
them away anywhere. I am about to ask her if any of the
other girls know that she is Jonno's niece. She must know
what I am thinking as she holds her finger to her lips as she
points to the room I now share with her and Chisimdi. I
almost wish I had chosen the other bedroom, with the rest of
the women.

I have no idea why I should keep their little secret now.

There appears to be no food in the dated kitchenette so I
quietly let myself into the bathroom. I struggle to clean the
mess from my face and hair, and I keep catching wind of the
smell. I remove my only pair of jeans and dump them in the
avocado-coloured bath, swearing to myself that I will clean
them in the morning. With wet hair stuck to my cheeks, I
tiptoe into the bedroom. Rebecca is still sitting in the living
room, in one of the armchairs, legs casually dangling over the
side, playing with a phone. *So she had one the entire time.*

In the bedroom, Chisimdi is stretched out on the mattress,
mouth slightly open as she sleeps. It must be past 1am, if she
has stopped working. I wonder if she noticed Rebecca had
even left the house.

Next morning, it is Keith herding us into the van. He looks at me, then looks away and spits on the pavement where the van is parked. Jonno's disappearance will be freaking him out. Rebecca is not rising this morning. They tell us she's *not feeling too well*. I know she probably sleeping off the beating from Keith, for having no clue on Jonno's whereabouts. I am aware of Chisimdi trying to catch my eye. I just know she's not a trap too. But I cannot talk to her here, crammed in the back of the van, other eyes and ears on us. We arrive at the factory at six on the dot, the sun already perched between high white clouds. As we file in one by one, there are no sacks of potatoes in front of us, but plastic crates. Some of us are looking around for guidance. Keith, and the other man, *Greg*, who works there, are waiting to talk to us. Keith explains that we will be out in the fields, picking out the potatoes from the ground. Some of the women will be pulling out carrots. We are to select the good from bad as we pick. The previous process was too slow and relied on more work hours just to get the vegetables out of the ground and sorted separately. I glance around at the other girls; Chisimdi is looking dumbfounded and again glances my way. We are led outside with the crates, marched alongside the factory, beyond where the chicken-sorting happens. Eventually we come to a field we haven't seen before. Chisimdi and I are shoved to the field on the left, some other girls are taken to a field further away. Keith shows us how to pull the carrots from the ground, brush off the dirt, and bunch them. We are then to put the bunches in the plastic crates. He walks to the side of the field, some distance away, and is looking at something on his phone.

"Where were you last night?" hisses Chisimdi. She has been dying to ask me this since we woke this morning, it's obvious.

I thought I was functioning okay. I thought my brain was handling the situation by locking it away in the back of my mind, where the hospital letters and unread emails are stored. I fall into her lap. She is my friend, she is real. I don't have to tell her much, only that our most gregarious girl didn't quite make it.

She has her arm around me all the way back to the new house. The other girls, I can tell, are desperate to ask what is wrong, but they refrain. They avert their eyes to the floor, or out towards the windscreen. I have told Keith I will not be working tonight. He doesn't argue. He doesn't want any drama, it seems. No wonder she was let off from doing the nights too. I use the evening to stretch my legs over the side of one of the armchairs, Rebecca-style, and plan what I need to do. Except that I can't think straight.

Visions of Ruby are materialising in my head; her face, her body reaching around the kitchen the first time I had properly noticed her, looking for food. Her confidence that she would be alright. It just makes me want to cry again, so I try to think of the most upbeat music I can play in my mind right now, to bring my mood up. I feel a stab of guilt as the other girls get ready for their nights with the men downstairs. I don't get to see the men, they use the separate front door down there. If I look out of the window from our top floor, I can occasionally see them; head down, hood up, playing with keys or phone on their journey to the door. Some of them look to be regulars, but I can't tell. My legs are swinging one at a time as I try to clear my head, try to hatch a plan of how to get to the authorities. We've never had phones, not since day one, and I didn't have much luck trying one of the men's laptops again. I think of how I can get my hands on Rebecca's phone, but she's out again tonight, perhaps back at the old house to collect more stuff. There is a knock at the door. I freeze. A punter has probably come to the wrong floor. I stand up slowly and try to peer around to where the front door is. I can see a plain-clothed man, standing alone. I don't think he can see me, so I debate whether to slink off to my room and ignore him. He knocks again, not aggressively, and I find myself walking to the door, prising it open a couple of inches, just so I can see his eyes. "The girls are in the building downstairs," I say. I hope it is a plain-clothed officer.

He shakes his head slightly. "No, I'm not after that."

I don't open the door any wider. I can feel that I am

frowning.

"I would like to speak to you, please."

My tongue is not finding any words. It is the police. It must be.

I open the door a few more inches and take in the suit, the white shirt. "Police?" I say.

He shakes his head, and now I am afraid.

I try to close the door on him. "I don't want to buy anything."

"Please, Yalina." He puts his hand between the door and the frame.

Hearing my name knocks me off guard. I am aware that I have frozen like a statue in the doorway. "How do you know my name?" God, I wish Rebecca were here tonight.

The man shifts from one foot to another. His white shirt is showing sweat marks at the armpits. "We have met before. You don't remember?"

There is something about this man that is familiar. I knew it when I could only see one third of his face.

"I visited as a customer before, at the other place, but it didn't happen. I got upset. You got me to chat to your pregnant friend instead."

Crying man.

"Oh."

"Can you let me in please? I need to talk to you."

I pause, and remembering that he caused no harm last time, open the door wide enough to let the man in. He steps through the door and removes his jacket. I gesture for him to take the other armchair, and he sits, smoothing his grey jacket over his lap. I wait for him to speak, but he doesn't for a while, just peers around the room, as if assessing it for damp.

"So."

He smiles weakly, and I wonder if he is going to cry again. "Let me tell you about my son."

I feel like sighing, rolling my eyes. *Has he come to tell me that his bastard son is a sex addict?*

I show my best listening face, and he clears his throat to continue. I hear a man cough downstairs. A punter? I wonder if Chisimdi is with him. She, in turn, is probably wondering if I have come up with a wonder-plan yet.

"My son was a brilliant boy. Dedicated to his family, especially his sister." His voice definitely has a wobble to it. I don't know how to comfort crying-stranger-men in suits. My brain is feeling foggy again. *Ruby. Ruby's filthy clothes. Ruby's darkened hands.*

"Are you ok?" he asks me.

"Yes. Are you?"

He nods, looking like he wants to continue with the story about his son. "Anyway.

Our son was taken from us. Last year. It was awful. Hideous." He is crying now. I wish I could send him to talk to Chisimdi again. I remember his eyes from before now; grey, fluid, kind.

"I'm sorry," I say.

He is staring at a spot on the floor; perhaps he has forgotten I am here. *Has he tried counselling?*

I am listening to him tell me that his son was a bit of a geek at school, straight A grades all the way to Oxford. He was doing *so well* there. He had a real talent for music, he was a classical musician. Started performing solo on stage. And then he was killed. A hit and run. Brain dead. Luckily he had opted to be a donor should the worst ever happen.

I am wondering whether I can go to bed straight after this man has gone. I am so severely sleep deprived that I feel sick again.

The man pulls out some papers from the jacket that is lying on his lap.

He points to a line on one of the pages where there is the squiggle of a signature, and tells me it's his son, George's signature.

I smile politely. I can only think of the mattress on the floor of my shared room. I need to sleep.

He pulls out a carbon copy sheet, a different, blue colour this time. He points to the very top. My name is there, printed out in capitals. He looks at me, his damp grey eyes misty and expectant. He points to the bottom of the page where there is another squiggle, and another below it.

I look at him and I cannot think anything, noting that the pages are mentioning again and again about the *donor* and the *donor organ.* There are two names printed next to the signatures. *Faiza Sheikh. Mo Sheikh.* Dated *March 2007.*

They are signing on someone else's behalf. They are signing for the *donor organ* to be transplanted into Yalina Sheikh's body.

Invisible stitches pull tight around my heart.

Chapter Forty-Seven

Richard

July 2008
Somewhere near Sheffield

I've told her. I just turned up and I showed her the papers, and I told her. She didn't seem to be listening at first. I was crying, she wasn't. Her eyes kept glazing over, as if she was somewhere else. I wonder if all the sex work does that to you. Trauma, of a sort. I wish I hadn't been such a coward, after that first time. I wish I could have just told her then, and then called the police. I don't know why I ran away. Nat didn't hear from me for weeks. I think she assumed the worst, poor woman.

Yalina hasn't yet asked how I found her both times. I think it was the shock. God knows what she has been through. Her family tell me how cold she was when she moved back home. Wouldn't talk to them, just stayed in her room, in bed. Her sister, who she was apparently so close to couldn't get anything out of her. They knew she was going to leave, run away. The mum had sensed it.

So tomorrow, I'm going back to the house, to tell her how I found her. How I managed to steal her phone out of her belongings in the hospital that day of the operation, when her family were too distressed to notice. How I managed to fit a tracker to her device, so I knew where she'd be at all times. Of course, it was one of those men who kept her phone, and used it for himself. Kept the battery running, though.

It was my only way of staying close to George, you see. My son. My wonder boy. She told me all about her musical obsession, about her piano playing. He passed it on to her through his heart. I will keep her close to me.

Chapter Forty-Eight

Yalina

1st August 2008
Somewhere near Sheffield

Richard has told me everything. I think I believe him. I want to tell Chisimdi, but I don't need anything going wrong today.

I dress for work, silently, and lead the way amongst the girls as we quietly pace towards the van. The sun is up early today, yet it lingers behind the trees on the peaks in the far distance. Chisimdi is eyeing me, as she does when she knows something is different. I clamber on to the floor and look straight at her, smile the greatest smile I can manage. She seems surprised, and grins back. I love those beautiful teeth of hers. She is mouthing *what?* at me. I pretend not to see.

The morning seems to last forever. We are in the field at around 9:30am, backs bent over, pulling at carrot tops when they arrive. Several cars are moving on the narrow road, which then disappear behind the structure that is the factory. Four or five men and a couple of women are walking over. The other girls in our field don't notice, don't look up. Keith spots the people first, and makes a sudden run for it, first towards his van, then staggering away in the opposite direction when he sees there are two coppers waiting there in the shadows. The other man, *Greg*, is on his phone, overseeing the potato field, chatting. He is caught unawares; pinned to the ground and handcuffed straight away.

Rebecca's image leaps into my mind.

The women all stop working, straightening their backs as they watch the commotion. The others in the potato field next door are looking over, hands shielding their eyes from the sun. They watch the man, whose name we forget, on the ground, writhing a little, dropping his phone. I wonder what the person at the other end of the line is thinking.

The two factory women, and poking woman are put in cuffs too, and their heads lowered into one of the plain cars parked near the van. Some men are calling to us, rounding us up like sheep. I can see fear in Chisimdi's eyes, but I am smiling at her, telling her with my face that it is ok, it is over now. We are all huddled together at the side of the carrot field; all the women from the two fields. There are three men who have gone inside to free the Chinese women in the chicken part of the factory. Moments later, two more men come out handcuffed. One is spitting and hurling abuse at the policeman who is holding him. The Chinese women file out, one by one. A couple of them are tearful. Their masks are still in place, many of them still wearing plastic gloves, insides of the chickens still smeared over their fingers.

I am comforting Chisimdi, she is rocking within the space of my embrace. All she whispers is "Adaeze, Adaeze," over and over. I hope it won't be long.

***

We are interviewed one by one, at the nearest police station. There are counsellors here for us, but I don't think anyone feels like talking more than we have to right now. I feel no loyalty to either of the men. In the past, when I fantasised about this moment, I had wondered if I would feel some sense of responsibility. There is nobody to protect now. I tell them about the past year; the night-time work, the lack of beds and food, the beatings. I don't tell them about the piano, that is irrelevant here; my own personal joy. We are

229

given accommodation in B&Bs for the next two weeks. The thrill of the smallest things is what is making us happy; the bursting heat of the power-shower in the immaculate bathroom. Clean towels. Bedding so puffy and soft you'll never want to get out of bed again. New, clean clothes. Warm, buttered toast. Chisimdi and I smile at each other over breakfast. We sit on matching chairs.

Richard tells me Rebecca was arrested at the new house, where he waited. She is still being held. Turns out she is seventeen, and cannot be tried as an adult.

Seems Jonno had a pretty strong hold on her, and she was forced into the prostitution at night too, same as the rest of us. I had wondered if that had all been a lie too.

"Some uncle," sighs Richard.

I think it has taken him a while to get his head around how our lives have been, all these months. The quieter girls; Lucy, Mary, they say they have been in this for years, Jonno and Keith at the centre of it all. They seem to be the most excited ones. Lucy tells me she has a little boy at home. She just needs the police to recover the passports, and then she can go back. I am watching the door, waiting for my own arrest.

Chapter Forty-Nine

Yalina

Late August 2008
Meersbrook, Sheffield

Rebecca has been released without charge. For this, I am happy; she is still a child in the eyes of the law. We don't get to see her, she is staying at another B&B in the city. I don't think I want to see her again.

We are at the funeral of Ruby. It is overcast, warm, but threatening to rain. The church is large, but feels colossal due to the lack of people. A couple of local looking strangers wander in at the back; it is always more interesting to find out who died when it's a young person. I hope they are not journalists. Due to time restraints, and finances, it was not possible to fly Ruby's whole family over. We are outside now, listening to the priest read a prayer. There are pigeons squawking in the nearest tree, unaware of what is happening just beneath them. Richard has paid for the entire service. We watch, silent as the small procession walks through the churchyard. There is not one coffin, but two. They found Petrova buried not far from Ruby, a little further back in the woodland; a different date. I did not have the stomach to identify her, even if it was just her clothing we were asked to examine. One of the other girls did it.

The coffins are plain wood, perhaps oak; expensive, and they are laid next to each other. I want to cry today, but I can't. My mind is raw, numb. I am watching the girls' coffins be placed into the ground, and I throw some dirt over the top. Ruby's mother stands at the front, arm linked with a man, Petrova's dad, I am told. Their heads are bowed. They don't seem to hear the noisy pigeons. I refer to Petrova with her most recent name as it's what I knew her by for those two days, but today she is *Lubna*. We learn that Ruby's real name is Lena. It is comforting to remember that the two girls were friends, and are now together, in a sense.

Later on, at the wake, Ruby's mother talks about *Lena*. She'll always be red-haired Ruby in my mind. Red haired Ruby with the booze and the polka dot clothing.

I drink some wine at the wake, it makes my legs so heavy and my head fuzzy that I can barely remember why we are all there. It hits me more than the lager and the vodka Ruby supplied me with that time. Chisimdi has noticed, she stands by my side to hold me up. Richard is laughing, and it makes us all relax. He has been telling us about his daughter Zoe, and his partner, Nat. Although I am drunk, my heart is singing. He has his arm around me at one point. It warms me right through. Skinny-legged girl is drunk too, she swings this way and that to the Nat King Cole song that is playing on the Cd player. One of Petrova's favourites, apparently. It is good to be reconciled with the girls who got sent to the other house. They drew the short straw, apparently, and were holed up in some basement flat in the Shiregreen area, just the two of them with a bunch of other girls from Lithuania. They had to perform for the men in the same area where they slept, sometimes in front of other girls who weren't working. It is helpful to me that we count our blessings. I black out in a chair later in the day. Richard carries me to his car, and to my room at the B&B. He asks Chisimdi to make sure I'm covered up well in bed, that there is a glass of water by my side. He is a man, but I trust him.

Chapter Fifty

Yalina

Early September 2008
Sheffield

Chisimdi is so anxious that she can't sleep. I know this because I can feel it. She is in the room next to mine on the corridor, and I can't hear a thing, but I know she's awake. I feel her tossing and turning, feel her watch the sun rise knowing that today could be the day. I am going through it with her. The police are going to do a 6am raid on the property they believe the baby is being held at. I meet her in the corridor of our B&B at the same time, cup of tea in hand for her. She says it has been more than two years since she last drank a cup of tea. She tastes it and smiles weakly, staring into the cup. It is such a luxury to have a kettle, tea cups and a miniature fridge in my own room.

I will be going to London with Richard next week.

Faiza and Mo are going to come up to visit. It may be strange, it may not be. I am not angry at them, they made a decision for me when I was unable to. They tried to save my life, my faulty heart. They succeeded.

I do not want to live with Mo. That won't be happening again.

We are pacing back and forth, back and forth in the living room downstairs. I have been given my phone back. The police are on strict instructions to call my number if they have discovered anything, good or bad. Chisimdi doesn't eat, didn't finish the tea I made for her. I encourage her to take a shower or read a book, anything to pass the time, but she won't. Her eyes are fixated on my phone on the table. After a while there is a knock on the living room door, and the proprietor of the residence pops her head around the door. She must be late fifties, pale, yappy like a terrier. Chisimdi's eyes are colossal, her arms frozen into position on the table. It is only Richard, come to see how we are. He has heard that Keith will most likely get life imprisonment for what he has done, even if it can't be proven he killed the girls himself. There are another nine men involved in the ring just in Sheffield alone, he says. One of them worked at the factory. Chisimdi looks as if she'd like to strike Richard right now. She shows no interest in what he has to say. She sighs, fingers drumming on the table, avoiding our eyes.

The call comes just after 10am. I answer the phone but I have forgotten to put it on to speaker phone as I promised. She is standing up now, gesticulating at me as I speak to the police.

I hang up. "They've found her. She's in Wakefield. She's fine."

She steps back and lets herself collapse against the wall. Her hands are in fists of triumph, held level with her head. I don't think she has the strength to hold them up any higher. It is me who is crying. Happy, hot rivulets of joy.

She's not allowed to see her yet. There are a number of procedures to adhere to first, the policewoman had said on the phone, not to mention DNA tests to prove it is actually Adaeze. Chisimdi, of course, thinks this is ludicrous, she *knows who her child is*. I offer to help the time pass by letting her come down to London with Richard and me, but she declines this with a casual waft of her hand. We are free now, in our newly donated clothes, so I take her to a cafe on the Meersbrook Road, half-way down the hill there. It is so strange sitting here, in this tea shop-come upmarket cafe. Last time I was on this road I also thought I was on my way to safety. They have tried to give the shop a royal theme, with union jack bunting and plates on the wall. We are not the only customers, there is a gaggle of females at the back, laughing and joking with each other. One of the women has a baby in a pram, which I did not notice until we had made our order of coffee and teacakes. We don't seem to get the same teacakes down south. It's a *northern thing*. Like battered mars-bars, not that we have had opportunity to try those yet. The baby squeaks, and the mother jig-jigs the pram a little. I know Chisimdi is looking over. I glance at her nervously and see she is smiling at the baby, whose gender is unknown. My friend's face is lit up. There are just days left to wait. We drink our coffee and stare out of the window, a sudden lack of things to say. I can see the little corner shop, just up the hill to our left, where I nipped in to buy something that day on my way to the city centre. I remember the man's face as he was paying for his food at the counter, the way he laughed when I had called him *Ali*. I know my biological parents wouldn't have wanted for me to suffer so much after my old ruined heart was exchanged for another, and they wouldn't have known what lay ahead. My life here is finished. I will miss the days and nights of comfort with my friend but it is time for my new life. And hers.

Chapter Fifty-One

Richard

Early September 2008
Islington, London

She's been here a week now, in my apartment. Zoe loves her, as does Nat. I hear the piano as soon as breakfast is over, and I am in the shower. She plays the music of George, scouring his music books, the old papers yellow with age. Each day she is learning another concerto or symphony. She wants to get a job teaching music to children, or refugees, she has said. *The sort of people who need everyone's help*. Lil won't do it for payment. She wants to offer her services for free. I can see the generosity of George in everything that she does. She stays in the room he used to stay in, but it's not strange. Some of his childhood toys are still assembled on the white shelves on the wall; Lego vehicles, books, a miniature trumpet. There are the black curtains with red and white footballs; very 90s - I'm not up to changing the decor just yet. If I go about my jobs in the flat; cooking, the washing, cleaning up, sometimes I can pick out a sound, a fumble coming from George's room and just about forget for a moment that he is not there.

Her parents came to visit yesterday, and her sister; it was good to meet Faiza and Mo again. Our previous meeting at the hospital last year was strained, although considering the stress everybody was under, it came as no surprise. We are all travelling to Sheffield for the court case together in October.

Yalina was offered the chance to give her evidence from behind a screen, but she said no, she wants to face them, see them squirm. Her own court case is in two weeks. I know she will be let off. It was self-defence.

Chapter Fifty-Two

Yalina

Late September 2008
Islington, London

Time is passing in strange ways. The nights are long, but perfect, enveloped in the thickness of the duvet and sheets of what-was George's room. It looks like a teenage boy's room but at least there's the double bed. Taking a shower is still a luxury, as is having breakfast. A whole eight hours' sleep a night would be the best imaginable thing, but my body has taken to either only giving me two or three hours a night, to going crazy and knocking me out for up to fourteen hours at a time. A lot of the time I wake up and don't know where I am. The relief that hits me is indescribable. I receive texts from Chisimdi most days. She was reunited with Adaeze a week ago. I'm guessing words can't explain that for her. She is sending me some photos in the post of the two of them together.

Today I am visiting George's grave. I have instructions scribbled down on a piece of paper of how to find the actual spot. When I get there, I see the space is immaculate. I wonder if Ruby and Petrova's graves will look this neat once their parents are back in their home countries. There is a lump forming in my throat at the sadness and impossibility of the situation; families too impoverished to fly their girls' bodies home. They will make memorials for them at home, I'm sure of it. There is a blossom tree with a plaque for

George, and a framed music book from when he sat his first solo concert. I crouch down and stare at the plaque for a good ten minutes, try to picture his face. I have only seen one photo of him so far. Dark blonde hair, a stretched grin framed with serious eyes. I leave the modest bunch of recently bought daisies at the base of the tree. I could only think of two words to write on the little card, and somehow they don't feel quite enough.

I play piano in the flat most days. It's a grand piano, no less, purchased for George's 18th. Zoe will sit next to me on the stool a lot of the time when she visits. I play whatever she requests; The Beatles, The Rolling Stones (she knows I am well acquainted with these) and of course, the classical pieces. The collection of music that George had acquired by such a young age still astounds me. She tells me he would play most of it without needing the music. I know she misses him, yet I do not feel like his replacement. They have made me feel so welcome. I have a family. I have known them forever; the missing part of the puzzle that has been clouding my mind now clicked into place.

Zoe shuffles along on the stool-for-one next to me, taking much of the space. For a moment, I am back in the house. Rebecca is squished next to me, the sun perched high on the clouds overlooking the purple patchwork fields below. There are shafts of light beaming through the floor-to-ceiling windows of the house, the faint sound of girls squabbling upstairs, each arguing over who will get to wear the high heels tonight.

THE END

Fantastic Books
Great Authors

darkstroke is
an imprint of
Crooked Cat Books

- Gripping Thrillers
- Cosy Mysteries
- Romantic Chick-Lit
- Fascinating Historicals
- Exciting Fantasy
- Young Adult
- Non-Fiction

Discover us online
www.darkstroke.com

Find us on instagram:
www.instagram.com/darkstrokebooks

Printed in Great Britain
by Amazon

55409393R00139